KANSAS
CHETOPA
BAXTER SPRINGS
D1206951
MO.
SALINE
Trading Post
CHOUTEAU
Salt Spring
OZARK UPLIFT
UNION MISSION
Illinois
TAHLEQUAH
Neosho
PARK HILL
Verdigris
Water mill
Arkansas
Cimarron R.
THREE FORKS
FT. DAVIS
FORT GIBSON
Burial of Cherokee Lighthorse
MT. VISTA
HONEY SPRING
WEBBERS FALLS
FORT SMITH
Canadian
Arkansas R.
WEWOKA
NORTH FORK TOWN
FT. COFFEE
EUFALIA
RED OAK
SKULLYVILLE
McALESTER
SUGAR LOAF
South Canadian
TEXAS ROAD
PERRYVILLE
JACK FORK MTS.
KIAMICHI MTS.
BOGGY DEPOT
FT. WASHITA
NAIL'S CROSSING
Boggy
Muddy Boggy
Kiamichi
Little R.
FT. TOWSON
Blue R.
FT. PRESTON
FT. McCULLOCH
COLBERT'S FERRY
Red River
TEXAS
ARKANSAS

THE BRIGHT FEATHERS

Also by John H. Culp

BORN OF THE SUN

THE MEN OF GONZALES

THE RESTLESS LAND

The Bright Feathers

BY JOHN H. CULP

HOLT, RINEHART AND WINSTON
NEW YORK CHICAGO SAN FRANCISCO

Published simultaneously in Canada by Holt, Rinehart
and Winston of Canada, Limited

Library of Congress Catalog Card Number: 65-11856

PUBLISHED, JANUARY 1965
SECOND PRINTING, MARCH 1965

Designer: Jack Jaget
81642-0115
Printed in the United States of America

For my mother

THE BRIGHT FEATHERS

Chapter 1

My name is Scrape Dawkins, just turned sixteen—Pete Dawkins' boy. I've got only one ear, from being dragged at the end of a tangled-up cow rope on the old Chisholm Trail up from Texas while chasing a longhorn. My mama doesn't know this yet. What's left of the lost ear is as small as a butter bean. The other is the size of a tow sack. Take a good look.

The main thing about being Pete Dawkins' boy is that Dawkins is dead, killed by Old Man Wallum's men. Jasper Wallum—a real coyote. He was the most hated man in our parts and would have been most anywhere else, I reckon.

This slapped-out drink of water beside me with a set of teeth like pitchfork tines is Scut Benton. He is grinning. His mama loves him like mine loves me. To Scut's left is Ham Esposita McGook, the dark silent one of the outfit, the Brain. He is short and wears a flat-crushed sombrero with a brim a mile wide.

Ham is half-Mexican and part-Irish. He is part-Irish because one time an almost pure-blooded Irishman brought a rejuvenating medicine show to the adobes of San Antonio and married a señorita. Then he left with his wagon and tonics while Ham kicked up his heels on a petate. No one knows what else Ham is part of, but it couldn't matter less to him. We call him Ham because he likes ham. He looks like a bullfrog.

Well, it's a windy star-snapping night on this old trail, back in the fall of '71, it is. We are standing by the skeleton-ribbed chuck wagon talking to Slick Pilifer, owner of the Turkey Foot on our way back to Texas from Kansas. We'd put in a good season getting missed by all the gun-slingers of Abilene and Newton, which was why we were still alive to feel the downward pull of our gun belts.

"I don't know," Slick says. His sharp eyes are on us. He'd always treated me square after I hired on when my old man died, but he never gave anybody an inch without looking around a turn of the road to see the next mile. He had to know first that there wouldn't be another mile—at least for a long time, that is.

"We've worn out Jesse Chisholm's Trail for two years," I say. "We want to go home by the old Shawnee Trail. It's still there and we haven't seen it. It runs right along with the Texas Road the emigrants use. We've been dodging Plains Indians for so long, we thought we'd go back through Indian Territory and see the country of the Five Civilized Tribes before the first railroad goes through. We wouldn't get home much behind you."

Slick says, "The Tribes got a rough shake when the government chased them out of the South, but after the Trail of Tears they did what they could to start over in the Territory. Then the war caught them up and they broke into the old factions again. It was worse than ever. The Territory was devastated, almost from one end to the other. I know. I fought there."

"We still want to go."

"I like you, Scrape," Slick says. "And I'd like you more if trouble left you alone. But it hangs 'round your door like a blue blowfly."

Sure, he likes me, but he won't take a chance on my leading Scut and Ham off for keeps, or even letting me go. He's a big man for the outfit. Leaning against a wagon wheel, he puts a cigar in his mouth and studies me the way he would the eyes of a Newton gambler at a card table in the old Bull's Head.

"I've got another reason," I say. "My old man used to drive cows up the Shawnee Trail to Baxter Springs before Jesse's trail was thought of. We talked of hitting it together someday. The railroad has just crossed the Kansas line and we thought we'd ride the train as far as it goes—to Chouteau."

"What about your horses?" Slick chews the cigar, his cold eyes in the leaping light of the fire not giving an inch.

"We'll ship the horses to Chouteau or spot some Texas outfit to take them on to North Fork Town. Maybe we can go from Chouteau to North Fork Town by stage."

"What about your saddles?"

"We'll keep them with us. We wouldn't part with these saddles."

"I've got a friend at Fort Gibson," Slick says. He grins suddenly. "The Fort's a little off the road, but maybe you'll meet him. He's a captain—fought against me in the war. I told you about him. He's not a bad Yankee. Well, you boys hit the hay. We're still not out of Kansas, so if I decide, you can head east at sunup. Where'll you go first—Chetopa?"

"It's the last depot in Kansas."

"Hit the hay," Slick says. "I'll think about it."

We move off toward a tree-lined branch for a drink and a caucus. After we fill up, we hunker under a high-limbed cottonwood tree. A clamor breaks out in the wind-blowing sky. "Listen to those trumpeter swans go south," Ham said.

"They fly high," I said. "They really yell."

Scut said, "Scrape, what do you think about Slick?"

If I had teeth like that boy, I'd open a scissors factory. "I don't know," I said.

"The way his face lit up when he thought of that captain he fought, he got a new lease on life," Ham said.

"He's always cooking up something," Scut said. "In spite of his cold nature, he'd rather prank somebody than eat."

"He thinks pretty well of us," I said. "I heard that mentioned in Newton."

"Then maybe we'll go," Scut said.

We are standing beside the railroad track in Chetopa.

We'd chased across the Neosho River to spend a few days at Baxter Springs, the end of the old Shawnee Trail, and now we were ready to strike out through the Territory on the Katy—the Missouri, Kansas and Texas Railroad, or, as most folks called it, the Kansas and Texas, the KT or Katy. From seeing Texas cows, which had been driven up the Shawnee Trail to Baxter Springs, we'd come back to Chetopa and railroaders.

It was a booming town, full of track layers, graders, and bridge builders. Everyone in the country came to the depot to see the trains come in or take a first ride. Some of the civilized Indians from the Territory, the Cherokees and the Creeks, wearing black or gray suits and plug hats, or brush jackets and boots, waited with dark-eyed women and children beside important railroad officials. Bare-chested and broad-faced Osages stood under gaudy blankets, while some wore single feathers and leggings and deerskin. Cardsharps and shouting traders crowded the tracks, and soldiers and government men with portfolios—all going into the Nations on the Katy line.

Stacks of rails and barrels of spikes stood along the tracks. Behind the chunky locomotive and the wood-filled tender stretched a line of cattle cars. Then came the flatbeds packed with lumber and machinery and steam sawmills, crossties and rails, scaffolding and pulleys and bridge-building equipment. Other cars were being loaded with horses and mules to go South to work on the right of way. With the railroad in Chouteau now, maybe someday the Katy would load cows there for the North. And maybe later they'd ship cows from Texas. On down the track two passenger coaches and a red caboose brought up the rear of the long string, like three buttons on a rattlesnake's tail.

"Texas critters are in those cattle cars." Scut pointed. "Ain't that a life for a stocker! They've trailed all the way from Texas to Abilene and to the Mississippi at Hannibal and now they're being shipped back. They've got Old Man Wallum's brand. I was told his cowhands will pick them up in Chouteau. He's called the Mohair King, but he sure keeps his feet wet in cows."

"You won't hold Wallum back," I said.

"Not the way he took over your ranch," Ham said. "That's the good thing about having one ear. Now you can hear only half of what he says against you. You spoke out pretty hard about him."

We have just moved down the track to stand by the caboose, when the conductor comes out on its rear platform. This individual is tall and spare and wears a straight-sided cap with a stuck-out bill. The ends of his black bow tie extend under the lapels of a dark coat, which is set with gold braid. He jerks a high-horned white goat down the steps for an airing. The animal has been shut up with the potbellied stove, and as he leaves the caboose, wagging his whiskers, his smell is rank. He has an oblong tag tied around his neck. The conductor must be cold-blooded, because as he joins us along the tracks he is shivering even in the mild fall evening.

"What's that tag for?" Scut asked him.

"That's where he's going." The conductor was suspicious. He ties the goat to the upright handrail at the steps. He looks coldly at Scut, as if he didn't like anyone in the world and Scut least of all. He left the goat to join two slouch-hatted men who stood on the opposite side of the track beside a straw-stacked wagon.

"It's lucky that Texas outfit took our horses to North Fork

Town," Scut said. "With this crowd and the railroad stock, we'd never get them loaded. If the Katy hadn't put on an extra run tonight, we'd never get started ourselves."

"We got to eat before we start," Ham said. "We ain't had a bite since last time."

"Go to Booger Red's Emporium," one of the slouch-hatted men who had crossed the tracks said. "It's the best place in Chetopa." He tried to edge us away from the caboose. A scar was on his cheek, and a cloudy eye made him look as if he wanted to meet our gaze but couldn't. A black-handled Colt .45 stuck from his belt.

"Where is this place?" Scut said.

"Down by the livery stable. Get along now. How about watching those saddles for you?"

"We'll tote them," I said.

We found this eating joint, which was built all on top of itself the way a crow's nest in the top of a tree is, with logs and scantlings poking in all directions. The stack rested on built-up corner blocks of stone as high as stilts.

"Hey!" Scut said. "Looks like somebody feared a rush of water from the Neosho."

The shack had been protected against weather with split tin cans which had been flattened and nailed to the siding. We looked up at an extending red-painted sign—Booger Red's Emporium.

Ham said, "If those sticks beneath that sign cave in, we're dead."

"If they don't cave in, we've still got a chance," Scut said. "We ain't eaten yet."

We crossed a creaking porch and opened a leather-hinged door. Once within the Emporium, we saw a line of tables spaced along the floor. They were opposite the counters and smoky stoves, and occupied by shouting railroad workers. We could hardly stick a boot into that hubbub because of the thick aromatic wall of garlic and cabbage. In the center of the floor stood a table, filled on one side with a row of big-hatted heads bent over their platters, but half-empty on the other.

Three vacant chairs are between what must be some sort of a foreign priest, who wears a black robe, and another, who turns out to be a black-bearded Mennonite from Russia. We dump our saddles beside the chairs and sit down. The priests are talking to each other in four different languages, not one of which is English. The big Russian in his flat hat wants to start a Mennonite colony in Kansas. We get this information later from Booger Red, who can't speak even her own language well but still knows everything that happens on the Katy between Chetopa and Chouteau and back to Hannibal, Missouri. The men of the cloth continue their conversation. They lean forward and turn their faces to talk across us, then they lean back and talk behind our necks.

Now appears what in the better greasy-thumbs of the cowtowns is called the piece de resistance—two hundred and fifty big pounds of red-haired Booger Red. In the hubbub and shouting, we hadn't heard her approach. She glowers, her arms and cheeks floating with perspiration. A towel hangs from the middle of her bosom. The smell of chittlings and collards follows her like a cloud. Her hair stands on end.

She snaps, "You want the regular?"

"Sure." Ham takes her in. "Two helpings. What is it?"

She snorts. "Aw, go rope a calf."

"It wouldn't be you," Ham said. "How did you know we're cowhands?"

"I wonder," she says.

"Grunt and growl," Scut says. "You sure are cheerful to strangers."

"My back's broke. And I'm busier than a stump of ants at a pie supper. And don't heap more burdens on me."

She leaves when she gets our order, which is the same for everyone in the Emporium, and returns with a chipped yellow bowl of red chile peppers and garlic pods and red radishes and sliced white onions. Then she hands out three platters of steaming hot chittlings and collards.

"Pass me that garlic," Ham says to Scut. "It won't smell any worse than what's in these plates."

Booger snaps, "Eat and shut up. If I need advice on my cooking, I'll ask you."

"Hey!" Scut said to an ox-train freighter who sat across the table with his bull whip, "what's that other smell in here, that long and everlasting smell?"

"That's Booger's beer cheese," the freighter said. He shoved his weather-beaten and rain-stained black hat back. "Booger's cheese makes limburger turn up its toes. A steamboat from New Orleans came up the Arkansas and landed by Colonel Chouteau's old trading post down near the Three Forks—trading supplies for furs and pelts and salted pigeons. Booger got her share—sausage from the old countries, cheese and pickled fish, and smoked oysters. Went down there herself. First time the stuff ever came part way back by railroad. Up till now Booger's sent her own wagon. No one knows what this cheese is, but if you hold your nose, it ain't bad. We call it beer cheese. Beer helps it more than anything."

"You mean it hangs on outside, like it does in here?" Ham asked.

"It hangs on," the man said. "So much a coyote won't get near you. If you want to be safe on the Indian plains, smear up with Booger's beer cheese."

A railroader in a red plaid mackinaw and a gray toboggan cap sat beside the freighter.

"You sure rushed the Katy across Kansas," I said.

He looked up from his cabbage. "We beat the other lines, and that's what counted. The first railroad to reach the Cherokee border got the franchise across the Territory." With this pronouncement, he ducks his head back to his plate.

"You mean it was a race?"

He looks up, surprised at being interrupted again. "It sure was a race. One railroad didn't get started, and the other got lost and ended up on the Quapaw reservation. On one stretch we laid four miles of track in a day. But those times are over; it's rougher in the Territory. Too many hills, too many rivers. But once we reach the Arkansas, we'll stick close to the old

Texas Road. Buffalo helped lay out that trail. They've got more sense than people."

Booger Red stood close. She puts down three bowls of pinto beans cooked with garlic. "You still got any of that beer cheese left?" Scut said.

"Oh God and little fishes." Booger jerked on the towel to mop her face. "Yes, I got beer cheese. But you ain't had the main course yet. That foreign cheese is a delicacy."

"You got smoked oysters?" I said.

"What about those pickled fish?" Ham said. "Speak up now; we're loaded with that cowhand money you hate."

"I got pickled fish and some that ain't with their eyes left in, and some in special oil unheard of yet." Booger Red looks about at her clientele and scowls. "But you won't spark a girl with that on your breath. Now eat your supper. In my place I ain't proud of anemics."

Our next course was three heaps of boiled cabbage and salt pork and black-eyed peas smothered in garlic. Everything in this Emporium is in garlic. Next came a steak which was big enough to reconstruct a cow.

"Hey, Booger!" Scut shouts. She comes back from the wall tables. "Do you know anybody named Leviticus?"

"I knew a Levi in St. Louis," Booger says. "He ran a hock shop. But he warn't a Leviticus. He was a Ginsberg."

"That's the only word I've understood from those preachers," Scut says.

Just as the men of the cloth left, Booger brought beer cheese and smoked oysters and pickled fish and sardines. The utter fragrance of the beer cheese and smoked oysters killed off even our reminiscences of collards and chittlings.

"Hey!" Scut looked up. "Ain't you going to eat tonight?"

"Soon as they thin out," Booger said.

"Be sociable and sit with us," Ham said. "Bring your plate over."

"I don't trust Texans," Booger said. "So don't try tricks."

Still, she seemed pretty proud we'd asked her, yet all of a

sudden she sighed like a tired wind and went back to the stoves.

"She's worked to death by these railroaders," Ham said. "She's plumb worn out."

As soon as we began to battle the beer cheese and oysters, Booger came back with two forks and a plate of collards. While she ate, I said, "That railroad man told us you followed the Union Pacific gangs all across the plains to Utah to meet the tracks coming from the Pacific. You were there the day they met."

Booger looked up. Above their wrinkled pouches, her blue eyes brimmed. "I saw them drive the golden spike that joined the nation."

"You served meals clear across that buffalo land?" Ham said.

Booger put her forks down. "And through the high mountains. I moved my cook shacks and tents from Abilene and on to Colorado at Julesburg, and into Wyoming. When you wake on a sunny morning in a cook shack and fill your lungs with rolling black train smoke—that's living. Smoke's got a smell of its own. I'm married to train smoke." She looked about the crowded Emporium. "But I'm tired; I'm getting old. I've got to quit my travels."

"You followed the Katy here?" Scut said.

"I was here first," Booger said. "I started with the first crews and was here waiting. Yes, sir. I think I'll settle down." She pulled out the towel and held it to her face. "Do you want to see my spikes?"

"Sure," Ham said.

Scut paid for the supper with a double eagle. Booger stood up and went to the counter and brought back the change, along with a heavy cigar box. She sat down and opened the box, and Scut began to draw a few sets of overlength whiskers on the stern government faces which decorated the paper bills and shin plasters.

Booger took six spikes from the box. She held one up. "This

is from the first crossties ever driven in Kansas—the Union Pacific. I was dressed in a boa and ostrich feathers and saw the first rail made fast to the ties." She held up another spike. "This is from the hot plains." She had one from Julesburg and one from Cheyenne. Then simultaneously she held up the last two. "This is from the Union Pacific the day they drove the golden spike, and this is from the Central Pacific."

Scut stopped his art work. "You must be the mother of railroads."

Booger pressed the tip of the towel to her nose.

"You sure are sentimental," I said.

Booger said, "I gave my whole life to railroading. But now it's time to stop. There ain't many places left for the rails to go."

"Why don't you move to Texas? That's good country. Everybody's going."

"With that war over," Booger said, "they all go to Texas. They give up land they've got to get more land. I've thought of Texas. Maybe some quiet little place."

"You'll find little places," I said. "But they ain't quiet."

"Well, we've got to catch that rain." Scut stood up. "You've been mighty good to us," he told Booger. "I'm going to kiss you goodbye on your noble forehead."

"You've got nice spikes," Ham said. "If you get to Texas, look us up."

When we got back to the depot, it is dark and the lanterns were being swung back and forth, making the rails beneath the cars gleam. The big-horned goat was still tied to the caboose rail. While the engine whistled and the bell clanged, the two men who had waited by the tracks began carefully to move a stack of heavy boxes from beneath the wagon bed straw. They carried them toward the caboose and helped the conductor place them inside. They called the conductor Kurbstone.

He stalks around in his blue frock coat and straight-sided cap as important as the admiral of a ship. But as he came out to the platform each time, the glance he gave us over his hooked nose wasn't friendly. "Clear out," he said. "Go up to the cars. In five minutes we pull out."

"Most everybody up at the cars is standing in the aisles," Ham said. "There ain't room for our saddles. The brakeman said we'd ride back here."

"Then I'm busy. Clear out for now."

We moved over to get comfort from the goat. Scut said, "Ain't nothing like a billy in a thunderstorm. We should have brought him some oysters."

We felt pretty good about making our first train trip, but if the steam-seeping locomotive ever did get started, it would be after midnight before we reached Chouteau, about fifty miles south of the Kansas border and about ten from the old trading posts above Three Forks, where the Neosho and Verdigris flowed into the Arkansas near Fort Gibson. There'd be a lot of unloading along the way.

When Kurbstone passed again, I said, "Is some of this railroad equipment going to Chouteau?"

He frowned. "No, not much from this train. We'll unload the construction men and horses at Big Cabin and leave the equipment behind at different work camps."

Up the track there was a ruckus beside one of the lamp-lighted passenger cars. Someone had cut a strip of red plush upholstery from a seat, passing it through a window to a long-haired Osage Indian in buckskin britches. He wrapped it around his neck like a scarf. When the brakeman saw him, he lit out full gallop down the track. The passengers leaned from the coaches and cheered him on. Someone threw one of those newly invented self-righting spittoons from a window. It didn't go anywhere. It just sat beside the tracks, rocking back and forth in a contented way, while the Osage ran.

Once more the locomotive whistled from its diamond stack, its lighted nose glaring down the rails toward the Cherokee Nation. South of that land was the Creek Nation and then the Choctaws and Chickasaws. The Seminole land lay west of the

Creeks, between the forks of the North and South Canadians, but off the line of the railroad.

We heard the overhead cry again. "Listen," Ham said. "It's more of those old trumpeters. They sure want to get south. They put a real chill in my back."

"They'll beat us south," I said.

The swans passed on—unseen and lost—only the cry remaining above the glinting rails. Near the engine the brakeman gave a last wave of his lantern.

The conductor untied the goat. He said, "Help me. Put him in the caboose. Then get your saddles."

We shoved the rear end of the goat up the steps to the platform, the conductor in his gold-braided cap still cold and important. He sniffed the air and said, "What's that I smell?"

Ham was nearest him, so he said, "It's not me. It must be this goat."

Inside the red-painted palace of the caboose we saw what we would ride to Chouteau in. It had a bench along each side, with seat-separating curlicues standing straight up. A potbellied stove, with its tall pipe extending upward through the ceiling, sat on a steel pad in the middle of the floor, a pile of fire wood before it. A pigeonhole desk was near one side of the door, which led forward to the passenger cars.

The conductor tied the goat to a desk leg. We lowered our saddles to the floor and sat down. On the side of the door opposite the desk, the boxes from the wagon were stacked. The conductor looked at us and back to the boxes. He went over with a red pencil and wrote "Dynamite" on each one.

"With those explosives back here, what if this train hits something?" Ham said.

"We won't tell no one," Scut said.

While we waited for the train to start, we sensed there was no love lost between us and this conductor. He sniffs the air near the goat and studies us. He throws more wood in the red-hot stove, then stands by the door and watches us and the goat and the dynamite. At last he looks at a big gold watch he takes from a vest pocket. He reads it and goes out the back door and down the steps to swing his lantern back and forth toward the engine. Ham and I watch from the platform. Scut had gone up front to look at the dynamite boxes.

The train lurches like a sky-bucking horse, and Kurbstone swings on. As soon as the steel rails begin to click, he sits down at the desk and shoves his cap back to put some figures in a book. Scut stands up from the seat and sways across the caboose to look out a window. With the motion of the train, he walks like a drunk man. Ham and I lurch to the back again and look out at the vanishing rails over the railed-in platform between the rear lamps. We are as unsteady on our feet as Scut.

When we come back, Kurbstone is watching from his desk. "Haven't you ridden on a train before?"

"No, sir," Ham says. "We sure haven't. It's all new to us. How fast are we going?"

"Maybe fifteen miles."

"You mean an hour?" Scut says. "I never went that fast in my life."

"We'll make twenty before the night's over," Kurbstone said. "We could make twenty-five if we weren't loaded and didn't have the stops." He sniffs. "Something smells."

I look at Ham. "It ain't us," I said.

"I'm not so sure," Kurbstone said.

He gets up and throws more wood in the stove and goes through the door to take tickets up in the passenger cars. When at last he came back, a scream of wheels on steel jolted the train. We got off to see what the trouble was. We walked up the tracks to where a group of men with lanterns gathered beyond the first coach. The construction workers from one of the flatcars were loading a body in a blanket.

"What's the matter?" I asked Kurbstone.

"The fireman slipped and fell going back to the tender for wood. We'll take his body on to Chouteau."

"Where'll you pack him?"

"Up in the engine. It wouldn't do for passengers to see him. Some Indians are still afraid of railroads."

The train started and rattled forward. It stopped once more and we got off again. On up the track in the flickering light of a dozen bonfires a group of section hands worked with steel girders and timbers to strengthen the bridge which crossed Cabin Creek. The locomotive inched forward and went half across. The railroaders unloaded more supplies and equipment. Then the train jerked on, leaving the men and the dark water behind in the pool of light. So far, we hadn't seen any of the Territory except this creek and where a dead man had been pulled from beneath the cars.

After ten more miles, we stopped. This was at Big Cabin, which Kurbstone said because of the Katy had got a post office last month. Over southeast on the meandering creek which we had crossed earlier, Cabin Creek, Civil War battles had been fought and dead men and horses had floated downstream to the Neosho. But all we saw at Big Cabin was a lantern or two. Then we make out a few shacks and log cabins and tents. There'd been another washout, and more graders and equipment were put off the flatcars. Once more the locomotive puffed away. The red caboose swayed and clattered on toward Chouteau.

But in spite of Kurbstone's cold-bloodedness, or because of it, the red-hot stove and its crimson pipe began to bring out more and more the smell of our supper at Booger Red's. It magnified it. The sweaty garlic oozed from our hides, and the smoked oysters and cheese threw up a fog you couldn't see through. The goat might have smelled as bad, but we couldn't tell for sure because we were smelling each other.

Kurbstone sits green at the gills at his pigeonholes. We couldn't blame him; he didn't have a chance against us and the stove and the goat. He gives a sick look at the dynamite and goes up to the passenger cars.

We made another stop to unload equipment and started again. At last the door opens and Kurbstone enters. If he was green when he left, once he stepped back into the built-up atmosphere, he turned gray. "Get your saddles," he said. "Your station is next."

"With all these slowdowns, we're getting there mighty quick," Ham said.

"We've made good time." Kurbstone ran a finger under his collar.

We stood up from the seats and hoisted our saddles. The train slows, and Kurbstone sang out with his station call, as if all the passengers from the coaches were in the caboose. He opened the back door. A stiff north wind, which had sprung up, swept our hot faces. We moved across the platform and down the steps.

"Where is Chouteau?" I said.

Kurbstone said from the platform, "Right there—beyond the tracks."

"It doesn't have a depot yet?"

Kurbstone moved quickly down the steps and swung his lantern. The train jerked on, with him swinging aboard by the handrail. There we stand on the black right-of-way, seeing only the rear lamps growing smaller and a shower of locomotive sparks flying high in the wind ahead of the train.

"This is crazy," Ham said. "So is that conductor."

"Everyone planned to get off at Chouteau," I said. "It's the terminus. But nobody else is here. This ain't nothing but trees. There's not even a lantern."

"It's the black middle of a wilderness," Scut said.

But something happened. Down the tracks the wheels screeched. The train had stopped so many times since leaving Chetopa that the ride had become a nightmare. But now it had stopped again. "We blamed that conductor too soon," Scut said with relief. "Which goes to show you shouldn't blame anyone too soon." He shouldered his saddle and we set out down the tracks. "The town's that way. The engineer just undershot the first time."

As we clumped toward the caboose, the train left. We

halted, watching the glow of the lamps glide down the dark path of crossties.

"If that is Chouteau, there ain't lights there either," Scut said.

We saw something white ahead, but in the distance we couldn't make it out. "It could be a signpost," Ham said. We started out and at last we saw what the white thing was. It was that goat standing beside the track. He waited as patient as if he had known us all his life.

"That old rascal Kurbstone," Scut said. "He really did it. Leaving three cowhands and a goat. When he went up to the cars, he must have got word to the engineer."

"We don't smell any worse than his character," Ham said. "Was that why he put us off?"

"You guess," I said. "I don't know where we are, but I'll get a match. Look at that goat's tag and see where he's going. Maybe this is it."

In the spluttering sulphur flare Scut said, "This goat done ate up where he's going."

"Then we're all for it," Ham said.

"That old high-pockets got us," I said. "What will we do? We can't leave the goat. Somebody liked him, to ship him on the Katy. We'd better take him."

"And get hung for stealing him," Ham said.

"He can walk same as we," Scut said, hoisting his saddle. "If we don't meet some tomahawk-throwing Cherokees."

"We're among civilized Indians," Ham said. "Slick Pilifer told me these Cherokees still have the old treaty and war factions—the pins some of them wear and the ain't-got-a-pins—but most of them don't go for tomahawking and scalping. They've got their own outlaws and lighthorse police, and since the war the best ones just try to hang each other legal."

"Some of these lighthorse in the Nations stand you up and shoot you," Scut said. "Others hang you. It's according to the Nation. Some of the Cherokees let you kill your own self—by stabbing."

"Ain't that fun," Ham said.

"What are we doing," I said, "Walking or talking?"

We put out down the track toward Chouteau. We guess it's there somewhere. It was pretty rough walking on the crossties in cowhand boots, toting saddles, stumbling in the dark on the sides of the rough roadbed or walking between the rails, trying to space our steps on or between the ties while all about us wolves and night birds make their racket. Nothing's as hard on a riding man as setting a gait he's not used to—especially on foot. We learned it the hard way. We hubbed it until we felt we needed a wagon greasing and sat down on the tracks to rest.

"What happens," Scut said, "when dynamite ain't dynamite? What happens when it's whiskey?"

"Those two men and that wagon by the caboose," I said, "the ones that wanted to watch our saddles. Old Highpockets got us away from that caboose so he could load whiskey to bootleg in the Territory."

Ham stands up. He pulls the goat's white whiskers. "You don't smell too bad in this cold air. I'm going to name you Leviticus."

Chapter 2

WHEN WE WOKE UP next morning in the Territory, the sun was poking its head over a hill like a red tom-tom, but we were in a bad way.

Last night Scut had sprained his ankle stumbling over a half-covered crosstie and we'd helped him off the right of way to camp and built a fire in a hollow. It was damp from the fall rains, but it broke the north wind.

When we woke shivering like all get-out without blankets, heads on our saddles and feet to the fire, a dazzle of sun hit the yellow leaves of the hickory-nut trees, and a couple of foxes sat laughing at the edge of the hollow. If we'd had coffee and something to eat, it would have been a fine day, but we had nothing to start on. We didn't even have drinking water, except what trickled between two mossy green-colored rocks.

Ham and I took our bowie knives and hacked off a hickory

crutch for Scut. It was a straight pole with a crosspiece on top, but all of us knew we weren't going anywhere that day, or eating, either. Scut's ankle was swollen double, so we scooped out a hole between the rocks to form a cold pool for his foot. Then he'd warm it by the fire for a spell.

While we sat and watched him, a sudden roar swept the air like a blast of hard wind rising. Thousands of passenger pigeons swept into the trees in short flights, alighting on the limbs and cracking the drooping branches. They were gray-feathered and slim-necked and sleek, shimmering in touches of blue and rose and brown as the early sun struck them. Others walked in long waves across the ground searching for berries and seeds and insects. The back line would fly over another to eat, then at last they all came to rest in the trees.

When finally the roaring wind moved on, we had been desecrated by droppings. But now we saw what might have started the sudden departure. Scut pointed. Someone had ridden into the hollow—a big black-masked man on a black horse. The noise of the pigeons and cracking branches had kept us from hearing him. He pointed a cocked pistol at us.

"One at a time," he said, "drop your guns and shell out."

We stood and dropped and shelled. Over four hundred bucks—all our savings—all we'd made on that cow drive to Newton.

Ham hurt. He licked his lips. "You're Big Bill Cookson," he told the outlaw. "We saw you in Newton."

If Bill wasn't the best outlaw in the Territory, he was one of the best, along with Belle Reed and her hoodlums. "Sure, I'm Big Bill." Cookson chuckled. "Have you boys had breakfast?"

"We ain't had a bite," Scut said. "We were ready to shoot a pigeon when you came up."

"Don't get too close with that crutch." As Scut hobbled forward, Big Bill pointed his pistol. "You boys build up a fire. I got some good vittles at Booger Red's place in Chetopa last night." He threw down a roll of foreign sausage and a round loaf of black bread. From his saddle pockets he took a sack of eggs and bacon.

"I guess it doesn't mean anything to you," I said, "that we've been on a cow drive and we're hundreds of miles from Texas. You've got all our money."

"I'm buying your breakfast, ain't I?" Bill Cookson took off his mask. He needed a shave, but he was a good-looking and a good-natured sort of cuss. "Pick up those pistols and lay them by that red sumac bush."

Then he lumbered off his horse. He took a skillet and some old eating irons and a fire-blackened coffeepot from his pack. He gave them to Ham. He sat down with his back against a hickory tree. "You boys do the cooking. I'll rest. What's wrong with your foot?" he asked Scut.

"I got a sprain," Scut said.

"Go to my saddle pockets." Bill Cookson pointed with his pistol. "I've got a bottle of liniment."

"What do you do—drink it?" Ham said.

"I get an awful kidney ache sometimes. Too much riding. What's that outfit?" He pointed the pistol toward the goat.

"That's Leviticus," I answered. "We took up together on the railroad, then we got put off."

"I see saddles," Bill said. "Ain't you got horses?"

"We'll pick the horses up at North Fork Town, down in the Creek Nation; that is, if we can pay them out of the livery stable after this raw deal."

"You won't have trouble," Bill said. "Not smart boys like you."

"How about lending us five or ten dollars?" Scut looked up from rubbing his ankle with the liniment.

"Not a chance." Bill shook his head. "I waited thirty minutes in the trees, until those pigeons came, to move in on you boys. So long as I outsmart you, the money's mine. Why didn't you put a guard out? You could have plugged me."

"We didn't think about it," I said.

"All things ain't heaven in the Territory," Bill Cookson said. "Next time you'd better think, or you won't grow up."

That breakfast was something anyway, and now Bill sits on

his big horse, ready to leave, grinning and looking down at us. It's all nothing but a big joke to him. "Well, so long," he says.

"Here's this horse medicine." Scut holds up the bottle.

"Keep it," Bill says.

"If we meet your old mama walking up the tracks," Ham says, "we'll tell her about your ailing back. Where'll we say you're going?"

"Tell her down around North Fork Town," Bill says. "I might camp out with Belle Reed's boys for awhile. Belle is sympathetic to men like me."

After riding about a hundred yards through the trees he drops our guns to the ground. Ham and I go after them and when we come back, Scut says, "I want a bath."

We went down to a branch below the hollow and stripped off on the bushy bank. "Who's standing guard?" Ham asks.

"Nobody," I say. "All we've got to lose now is personality."

There was a rock bottom in the deep water and we were scrubbing up pretty well when with my good ear I hear these near-by giggles. I ease to the bushes, and up there, kneeling on the bank, are the three prettiest dark-eyed girls I ever saw. They had bright devilment shining on their laughing faces while they gathered our clothes into bundles. I gave a shout and in a trail of laughter all three ran away. We came out of the branch and what we had left on the bank were three pairs of boots.

"Scrape," Ham said, "you're the smart one. No, we won't stand guard; we just got personality left. Well, they almost got that."

Now we are in a pickle. Those three civilized little Cherokees are laughing fainter and fainter off in the distance, and all we can do is sit or stand, or sit.

"We ain't walking a railroad track dressed this way," Scut said. "Not me and this crutch. We might meet Bill Cookson's mama."

"I'm not sitting in boots all day," Ham said. "I saw basket weavers work in San Antone. I'm making some clothes."

A heavy growth of rushes stood in the shallows, so we

waded in and did our gleaning. Soon Ham turned out three knee-length skirts. The only thing was—he'd started his work by tying one long rush around our middles and had built the garments on us, and once dressed—we couldn't get out or in.

We skulked back to the hollow. We didn't have anything left to eat for the day but half the foreign sausage Bill Cookson left us and, after our eating binge in Chetopa, we didn't want it.

Scut said, "Scrape, trouble sure hangs 'round your door."

"All three of us are in this. It ain't just me."

"We've sure seen the Cherokee country," Ham said. "One creek and a hollow."

To the south we heard a locomotive whistle wail. "Do we want to flag that train back to Chetopa?" Scut said.

"No," I said. "Not dressed like this. I've got respect for humanity."

A medium-sized dark man strode into the hollow. He was middle-aged and wore buckskin pants, a red flannel shirt, and a brush jacket. In one hand he carried a slungshot, and from the other half-a-dozen dead squirrels dangled by their tails. The man's hair was long and glossy black, sweeping down to his shoulders. He came straight to us and held up the slungshot hand in greeting.

"How, John. How, John."

Scut stood up on his crutch. "What's this John business?"

The Indian laughed. "Aren't all white men called John by Indians?"

"What game are you playing?" I said. "Are you a Cherokee? You must be pretty good with that slungshot."

"It takes practice," the man said. "I'm Willard Law."

Scut said, "Our names don't matter."

Willard Law glanced at our raiment. "What is this?"

"We don't know yet," Ham said. "We were swimming at the creek and somebody stole our clothes and guns."

"Railroad workers?" Willard Law asked. "There's a construction camp down the tracks."

"Girls," I said.

A sharp gleam came to Willard Law's eyes. "Girls?"

"Three little Indians."

"How old were they?"

"About fourteen. Pretty as pictures—one especially."

"H-m-m," he said. "I'm just walking around today. Want to come with me?"

"In these get-ups?" Ham said. "Even as hungry as I am, I wouldn't be caught dead in a grocery store."

"Come on," Willard Law said. "And bring your saddles. No one will see you. I've got a visit to make down the creek. Where did you get the goat?"

We told him. He laughed. "Maybe I can help find your clothes."

It wasn't until he started along the bank that we knew him for what he was. He wore moccasins and without appearing to try, he moved surely and silently, stepping on flat rocks or on certain soil where no trail was left, or twisting his body to avoid trembling a leaf on a tree branch. Being middle-aged didn't hinder his sureness. Sometimes we'd catch his eyes on the trees, and there would be an owl or a nighthawk on a limb.

"Do you know the nighthawk?" he says. "It's kin to the whippoorwill family. The nighthawk doesn't sit across the limb; it sits lengthwise with it."

The trail wound beneath sycamore and oak and ash and cedar, their leaves changing color, the green of the cedar duller or purple with berries, now that fall had come. "Did you ever know a Cherokee?" Willard Law said.

"Not directly," I said. "We know Comanches and Kiowas better. When she was a girl, my great-grandma got scalped by Cherokees back in Carolina. But she lived to raise a good family—twelve kids it was. She wore a lace cap on her head and always sat by the fireplace with a cup of tea. I've heard tell of her."

"There's no more of that," Willard Law said. The wind blew the black hair about his shoulders. "It was bad enough among our own people during your last war. Nation turned against nation and family against family. I know what it was. I killed a Cherokee in battle. I found his body later—my own brother."

"Who'd you ride with?" Scut asked.

"Stand Watie. The best of the Cherokees, the last general to surrender the Confederate flag. Yet I'm glad it's over. There must be a better way for all men."

We came to a clearing which opened across the creek. Beyond the narrow, swift-flowing water an old man and a woman sat before a log cabin. They wore blankets about their shoulders and sat in rocking chairs under a big pecan tree. "My father and mother," Willard Law said. "They could live with me, but they like the old home place. They found it after the Trail of Tears, when we were driven from the South."

"You don't expect us to go over there?" Scut said. "Not dressed this way."

He said, "Wait here. I want to take them the squirrels." When he came back, he said, "Let's go to my place."

We walked down the creek, then cut over a hill to a wide flat valley. Below the hill a large white house sat among the trees, the outbuildings painted white and the smooth furrowed fields of the farm filled with high corn shocks and yellow pumpkins. The tree lines of an orchard spread beyond the house. Cattle ranged on a distant prairie.

"Those cows aren't longhorns," I said. "What are they?"

"It's a small herd. High on Durham blood. And I run some blacks with them."

"We've got Durham upgrades in Texas, but they don't look that good."

"When we get lunch, we'll ride out. Today there's a roundup in the district. We'll tally about noon. Are you good tally men?"

"Slick Pilifer lets us help," I said. "If you get by Slick, you're passable."

"Maybe we'll use you—to keep down suspicion on the part

of the factions. It's best to have a few outsiders help as tally men."

"I ain't counting brands in these clothes," Ham said.

"We'll get your clothes," Willard Law said.

"Have you got a brand book?" I said.

"Here." He reached into the side pocket of his brown brush jacket. The book was red and leather bound.

"I can't make head or tail of this writing," I said.

"Did you ever hear of Sequoyah?"

"No."

"He was one of our people. He invented our alphabet before we were dispossessed in Georgia. You're trying to read Cherokee. Don't pay attention to the writing, watch the listed brands."

"What about those clothes?" Scut asked. "And my ankle's hurting. Even in this sun I've got chilblains."

We are standing by a good-sized plum thicket, its leaves all orange or yellow or lost in the early autumn. Again that queer expression of laughter and keenness lurks in Willard Law's eyes. The wind blows his black hair. "I'll get your clothes," he says. "Wait here."

We watched him go to the farm house. After about fifteen minutes he came from the wide door and walked to an outbuilding. He came out with three bundles. He went to the well house and came out with another.

When he joined us, he put down the bundles, saying, "Get your clothes on. I've brought a sack of steaks and we'll eat before roundup time. Today the sun's on my back. I want to eat outside." He wore rough boots now instead of moccasins, and a wide-brimmed slouch hat.

"Those must have been your girls," I said.

"Two of them are. The other's my niece. They're students at our Park Hill Seminary. They're on vacation for a week and all are kicking their heels up."

"Whose is the prettiest, the one with the longest and blackest hair?"

"She is mine."

"What's her name?"

"It's not her name, but in our language we call her Moonlight."

"Then take a good look at me. When I grow up, you might have a one-eared son-in-law."

Willard Law laughed, "You'll have to ask her."

After we ate, a slightly built Cherokee from the farm drove four horses to the plum thicket. One was saddled and the others had extra blankets on their backs. We threw our saddles on and got ready to ride.

"You were talking about a construction camp," I said. "How far is it?"

"About a mile south."

"We'll go there about sundown," I said. "If they run a special tonight, maybe we can flag it for Chouteau."

"Why don't you stay with me?"

"We might get in trouble with those females," Ham said.

"It's not likely," Willard Law said. "I locked them in their rooms. They'll stay there until morning."

"We've got to get on to North Fork Town and our horses," I said.

We rode toward the westering cow dust and the galloping horsemen. "Man, this is living again," Scut said.

We put in an afternoon's work at the branding fire, Ham and I helping Willard Law as tally men while Scut sat his horse and rested his ankle. Ulysses Sandys, one of the other faction from down near Chouteau, was at the fire, too, helping to tally. He was a light-complected man, broad-shouldered and suspicious of everyone.

The Cherokees were reckless riders, cutting cows and calves and yearlings out of the one big herd and, after what necessary branding and doctoring was done beside the fire, driving them toward their own individual brand group. When we finished work and the prairie was clear of cows, the roundup chuckwagon put out toward the railroad.

We rode back to the wide yard of Willard Law's house to leave his horses. "Won't you stay with us tonight?" he asked. "My wife would like to meet you."

"No, sir," I said. "We've got to go on. When the chuck-wagon comes by, we'll hop a ride to the construction camp. Maybe we can catch the night train."

We hadn't told him about Bill Cookson, since we didn't want him to know we were flat broke and have him offer help. Once more the giggles of the creek sounded and I looked up to see three girls laughing down from a second-story window.

Willard Law frowned. "You see how fruitless my punishment is."

The girls moved farther back from the window. There was more laughter, then singing.

> "Like Roses bright we hope to grow,
> And over our home such beauty throw
> In future years—that all may see
> Loveliest of lands,—the Cherokee."

"What's that song?" I asked.

Willard Law was laughing. "One of their school verses."

"Remember," I said, "I might ride back some day. Good-by."

"Sta la," he said. "We say good luck."

We were up early next morning to set out down the track. There hadn't been a night train, so we managed to get put up in the railroad construction camp by washing pots and pans for the cook. In return we were given a dipperfull of mulligan stew, a slice of stale bread, and some sour hashed-brown potatoes which weren't brown but only sour. We slept in a blowing tent, covered with a pile of tow sacks.

Two plank shacks stood near the right of way. Last night they had been filled with liquor drinkers, gamblers, Indian girls, and cow-town and railroad touts. Outside of one drunk man getting kicked on the head by a mule, two brawls, and a knifing, nothing happened.

The new morning in which we are standing on the tracks is so dewy it looks as if the whole world is dripping, with every gay bird in the high trees singing its praises. Overhead, the wide-winged bald eagles soar. Everything sparkles in the sun like a million blinking eyes. The steel rails are wet and shiny.

"What will we do?" Scut asked. "Stand here and wait for the noon train?"

"Let's hoof it," I said. "I don't want another railroad hand-out."

"We're close to the Three Forks country," Ham said. "Flat broke and no future. Those old trading posts are down near the mouth of the Verdigris; maybe we can get a job unloading beer cheese."

We gave a look down the narrowing rails and hoisted the saddles and struck out. After a mile a flock of yellow turkeys walked toward us. "Looks like we can eat," Ham said.

"Not this boy," I said. "They won't hang me for killing a Cherokee turkey."

"Willard Law was talking about yellow turkeys," Ham said. "When the Yankee soldiers raided down in the Creek Nation, they caught a big flock and picked them on horseback. The Texas Road was yellow-feathered."

"How far are we from the Road?"

"That one-eyed cook said it's five or six miles east."

"Let's hit the timber and strike east. On the Road we might catch a covered wagon to ride in, or meet somebody with extra horses. It may take longer to reach Chouteau, but it will beat counting crossties."

"Give Leviticus a shove," Scut said. "He's stalled by turkeys."

We got off the right of way and walked through the bright trees. Now and then in clear shady pools we saw blue herons and snowy egrets standing, and there was always a deer or some other animal close by. After an hour's walk in the balmy air we got pretty thirsty.

We go down to a bold spring in a hollow and all three of us stretch flat out to drink. Our heads pop up and we look at each other over the water, as knot-eyed as three frogs at a special committee meeting.

"It's salty," Scut says.

"Sure," I say. "Look where salt dried on the rocks. This is a salt lick. Ain't it funny what salt does for a place—how it helps open a country. I heard that Indians and traders went to Chouteau's place to load salt hot from the kettles. Folks from Kansas and Missouri and Arkansas and all the way through the Territory used this salt."

It was relaxing to do nothing after a cow drive, in spite of our setback in the Territory, so we decided to sit a spell by the spring and take things easy. We cracked pecans and walnuts on the rocks and listened to the whistle of the faraway train. After an hour we were getting ready to move on toward the Texas Road when we heard voices. Horses trotted through the trees.

We thought the riders might come to the hollow, so we stood up. But they went on without either side seeing the other. We left the lick and after a mile walk through the trees, we came to a clay-chinked log house in a clearing. An old, dried-up Indian in a shapeless black hat sat on the porch between two yellow dogs. He was eating potato cakes, which he shared with us. They were made of corn meal and sweet potatoes. His face was wrinkled like an old persimmon.

The turkeys had followed us through the woods. Now they flew to the roof of the cabin. "Why do they walk that railroad track?" Ham asked the old man.

"They never see train before. They go every day. After engine pass, they come home. Two men from that train here to look for you."

"Us?" Scut said. "When?"

"Just now—they ride off."

"They must have been on the horses we heard," I said.

"Can we get a drink?" Scut asked. "The water in most of these springs is salty."

The Cherokee got up and led us behind the cabin to a well.

He had some drinking gourds hanging on the upright supports of the pulley beam, and a wooden bucket hung at the end of a rope suspended halfway down. A V-shaped, hand-rived ash hopper stood near by, the lye from the watered ashes dripping into clay pots.

"How do you know those men meant us?" I asked.

The Indian shrugged. "They want three boys with three saddles and white goat!"

We pulled the bucket up and dipped the gourds. "What do they look like? Do you know them?"

The Indian nodded. "One rides in little red wagon at end of train. The other cooks at railroad camp."

"You mean a one-eyed man?"

"Yes. They want you because you steal goat."

"We didn't steal this goat. The conductor put all of us off the train. We've been walking ever since."

"We'd better think this out," Scut said. "What do you make of it?"

Ham said, "It's got me beat. I don't know what Kurbstone is trying to pull." He asked the Indian, "Can Cherokees hang us for stealing a goat? The Katy will have the whole army after us."

"Another man laugh about you. He stay here last night."

"Who?" Scut said.

"He laugh at money you give him."

"We didn't give anybody money. Man, we ain't got a penny. We're flat broke. We live on the charity of the land—potato cakes, pecans, and yarbs."

"He make big laugh at whiskers you put on man." The Indian pulled a grubby five-dollar bill from his pocket.

"I'll be," Scut said. "I decorated that five-dollar William in Booger Red's place, along with the shin plasters. That skunk Bill Cookson hides out with you," he told the Indian.

"Him good man. Him live on charity, too."

"What are you going to do?" Ham asked. "Tell people we've got this goat? The goat didn't matter to Bill Cookson."

"Let's get out of here quick," I said. "Hit the Texas Road and head south. It's a good thing we didn't wait for the train this morning."

"How long have you lived here?" Ham asked the Indian.

"Almost always. Since we left the old home. I see many suns come over these old hills—many moons."

Scut said, "Have you ever been out again?"

"Sure. Many time to Pittsburgh."

"You mean Pittsburgh, P-A."

"Yes. Up by Cincinnati. Pittsburgh big smoke town. Factories make good salt kettles. We needed many kettles at Chouteau's salt works."

"Good Lord," Scut said. "How'd you ever get to Pittsburgh?"

"Steamboats and flatboats. Go with men from salt factory down the Neosho. Make trip back down Ohio and Mississippi and up Arkansas to Fort Smith. Then have bad times, river up in big flood, have to bushwhack."

"What do you mean, bushwhack on a river?"

"Poles no touch bottom. Catch bushes and tree branches on bank—pull boats back."

"I'd rather make a cow drive," Ham said.

"You want conihani—hominy?" the old man asked.

"We've got to go," Scut said.

We left the old Cherokee sitting on his porch and struck on east at a good pace. After a mile or so we heard an up-and-down howl and screech that was weird enough to wake the dead. Scut's hot face grinned in relief. "Well, we made the Texas Road. But that wagon sure needs greasing."

Another hundred yards brought us to the road. But before going into the open we looked out cautiously from the trees. We didn't want to go too far all at once and have Kurbstone and the cook ride lickety-split upon us.

The road was about a hundred yards wide, but toward the north and south it broadened to several hundred yards. This far up in the Territory it was part of the old Trace the Osage

Indians from the Three Forks country had used to carry their furs and pelts to St. Louis before the time of the French and the other traders who later set up at the Verdigris landing, and before the civilized Indians came west.

Some of the ruts of the road were knee-deep. And we later learned that the very ruts had made the road wide. When they got too deep for travel, teamsters had driven their oxen or horses or mules to one side and cut new ones. Then the old ruts filled up and in time the road was back where it started, after wandering all over to the tall trees on the opposite sides, or starting once more from the middle.

This creaking covered wagon passed on, pulled by two half-starved mules, its tar bucket under the rear axle swinging empty. Behind the wagon, a line of big-hatted freighters with their popping bullwhips strode beside their ox-drawn wagons.

"Doggone," Ham said. "Look at those sheep."

Coming up from the south, from Texas, it seemed that a cotton crop moved—thousands of white sheep. The shaggy sheep dogs ran over their bunched backs, or ahead to sit and wait, while others stayed behind to nip at the broadened drag. Following the sheep a lean herd of Texas longhorns plodded, the cow-wise point riders of the long line dusty and sure and sweat-streaked. On the road beyond the strung-out big-horned herd, the heavy cow dust hung above other covered wagons headed south.

"I've seen what my old man did," I said. "He and Ma came down this road from Baxter Springs in a wagon when I wasn't a riffle in a whirlwind. Then he drove cows back north. He must have been a fair cowhand."

"Great Lord!" Scut said. "Think what it must have been when those early settlers went to Texas before it was Texas. Only then they drove sheep and cows and hogs south—now these herders drive north."

"Thousands of wagons. This poor old road. The devil himself couldn't plow it deeper."

"The railroad will end it," Scut said.

"I don't see old Highpockets," I said. "So let's put out."

"Sure," Scut said. "But look at those horses."

We'd been watching for Kurbstone so hard we hadn't noticed what stood almost beside us. Under a heavy stand of red and yellow oaks were three well-kept black horses. "They're not tied," Ham said. "They must have run off."

"Look at the brands," I said. "They must belong to Ulysses Sandys, that pin-faction Cherokee who was at the branding fire with Willard Law."

"Scrape, you old rat," Scut said. "You see daylight. We'll take these horses to Chouteau and maybe Ulysses will give us some eating money."

"Then throw that crutch away. Hold Leviticus. I'm going to them."

The horses stood steady, and in no time they were under our Texas saddles. We didn't have bridles or blankets, since they'd been sent on to North Fork Town with our own nags, but we mounted up and moved out on the Texas Road with Leviticus. We felt mighty good again, on horses once more, all trouble behind.

"Willard Law is a fine man," Scut said. "We met some fine people."

"He was educated at a college in Tennessee," Ham said.

We didn't see Highpockets as the horses trotted down the crowded road, so we stopped a covered wagon which was beyond the creaking one and asked the man if he would wait and give the other wagon some tar. Its cry hung over the road as discordant as a whooping crane's. The man said he'd have stopped earlier if only he'd known where the howl came from, but in the still air it sounded from one direction as much as from another, until he thought a dozen wagons or every wagon on the road needed greasing.

Soon we were joined by the other wagon and its driver. He looked frazzled and worried. His wife wore a faded sunbonnet. She was frizzle-haired and anemic. "How far is it to Texas?" the man asked as he climbed down.

"What place in Texas?" Ham said.

"The first stop. I ain't heard nothing from this woman but Texas in five years. How far is it to Red River?" He walked with the other driver to the full tar bucket. "That's a fine goat you've got."

"His name's Leviticus," I said.

"From the Bible, I take it."

"It's from the Bible."

That wife stuck a six-foot neck around the side, and so did a five-year-old boy. "Now, that's nice. I allus said—boy, how come you've got only one ear?"

"A cow chewed it."

"Oh, mercy!" the woman said.

We left the two drivers and rode on and passed more wagons and freighters and met more late Texas herds driving north, heading for Baxter Springs. The road ran between dense trees and hills, or now and then dipped to splotches of wide prairie. The balmy air still clung like a soundless bell, and the road angled nearer to Chouteau.

Then after a couple of hours we heard behind us the gallop of onrushing horses. We turned in our saddles, suspecting anything, fearing Highpockets and the cook, but instead we saw six soldiers with their pistols drawn and pointed and that old potato-cake Cherokee.

They rode upon us like gale-driven leaves. When the Army chased after cowhands, it didn't fool around—not with those pistols over their horses' necks. Seeing the old Cherokee, our first thought was that they had come for the goat.

But before we knew differently, we were prisoners.

Chapter 3

SO MUCH BAD LUCK had dogged us since we left Chetopa that, after our artillery had been taken from us by the soldiers, we couldn't do anything but sit in the saddles dumfounded.

Willard Law, when he told of the nighthawk, had laughed about a race of little people the Cherokees had brought with them to the hills. They were about two feet tall. They hid among the trees and on the bluffs, sometimes prankish and sometimes ornery. They rolled rocks down on fishermen, making them leave the creeks or move downstream, and at night they sat in the hills and held council around logs of fox-fire. Any man with common sense wouldn't put any truck in this talk, but with all that had happened to us in this Nation, I was ready to believe it now.

So we are sitting here on this thoroughfare to the South,

hands and arms high in the air, being surrounded by covered wagons whose drivers all pull up to see the show, with half a dozen slack-mouthed sheep herders joining in. This slant-eyed, hook-nosed captain is reining his horse by quick jerks to place him head-on to ours to watch us eye to eye. He wears a black hat with one side of the brim turned up. His coat is blue and wide yellow stripes run down the outside of his britches to his thigh-high boots.

"Well," he says, looking us over. "Do we hang you now?"

"Listen," Scut said, "you're as bad as an outlaw. You got to have charges against us. We want a habeas corpus to get out of this."

"You'll get out at a rope's end." The captain took off his gauntlets and began to beat them on his right leg.

Ham said to the old Indian, "You sure double-crossed us. We thought you were our friend."

"No double-cross," the old Cherokee said. "For many years I scout for Army. We look for stolen horses. We ask people on road. They say come this way."

"You can just keep going," I said. "We're taking these horses to Ulysses Sandys at Chouteau. We worked with him. These horses have his brand—U. S."

This captain and his men begin to laugh. "That U. S. means United States," the captain says. "You're running off with U. S. Cavalry horses."

"You mean these don't belong to Ulysses Sandys?"

"They don't. They were ridden off by three deserters from Fort Gibson. Now, where did you help those soldiers go? What did they give you?"

"Listen," Scut said, "you talk like a crazy man. The last thing I want to do is get mixed up with the Army."

"From now on," the captain said, "whether you like it or not, you're in the Army. Let's get on to Chouteau," he told his men. "We'll make the Fort tomorrow."

So here we are, riding down the Texas Road, surrounded by an armed guard, and it's really armed. But our big worry is to be caught riding into Chouteau with Leviticus. If Kurbstone saw us, there wouldn't be a chance to escape him—not with this army about us. We rode pretty morose. The captain and three soldiers rode first, then the Cherokee and I, Scut and Ham, and the rear was brought up by two privates. About the only taste we had for the Texas Road was the dust in our mouths.

The captain's name was Jamison. At last he turned off the road to cut through the woods to Chouteau. A quiet rustle swept through the trees and a few leaves fell. Then a whipping wind began to howl out of nowhere, hard and gusty even in the shelter of the woods. It was getting late in the day and the shadows darkened. Far beyond the tree trunks we glimpsed the campfires at the Chouteau terminus. A few weeks ago no town at all had been here. At last we neared the leaping fires.

Along the right of way and running back to the cleared tree lines, were the two rag towns—the collection of tents and tarps and plank and log shacks. The fires blazed before the tents, the red sparks flying. Captain Jamison slapped a gauntlet on his leg. "The fools! They'll burn the town. Look! Some of the tents are smoldering." Even as he spoke, people scurried about with buckets to throw water on the flames.

We made our way through the rag town on our side of the tracks and rode between two plank shacks. One served as a depot, with a lantern swinging outside. It was lighted inside by two lamps. On ahead stood the mess shacks for the construction crews. Piles of railroad equipment, lumber and implements, and stacks of rails and crossties lay cluttered along the right of way.

Then as we rode, the captain became silent. He no longer talked to the soldiers or spoke in confidence to his sergeant. In almost a few moments—so quickly it happened—he seemed to slump in his saddle, his head lowered as if in thought. We rode down the track and came to a long open shed with a broad platform across the front. The interior was filled with army supplies. A few soldiers loafed about inside and two others stood guard with their rifles at the open door.

The captain dismounted. He climbed to the platform and went inside. In a few moments he came back. "We'll eat in their mess." He walked on down the track, leading his horse, the rest of us riding behind him.

The soldiers climbed down at a bare-fronted shanty. We prisoners didn't know whether we'd be shot or starved to death before we were hung, so since we hadn't been given an order, we stayed put. "Get down," the captain snapped. His slant eyes looked us over. "What the devil do you do with this goat?"

"You can't hang us double for him, can you?" I said.

Inside the shanty a mess table stood. This dining room was ventilated on the north and south by someone having propped up the opposite hinged ends of the plank walls. A bald-headed blue-eyed cook in greasy underwear tops stood with his belly hanging over a coal-oil stove.

"What you cooking?" Scut said.

"You got any beer cheese?" Ham asked.

The captain said to the cook, "If I caught you at the Fort in this condition, you'd wear a ball and chain for a week."

Now that he was back in an army bailiwick with someone else to boss, he seemed to be what must have been his old self again. He slouched about, putting his forefinger on every plank and pot and pan in the place, hoping to find dust, but the way sand and gravel blew through the open ends, the man didn't live who could tell if he did or not.

But the slouch he walked in—it wasn't what you'd call a slouch, it was a quick nervous movement, with one shoulder going out first and then the other—the dark face and hooked nose made him look like a bird of prey. But the queer slant of his eyes put something else in his face and made him look human. He was under some sort of pressure, but he was so much a handbook officer about not eating with his men that he stood up to eat alone when we were served our own army grub and sat in luxury at the splintery mess planks, with a garbage bucket at one end.

We had a sumptuous military repast—hardtack, a gluey pock-marked spud boiled in its hide, a slice of half-burned, curled-up sowbelly, black beans and rocks, and brown coffee grounds simmered in a spoonful of hot water.

"Hey!" Scut said to the cook. "You got any scraps left? We got a goat outside."

"I got more of what you ate."

"Well, his stomach should be as strong as ours. Fix up a batch—double on the hardtack."

"Did you like that coffee?"

"Sure," Scut said. "Where did you dig it? Give us a boilerful. It's a bad windy night for a goat."

The captain put his empty plate on the table. "Where's your pistol?" he asked the cook. The cook turned and took a gun from a shelf. "Guard them." The captain pointed to us. He called his men outside.

"What are those quartermaster supplies in the other shack?" I asked the cook.

"It's a new plan they figured out in Washington." He pointed his pistol at us. "They're always figuring. They figure one way one day and another the next. From now on supplies for the Western forts will be shipped on the Katy to the last terminus, then freighted. Fort Gibson and Fort Smith are closing down—that's part of a big economy move by Congress. They're figuring too, like the Army."

"Good Lord," Ham said. "I've heard of those forts all my life. Now they are going."

"Nothing in the Territory will be the same with the railroad," the cook said. He opened his underwear top to scratch his hairy belly button. "Even these Indians will change. This terminus is already loaded with touts and gamblers and the hardest outlaws in the West—Indians, whites, and freed Negroes—brawling and drunk. Two men killed last night. A few dance-hall women have been smuggled in from the Kansas cow towns, and some of what you might call renegade Indian girls, picked up mainly by gamblers and bootleggers. It's going to be hell and high water hereabouts. You can say good-by to the Territory. You know those old trumpeter swans?"

"Yeah," I said.

"They're getting fewer each year. They go south with the railroad. It's about over out here."

The toothless old Cherokee sat before his uneaten hardtack. "The swan, the pigeon, the prairie chicken—they all go. The deer goes—everything goes—only same moon comes up. Only same winds blow."

"They'll bring the Army back," the cook said. "Sooner or later. The Indian lighthorse can't control these whites. Already they howl for free land. The railroad makes it theirs."

"Don't you want a home?" Ham asked.

"I got a home right here," the cook said. "But it ain't the old army."

"A hundred years from now," Scut said, "all you soldiers will still be howling about the old army. It just goes back to what you were brought up in."

The big-chevroned sergeant came in the door. He gave us a real Kurbstone look. "You boys will be kept in a shed tonight. You'll have a bucket of water and blankets. Let's go."

"We ain't fed our goat yet," Scut said.

"Take him with you, or leave him outside."

"We'll take him," I said. Being shut up for a night even with a goat was good news. Being kept in a guardhouse would be the best way of missing Kurbstone, if he was here.

"What are you brave soldiers doing tonight?" Ham stuck out his chin. "Going to hear Jenny Lind at the opera house?"

The sergeant said, "Us brave and fearless soldiers are patrolling these tracks till daylight. Our noble captain has even called upon the supply boys to shoulder their big pencils to help. There were killings over half-breed dance-hall girls and card games last night, and once more it's stacking. The Cherokee lighthorse shouldn't be asked to handle this mess. But the pigeon brains in old D. C. don't think of that. Now, let's go."

We went out into the wind. On either side of the long rail lines the yellow lanterns swayed from the fronts of the distant shacks, a moving flicker which stretched in the dust almost as far as we could see. Yells sounded, and far people moved. In the rag towns a tent burned, and then another. A shadowy group of riders passed the shack, moving toward the lights. "Cherokee lighthorse," the sergeant muttered.

We are led from the tracks to this place of detention, and after sleeping under tow sacks last night at the construction camp, the wool army blankets are welcome.

That bald-headed cook knew something. A wool blanket meant home.

"Listen," I said to the captain when we reached the Texas Road next morning on our way to Fort Gibson. "We didn't steal these horses. Why don't you keep them and let us go? What good does this do you?"

"I represent the government," Captain Jamison said. His eyes were circled darkly from no sleep, and so were his soldiers'. "Listen to me, son. You're a cowhand. You have your own brand. I represent the U. S. brand."

"I always heard that the Army was the servant of the people, not the master."

"In your case that's what a court-martial will decide."

"It sure will," Scut said. "A kangaroo court."

"I will have nothing to do with that," the captain said. "Nor will the Army. It will be a fair trial."

We rode most of the morning down the Texas Road through a bright land of rolling woodlands, the wind hard and beating, the weary heads of the freighters' oxen and the teams of the covered wagons moving always southward. "You know what I'm thinking?" Ham asked.

Scut said, "I didn't know we had anything left to think with."

"I'm thinking how quiet it was in that hollow on Willard Law's place. How quiet this old Cherokee was when we found him. Then, wham! All we came to is death and destruction."

"It ain't over," I said. "Don't get your lip down."

"You got long time to live," the old Cherokee said. "They take you to Fort Smith for trial."

"How do you know that?" Ham said.

"I go, too—big witness about these horses. Then government men want to know what I think of railroad in Territory, and Comanches and Kiowas on the plains. Maybe I go to Washington to see big Congress people—big White Father want me."

"You sure run this country," I said.

"I run nothing no more. Everything go 'round and 'round. Whole country after war one big mess. Before war, one big mess. Always one big mess. Always a treaty. In old days Indian lose coat, then treaty again. Lose shirt, then one more treaty. This time lose pants. Some day they give our land to white men or wild tribes."

"What happens to those dogs you left at home?" Scut asked.

"They run into hills."

"How do you get them back?"

"Blow big old horn three times. Then here they come."

"If I was you," Ham said, "I'd just sit on that porch and pray for rain."

"Rain no come again. Railroad stop it—evil spirit. Big cloud and rain come to other side of tracks but stop there."

"Now, listen," I said. "You don't mean that two steel rails—"

Captain Jamison jerked his head toward us. "Yes, that's exactly what he does mean. Leave the old man alone."

"Yes, sir! Captian, sir!" Scut said.

The captain stopped his horse and turned. His dark eyes flashed. The sergeant and the privates got as tight-faced as five drum hides.

"Son, what's your name?"

"You're a long time asking for it. That must be the army in you. My name's Scut Benton, and I smell like a cowhand and a goat. My boss is Slick Pilifer."

"Slick Pilifer?" Captain Jamison said.

"That's right. He said he knew an officer at Fort Gibson, but it sure couldn't have been you."

"I see." One of Captain Jamison's shoulders went out in a hunch. "Well, I've got a good idea. Until the court-martial, I'm going to let you enlist in the Army. We need new cannon fodder. I'll say a good word for you at the court-martial, provided you enlist."

"We ain't old enough," Ham said.

"You're old enough for me. After a few days at Gibson you'll be older. You'll be glad to enlist. Remember that." He turned his horse and started down the Texas Road.

Ham said to Scut, "Well, you've done it. You'll get Slick hung along with the rest of us."

The Cherokee said, "Don't worry. Him good man." He leaned forward in his saddle. "S-s-t. I no tell him where you got that goat."

I said, "When I think of what my old man did on this Trail, I could might nigh bawl."

The rolling tree-clad hills we rode through were as varied as ever, some still green and others broken with hundreds of shades of bright colors leaping from every cut and hollow. The covered wagons with the tight faces above the wagon seats rolled on, and more longhorn herds still trailed north for Baxter Springs.

At noon Captain Jamison turned into the trees. "We have about thirty miles to go today—as the crow flies. But we can't fly, so it will take longer. It's time to eat." His men were chuckling about something, and so was he.

While we hunkered beneath the branches to eat, we saw an army paper he had signed for the hardtack and bean cans he took from his saddle pockets, and it said "rats." It was. We ate with deliberation, then mounted up and rode on down the

Texas Trail. We were in the heart of the Three Forks country, where the rivers came together. The road ran near the course of the Verdigris and the old trading post landings we'd heard of.

The Cherokee said, "Go west to Verdigris, you see old water mill under bridge—old trading post country—many trading cabins long time ago when this was Osage land before Cherokees come. Government take their land and give it to us—treaty again. For long time, Frenchmen meet here to trade for furs and pelts. That many years ago. But steamboats, when they come, no go beyond reefs. Traders build shipyards, make own flatboats. Creek Agency that way, too, south of Arkansas. Old Tullahassee Mission school for Creeks that way. Old Tulsey Town way over there."

"How come Creeks to be up here in Cherokee land?" I said.

"No. Their land south of Arkansas, ours north. Our Nation runs southeast to Fort Smith. Their land south from Arkansas to North Fork Town, west along North Canadian."

"You Indians sure got dealt a mix-up," Scut said.

"It worse now. All north Indians shoved here. Now they take our land."

Later the Cherokee said, "We get pretty close now to Big Drunk's place. It that way across Neosho." He waved a hand to the east. "Wigwam Neosho."

Scut said, "You mean Sam Houston, our beloved first Texas president?"

"Yes. He come out of Tennessee and marry a Cherokee—Jesse Chisholm's aunt. Old Jesse name your cow trail. Jesse smart man, too. He rescue Mexican boys from Comanches, rent them for twenty-five dollars a month to explorers. Jessie die of cholera."

"Did you know Sam Houston?" I asked.

"Help him build cabin when he come here. Help him unload keelboat full of whiskey kegs. Him called Big Drunk, but he smart, too. Stay most of time near Fort. Sell whiskey to white friends. Live pretty high, but try to sell Cherokee land to friends in Washington."

"Anyway," Ham said, "he saved up something for Texas. He went pretty strong down there."

"Him smart man," the old Cherokee said. "Like John Ross."

We rode from the rolling hills to the ferry on the Arkansas, between the mouths of the Verdigris and Neosho. As we approached the river where the long string of wagons and freighters was drawn up on the narrowing road to wait for passage, Captain Jamison turned his horse into the trees. We rode slowly, half hidden from the road by bushes and tree trunks. At last we stopped.

"This spot is as good as any," the captain said to the sergeant. "I want to see if the deserters come this way. "We'll wait as long as we can to see what happens."

The soldiers pulled their horses closer to the road to check the wagons and horsemen as they neared the ferry. Captain Jamison remained with us. "Hey, Captain, sir," Scut said. "You ain't going to stop those renegades from becoming good Texas citizens, are you? We found our first president in this country. We might need some more politicians."

"You've got enough now." Something decisive lurked in Captain Jamison's slant eyes as he studied Scut. "By the Articles of War, I can't lay a hand on you. But one of these days you'll call me 'Captain, sir' with pleasure."

"Yes, sir!" Scut saluted. "Yes, sir, Captain, sir."

We moved toward the river. Wide flatboats moved heavy pilings up the Arkansas toward the location of the bridge the railroad was building. And when the tracks crossed, another new terminus would pop in the Territory—the white touts and outlaws, the gamblers, the women, the construction men.

Below us the ferry made its slow and patient swaths across the wide water, wagons and horsemen crossing for the south, other wagons and horsemen returning. Downstream a herd of longhorns swam northward, their noses held above the water and their wide horns gleaming wet, the big-hatted cowhands on shaggy ponies swimming beside the cows, pointing the line of the herd, and others forcing the drag into the river.

"Good Lord!" Ham said. "Look there!"

From the north, among the wagons and the standing and waiting women and short-shirted children, Highpockets rode at a gallop. We'd feared that rattlesnake all day. He rode on to the ferry landing, inspecting every wagon he came upon, then his horse galloped back the way it had come.

I looked at Leviticus and rode over to Captain Jamison. "Listen, we've got to get this goat to Texas. With what's come up, we can't take it to Fort Gibson and Fort Smith and have it held forever while we get tried. I see some Texas cowhands on the road. Can I go talk to them?"

"Go ahead, but don't try to leave. I'll have a pistol on you."

When I came back, he snapped, "What luck?"

"It's good. Those boys have been driving burnt cows up from the Choctaw Nation, and they know a little old woman at the edge of North Fork Town. She's got some nannies and no billies. Her name is Mrs. Treadways. They'll leave the goat with her to keep till we get there, or if they hear we're hung at Fort Smith, they'll write her and see it gets to Slick Pilifer with a card around its neck."

"The letter edged in black," Scut said.

Below us, the land-hungry jam at the ferry began to clear. I drove Leviticus to the road to the cowhands, but Captain Jamison and his outfit followed. "As soon as you're rid of the goat," he said, "we'll go on to Fort Gibson."

We left the road and started over the east fork which led to the Fort. There'd been heavy cane in the low malaria places during the day, and now as we traveled among the creeks and bogs, it became denser. At the fork, we'd made an almost right-angle turn from the main Texas Road. Before long the old Cherokee waved his hand to the north. "Wigwam Neosho up that way now. We make big ride around it today."

"If Sam Houston's ghost is floating above these canebrakes,"

Scut said, "I wish it would let me smell his bottle. I'm getting mighty discouraged. No wonder so many soldiers died of fever. There's nothing to live for here."

Among the escort there was an outburst of laughter and guffawing. We were only a few miles from the Fort. The road curved like a strung bow back to the Neosho, as if the river had been its string. We had only a short distance left to go, and the horses, knowing they were near the Fort and the stables, quickened their pace.

"I dread tomorrow more than any day in my life," Scut said. "If we join the Army, I don't know which would be worse—that or hanging. I never had a future ahead of me, but I sure like to wake up every morning standing beside a chuckwagon and seeing nothing but space and the sun ahead. I'll die in one of these closed-in forts."

"Captain Jamison's been holding back on you," Ham said. "Beginning tomorrow, you'll stand by a flagpole to salute and say 'Captain, sir' all day."

"Sure," I said, "and they've got a gristmill there. I hope it ain't one of those long-pole turn-around things a horse pulls. If it is, you've got another job. They'll have enough corn bread to feed the Territory."

"How do you get a habeas corpus?" Scut said.

"The best way is to stay where you live," Ham said. "And have a judge for your grand-daddy."

"We won't be at this place long," I said. "The sergeant told me that Captain Jamison will go to Fort Smith by steamboat and take us with him. With the Fort closing, he's got some sick soldiers to move, and a lot of special ordnance and a dozen bales of all those government and army records. In case the fall rains begin, they don't want those litter-case soldiers to bog on the roads in Army ambulances."

"I ain't ever been on a steamboat," Ham said.

"I ain't even seen one," Scut said. "Riding a train's new to me."

"How long will this voyage take?" Ham asked.

"It's about seventy-five miles to Fort Smith by river. The sergeant said it will take about three days. The boat will lay over at Webber's Falls for cargo, then stop and load up at other landings, like Skullyville."

"We didn't see much of the Cherokee Nation," Scut said.

"We'll still see it. It's still Cherokee north of the Arkansas to Fort Smith, and if we don't get hung or shipped to Montana with the Army, on the way back it will be Choctaw until we reach the Creeks at North Fork Town."

"For the first time in my life," Scut said, "I wish I was a goat."

Through vine- and grape-grown woods the road descended to the waters of the blue Neosho and the Army ferry. As we neared the crossing, we saw old rotten logs among the trees—the remains of those which had been felled for the barricades of early times. By now the day was almost gone, but across the river on the hill would be the shadowy stone buildings of the Fort. Flares and lanterns burned at the ferry stop.

In all the saluting and 'Yes, sir, Captain, sirs' we rode our horses aboard the scow. We know it now—at last we are really prisoners.

"Yes, sir, Captain, sir."

Chapter 4

IN THE BRIGHT SUNLIGHT next morning we saw what the Fort was like, from a guardhouse window, that is.

The stone buildings were within a picket stockade which had a blockhouse at each corner. Slate-roofed barracks stood on the hill, and frame buildings for officers' quarters flanked the big stone house of the commandant. There was a long stone stable, a commissary and hospital, and all the stone headquarters buildings. Between the officers' quarters and the guardhouse the parade ground spread, where two early fagged-out soldiers in ball and chain policed the area to pick up everything that didn't move. From a high pole the Stars and Stripes flew. It was peaceful to stand by the window, looking out to see the Fort come awake, now that we had recovered from the nerve-shattering blast of the bugle reveille which woke us.

"Looks like our future is right ahead," Ham said, "with a ball and chain."

"Do you want one or two?" Scut said.

Instigated by Captain Jamison, the preliminary court-martial with all its charges was put up against us last night. This sleepy side-whiskered colonel who sat at the main rectangular table in the adjutant's building listened to all the testimony. Captain Jamison spoke of the circumstances of our capture. The soldiers who had ridden with us from the Texas Road and the old Cherokee were his witnesses. The rest of the board was made up of one other captain and three lieutenants. There wasn't much rank left about the Fort—it was going, going, gone.

Scut and Ham and I are to be held for the disposition of a future court at Fort Smith, on charges of being caught in possession of three government horses, having disposed of three clumsy McClellan army saddles, which no Texas cowhand would have sat in anyway, three bridles, three saddle blankets, and other accouterments, and under further suspicion of having assisted, aided and abetted the escape of three deserters from said Fort Gibson. We will be taken in custody of Captain Jamison to Fort Smith by steamboat.

At the conclusion of this preliminary hearing the slant-eyed captain stands up. "Colonel, sir, if I may say so, and since the prisoners will be in my custody on the river, could they be remanded to me now?"

The bag-eyed tragic colonel, who belches and dozes and yawns in his chair like an old army man, and who needs a good dose of baking soda or bismuth and pepsin to set him right, looks up and nods. "These proceedings are closed. I leave for Fort Sill tomorrow. With what men are left, Captain Jamison, you will bury the old post." He stands up. He stumbles around vaguely, a lost look in his eyes, and leaves the room. These officers sure liked their glory, to give it up so hard.

This morning as we look out on the bright flag from the

guardhouse, a squad of soldiers led by a big-chested drill sergeant marches toward the window. Scut said, looking through the bars, "Here's where I get it paid back for those 'Captain, sirs.' "

As he bulked against the guardhouse wall, the bull-jawed sergeant was briefly lost to view, then he appeared again as he unlocked the door. When it swung open, we could see what in particular had stood out about him, even at the distance across the parade ground. He had this heavy jaw like a double-sized bear trap and a pair of small tight buttocks which lumped out behind like a couple of cantaloupes. Otherwise, all we see are big chevrons.

The bear trap opens, and he bellows, "March out to breakfast. Then to the latrine. Fuh-hor-wud, harch."

"I want to go to the latrine first," Ham says.

"Take him," the sergeant growls to a waiting private.

With the sergeant, Scut and I march out the door. The valley of the foggy Neosho lay beyond, but in this new mental condition which numbs our minds we wouldn't have known the tree line of the misty river from the wavering smoke of a prairie fire.

We march over to this mess barracks. It has a stone floor and plank tables. Ham joins us. Moist cooking smells come from behind a walled-in counter. We are given kits and follow a group of shuffling blue-uniformed soldiers past an opening. As we go by, food is slapped into the kits. At last we come with the sergeant to a table where we sit to eat and to be stood over and guarded. The breakfast consists of sowbelly, scrambled eggs, oatmeal, and Chouteau-style hashed-brown potatoes with gravy—only the gravy has been dumped on top of the peach preserves and eggs and oatmeal. Everything swims together so it can drown collectively and not individually, which is true democracy at work.

When breakfast is over, we march with the sergeant to a stone building and Captain Jamison's office. He sits behind a wide desk. As soon as we come to a halt, the sergeant yells,

"Het-shut!" We don't know what he means till we see him rare back with his chest stuck out like a curved whiskey keg, with both eyeballs rolling. We stand likewise.

"At ease," Captain Jamison says.

So we are at ease in everything but our thoughts. Three files of papers are stacked on the desk, lined up straight before us and waiting, and before each stands a mile-high pen in a round inkwell. The captain's slant eyes drill our own, two at a time.

He snaps, "You understand the charges of last night. It's not the Army's purpose to sentence you until a court-martial proves you guilty. Meanwhile, for your own good I have this to suggest." He shoved the papers forward, tapping a pencil on the desk. "Sign here. It may lessen your punishment. The Colonel and I will ask for leniency."

"Hey!" Scut said. "You can't railroad us into the Army."

"In this Fort, begin your remarks with 'Captain, sir,' " Jamison snapped. "Repeat to me," he told Scut, " 'Captain, sir.' "

"Captain, sir," Scut said. He jerked and came to het-shut again without knowing it.

Captain Jamison tapped his forefinger behind the papers. "Sign here."

We didn't have a leg to stand on—not a witness. We signed.

"You're in the Army." Captain Jamison's voice crackled. "Sergeant Nematode, get them outfitted."

In another stone-floored building we stand before a wide supply counter and shelves which are filled with hats and caps and clothes and leather smells. At the counter a seedy, sandy-haired corporal leans on a worn-out elbow with his head bent over the cover of a yellow Police Gazette. This dancing girl who is in tights looking back archly over her shoulder is as big as a cow. At our interruption the corporal glances up with irritation.

"Recruits," Sergeant Nematode growls.

The corporal straightens. He raises a pale eyebrow. "Fresh

meat," he says. "Well, we got two sizes—too big and too little. Which do you want?"

Before we answer, our mouths are stopped by a gale of flying caps and blue britches and shirts and underwear and shoes and coats. "Put 'em on," the sergeant says. We strip and do it.

In the new regalia I come out loose on top and tight on bottom. Scut is baggy, and Ham is bound as tight as a drumstick on a range-running rooster. These caps look like three tin cans which have been hit with a sledge and mashed frontwards on top. "Het-shut!" Sergeant Nematode walls his eyes. "Bu-hout fa-hace! Fuh-hor-wud, harch!"

So we harch down to the hospital. It is a two-story frame building with a wing attached. Again we strip. We come to het-shut before the surgeon in our birthday suits. We are measured up and down and sideways and open our mouths and say 'ah' and bend over and cough and come to het-shut again. Then this bald-headed, black-whiskered inquisitor with the pallid face comes toward us with a hypodermic a foot long.

"Hey!" Scut says, turning pale. "Ain't that for a horse?"

When we get innoculated and scraped and vaccinated and dress again, we harch out to the parade ground. Ham can't move in his tight pants and my fatigue coat drops below my knees. From an upper window of the headquarters building the colonel and Captain Jamison look down laughing.

Sergeant Nematode bellows, "Squad, hu-alt! Hut two!"

"Hey!" Scut says. "How many make a squad?"

Sergeant Nematode growls, "From two to twenty—as many as I want. There ain't no rule." A crazed look spreads to cover his features. His eyes roll. He throws his head high, "The sum of the General Orders you are to be told by me were first instigated in the Army of the United States of America in the time of General George Washington. The purpose of these orders is to instill in the mind of the enlisted man an awareness of the soldier's duty at all times for the welfare of the su-her-vice. You will learn and repeat these orders to Captain

Jamison within two days. Ge-hurn-eral Order Number One—" and he was off on walking our post and calling the corporal of the guard in time of trouble if he was awake, and protecting government property. His voice blasted our ears like a cannonade.

When this exercise in elocution was over, we took up marching on each other's heels. More soldiers from the guardhouse were called out for exercise and we did close-order drill. Turning in our tracks with our tongues out and that experienced squad of felons going backward and forward and sideways, we always ended up somewhere else than where we were supposed to, like a covey of quail which had been scattered by a shotgun blast. Then we legged it back to the sergeant to get in ranks again.

"I wish I had a horse," Ham panted.

"Suh-hi-lence in the squad!" the sergeant bellowed. "Hut two, three, four! Hut two, three, four! To the rear! Harch!"

I come face-to-face with Scut. "How come you're looking at me?" he asks.

With Scut slamming head-on, all I do is grunt. "You're supposed to be going the other way."

After chow we hit the grit again. About midafternoon, while our feet were still slapping the face of that same monotony and we dripped sweat all over, there was a sudden commotion on the road from the ferry. Sergeant Nematode called a halt. The Colonel had left for the Wichita Mountains; the Indian traders and squaws who had been in and out of the stockade all morning had gone. Now that we stopped in our tracks, as tired as three saddles after a cow drive to Abilene or Newton, the parade ground was quiet.

We watched the road. What appeared to be a company of Cherokee lighthorse had drawn up below. Two riders supported another who slumped in his saddle. When at last all had stopped, a yellow-leg shot forward, his horse stretching into a long gallop as it raced up the hill.

Sergeant Nematode waited at the gate with the sentry. The cavalryman pulled his horse up. "A lighthorse is hurt," he said. "Get a litter."

Sergeant Nematode gave an order to one of the prisoners. He said to the cavalryman, "Tell Captain Jamison to come."

The cavalryman spurred his horse to the headquarters building. When the captain appeared, he grabbed the reins of the horse and galloped through the gate. All lighthorse had dismounted. Captain Jamison swung out of the saddle and knelt beside the man who had been stretched on the ground.

The soldier came back with the litter. "Follow me," Sergeant Nematode said. He ran down the hill, the two cantaloupes following, the rest of us trotting behind.

We loaded the injured lighthorse and carried him back up the road. His chest and stomach were almost blown away by a shotgun. As he looked up at Captain Jamison, who rode beside him, a grim smile hovered on his dark face. At the hospital wing two orderlies took the litter. We came back outside and fell to in squad formation again, just so we wouldn't hear the sergeant's bull voice give the order.

Sergeant Nematode appeared and shouted, "Dismissed!"

"What's ailing him?" Ham said.

That night after retreat and chow we went out to the parade ground. When earlier the flag had been lowered, that band was really pitiful. Even cow-town bands were better. Now that the Fort was being abandoned, not more than six or eight pieces were left to play. In past times the Fort had boasted the best band in the Army, and it had marched off to the war with Mexico, its proud colors flying.

It wasn't because we were ambitious to succeed in our new calling that we went out after chow; we had to figure some way not to step on each other's heels. We were used to riding and boots, and not wearing shoes and putting up with walking. We hadn't worn shoes since our proud mamas took bootees off our feet.

"I can't walk," Scut groaned. "I never knew everybody took different-size steps. Every muscle in my legs quivers. My heels are raw as beefsteak."

So we stuck our pants legs into the tops of our heavy wool socks the way some of the regulars marched and we pulled down our forage caps and lined up behind each other. We started off, measuring our steps exactly. After an hour we called a halt and sprawled on the ground to rest.

I told Scut, "You ain't too bad, but you pick your feet up like a hill man jumping rocks. Then those satchels come down on my toes."

"You can't talk," Ham said. "When you step out, you hop like Old Millie churning for butter."

"Then your name must be perfection," I said. "You're like the last steer in a cow drag. I skip and jump all day to keep off you, but there's always a hind leg dragging."

Scut stood up. "Let's go," he said. "Fu-hall in! Ten-hut! Haw-wud, harch! Hut two, three, four! Hut two, three, four!"

So we are off and around for more training. After we go a time or two, Captain Jamison walks up in the shadows. Scut sees him first and yells, "Halt! Hut two." We stand rared back at attention.

"At ease," Captain Jamison says. "What's the meaning of this? Speak up."

When we told him where and why we hurt, he said, "Tell the surgeon's orderly to give you some liniment. Why do you have this trouble? Not all men do."

"We weren't made for infantry," Ham said. "We've ridden horses all our lives. We don't space our steps right."

"Sit down," the captain said. We had halted by some packing crates. He sat down on one, so we sat beside him.

"How's that wounded man?" Scut asked.

"His condition is poor."

"Will he die?" I said.

"I'm afraid so."

"How did it happen?"

"The lighthorse of the Creeks shot him by accident. Lately, things have been bad in the Territory, especially among the Creeks. Outlaws, horse thieves, whiskey peddlers. Then they've had a dispute at their agency over the payment of annuities —a part of the old faction trouble of the Nation—just as the Cherokees have their factions. The Creeks have increased their lighthorse to a small army, but many young men are not experienced. One company set an ambush for horse thieves, and the first of our own lighthorse fell into it."

We couldn't figure why he wanted to sit and talk, but he was a captain and that was his business. He said, "It was the Cherokee's son."

"Where is the old man?" Scut said.

"Sitting by the cot in the hospital."

"That's bad," Ham said.

"What do you mean by that?" Captain Jamison said sharply.

"I'm just sorry. He's a nice old man. I don't like to see this happen to him."

"It's not the fault of the Creeks. It could happen to anyone."

I said, "That doesn't make it any better for him."

"Who is this man you work for in Texas—you said his name is Slick Pilifer?"

"Yes, sir."

"How large a place does he have?"

"It runs clear across the country till it hits Old Man Wallum's spread."

"Part of Wallum's land used to be Scrape's," Scut said. "Wallum stole it after he had Scrape's dad shot down."

"Oh," Captain Jamison said. He asked me, "What did you do about it?"

"Nothing," I said. "What could I do? There was a legal hearing, but it was Wallum's judge. It's Wallum's county. Slick is the only man who stands against him."

"Do you know what the old skunk did?" Scut said. "After

that so-called hearing he rides out to Scrape's ranch with the sheriff. He brings a deed to the land. The sheriff puts Scrape and his mama off."

"Who signed the deed?"

"Wallum said my mama did."

"Wouldn't that be legal?"

Scut said, "What if she signed it X—her mark—after going to Texas from the East, where she was the first woman to graduate from one of those big colleges? Would a faked X be legal? She didn't get a diploma by walking up the steps to a lighted stage not able to sign her name."

"Does Slick Pilifer know this?" Captain Jamison said.

"I never told him," I said. "I needed a job and I wasn't crying for sympathy. Some day I'll settle with Wallum, but back then I didn't have anything to fight with."

"H-m-m." Captain Jamison got up and walked back and forth in that queer slouch. He sat down again and said, "Has this Slick Pilifer done pretty well after the war?"

"How'd you know he was in the Army?" Ham asked.

The captain, looking at the stark buildings of the fort, was silent. At last he said, "Most men were."

"When we left Kansas," I said, "Slick said he knew an officer here. But he must have been shipped out."

"Everyone's being moved," the captain said. "It's over."

"You ought to hear some of the yarns he told about that officer," Scut said. "He was a character."

"I see. What was his name?"

"I don't recollect, but he must have been a crazy devil, as crazy in his own way as Slick. Do you want to hear one of those stories?"

"Yes. I'd like to hear how he told it."

"Well, this happened about midway of the war. They were both lieutenants with their own raiders, and they'd been chasing each other through the Territory for two years. It sounds crazy, but in trying to outsmart each other, they'd got to be good friends—just in their own minds, that is, trying to figure each other out. It made something different out of always chasing and killing. One day by accident they both got fooled and led their outfits slap-dab together. They hit the bushes, and their men turned tail and left. There they were, just two old friends pot-shotting at each other across a dogwood thicket."

"Who won?" Captain Jamison said.

"Shucks, that was just the beginning. They got away from each other that night, but next day both came looking again. This foolishness kept up for two weeks, the two of them just hiding up there in the dogwood hills all day and shooting."

"That was needless."

"Then Slick figured that each was trying to show the other up. He did some shrewd calculating."

"He did, did he?"

"Every time one fired, the other fired back. Then Slick hatched out his scheme. He knew this man was smart and mighty curious. So one day after Slick was fired at, he yelled like he was hit and didn't fire back. Then he settled down to wait. He waited an hour, and then another, but still that lieutenant didn't show. Slick waited all afternoon, but by then he got afraid. He figured that the lieutenant was wise to his scheme and was waiting to pot him when he left at night. Slick wouldn't have left that thicket for a million dollars. He'd banked on the lieutenant coming down in mercy to look after a wounded man. Just about sundown, when Slick was really worried crazy, the lieutenant comes slipping from tree to tree. Slick had him covered, and they sat down and talked and had a cigarette. They agreed to call off the shooting matches."

"Well, which did Slick say won?"

"Won?" Scut said. "Slick wasn't talking about who won. He's got a funny sense of humor. He always laughed about how afraid they both were. They saw a lot of each other later, even in war, always up to the same pranks, but not as serious."

Just then a bugler began to blow taps—the lost day call—a long and lasting cry that drifted far away and held to hover above the valley of the Neosho until the last mellow note was lost. Captain Jamison stood, facing the west.

"That's one bugle call that goes all over me," Ham said. "Just like those trumpeter swans. It's not like reveille."

"I'm thinking about that old Cherokee scout," Scut said, "sitting up there by that hospital cot."

"Goodnight," Captain Jamison said abruptly. He started to leave, but turned. "You soldiered well today."

He walked up the slope to the hospital.

There's nothing like praise to make a man struggle to rise above his hardships, and Captain Jamison's good words to us that night, more than the perils of a guardhouse, decided us to do our best in the army and be helpful.

So it is with this spirit of forgiveness in mind that a couple of days later we are marching about the parade ground with Sergeant Nematode's felons. A smoky haze smudges the valley, and halfway down the road the Cherokee lighthorse are camped, the smoke from their fires mingling with the grayness of the distance. A corporal double-timed from headquarters. Sergeant Nematode ordered a halt.

After a conference with the corporal he turns. "The Captain wants three volunteers to report to headquarters for special duty. You'll be excused from two days' drill."

Those blank-eyed squad mates stare straight ahead. They are completely indifferent to advancement. I nudge Ham. "Here's our chance. If we get in good at headquarters, maybe they'll make us corporals."

"Silence in the ranks," Sergeant Nematode growls. "Volunteers, speak up!" That remark showed how contradictory army orders were, especially from this sergeant with his pair of cantaloupes.

"We'll volunteer," I say.

"Fall out!" Sergeant Nematode turns us over to the corporal. Then he goes marching away with his squad like a big-chested drake leading goslings.

"Let's go," the corporal says.

Scut says, "That ain't no way to give orders. You want us straight out or sideways?" We pick sideways to keep off each other's heels and march up to headquarters. The corporal leads us to Captain Jamison's office.

He looks up from his desk. "Did you three volunteer for this duty?"

"Ain't we supposed to?" Scut says. "We want to get somewhere."

"You'll get somewhere," the captain said. "We want the stables cleaned."

"Oh, my Lord," Ham says. "Scrape, you did it again."

"Haven't you learned in the Army yet," Captain Jamison said, "never to volunteer for anything?"

"It's just dawning," I said. "Do you mean it takes two days to clean that stable?"

"The way I want it, it might take three. Your implements are already there. Corporal, take over."

We march in a military manner to the stable—a low stone building. If it's an inch, it's a hundred feet long. The shovels and rakes and pitchforks stand against the wall. Scut groaned. "Why do horses eat hay and oats?"

"The team's over there." The corporal pointed. "When the wagon's filled, I'll show you where to take it."

At the end of two days we had the old post garden fertilized. But that didn't make sense, since all the men were being moved out and nobody would be left to smell the roses. Still and all, that was about the cleanest and best-scrubbed-out stable in the Army. This fort would always be remembered for two things: the cleanest stable before it closed and the best band.

When we reported to the corporal that the work was finished, Captain Jamison came for inspection. "Ten-hut!" Ham yelled. We stood inside the stable at attention with our implements. Captain Jamison walked around the stalls hunching his shoulders and touching everything as if inspecting a dining hall. "H-m-m," he says, looking here and there. "H-m-m. At ease."

"Captain, sir," Scut said, "ain't you got a horse doctor on this place?"

"Not any more."

"You've got a floundered hoof on one horse those deserters rode, and a sprained fetlock is pretty bad on another. There's one case of wind galls."

"Where are the horses?"

"Those last three in the corner. We put them away from the others."

Captain Jamison made his inspection of the horses. "Good. Can you look after them?"

"We've been doing it," Ham said. "That's our calling—horses and cows."

"Get what medicine you need at the dispensary. If you need the surgeon, let me know."

"Is that wounded Cherokee better?" I asked.

"No. I'll leave for Fort Smith a few days early to take him there with other hospital cases. I've notified the steamboat at the Verdigris landing. It will be here Friday."

"So we live to get hung," Scut said.

"It's possible," Captain Jamison agreed. "But tomorrow I begin to pack the post records. I'll need crates and boxes. I want you to build them."

"You mean no more Hut two, three, four?"

"Not at this Fort." He glanced down the hill. "What happened to the horse we had staked in the trees?"

"We shot and burned it," I said. "It had glanders. You wouldn't want these horses here to come down with glanders. You'd lose the whole bunch."

Captain Jamison said, "The horse was under observation. I wish I could impress you with one thing. You should have gone through channels. There's a right way and a wrong way to do things."

"And there's the army way," Scut said. "But glanders

doesn't wait for channels. I've seen a whole horse herd wiped out in no time."

"You destroyed government property."

"Do you mean we get another court-martial?"

"No, but I want to save you from one at some future date. Tomorrow, take the morning off and report at noon to begin work on boxing the post records."

"Just one thing," Scut said, rolling his knee-length coat sleeves around his wrists. "Don't ever promote me to more than a private. I don't feel I can even accomplish those duties. I've lost ambition."

Getting ready for the river trip, we didn't have time for idleness. It was hard work from reveille to retreat, and sometimes even later, nailing up crates and packing the Fort's record boxes in the commissary.

But more than work hung over the closing of Fort Gibson. It was when what was left of all those who had soldiered here turned out each day for retreat. The flag was slowly lowered, to be caught and folded by Sergeant Nematode while the band played.

The first log fort had been built in the lowland, then moved to the hill. It was abandoned and reopened and added to with stone buildings in the changing times. It had protected the Cherokees from the Osages and guarded the other civilized Indians who had moved west. Now only the buildings would remain.

One night Captain Jamison came to the commissary. We'd been ripsawing and crosscutting to put the last crates together from a pile of saved-up lumber. We made so much racket with the pounding we didn't hear the captain and didn't know he had come until we saw his boots before us. Ham throws down his hammer. "Ten-hut!" he bellows.

"At ease," Captain Jamison says. He looks at the boxes. "Have you about finished?"

"It will take another hour," Scut says.

"Report to headquarters in the morning. I want a cemetery detail."

"Has the lighthorse died?" I said.

"No. But I want the last few graves in the cemetery put in order and markers set. Have a wagon ready." He kicks at the scattered lumber and sawdust and looks at the boxes. "I can't fault you on this job."

"We're trail drivers," Ham said. "When we do a job, we rip it."

We put out next morning in the seat of the transport wagon with Captain Jamison riding beside us. After crossing the river on the ferry, we turned east away from the Neosho. "Where does this road go?" Scut called to the captain.

"To Park Hill and the Seminary. The old Union Mission was there. It had the first printing press in the Territory. The road which branched off goes to the Cherokee capital, Tahlequah. Tahlequah has the National Seminaries."

"Scrape's got a girl at the Park Hill Seminary," Ham said. "As soon as you make him a general, he gets married."

"Do you know a Cherokee girl?" Captain Jamison asked sharply.

"In a way I do. Willard Law's daughter."

"Oh," said Captain Jamison.

"Do you know him?"

"Yes," Captain Jamison said. "I fought against him."

"Will you tell us about those Pins and factions?" Ham said. "It's a big mix-up to me. We tallied cows at Willard Law's, but when we asked the Cherokee cowhands about the Pins, they wouldn't talk."

The captain said, "The factions grew out of the removal treaties. Some of the Cherokees thought they should hold their old lands in Georgia and Tennessee and the Carolinas, and others thought that with all the pressures of the white man, it would be better to start over in the West. This faction signed a removal treaty without the consent of the other, or of the chief, John Ross."

"That's the name the old Cherokee mentioned," Ham said.

"Later in the Territory most of the treaty signers were assassinated. It was that way with the Creeks. A Creek law provided that anyone who signed away tribal lands could be executed. This was done. Chief William McIntosh and others were killed in Alabama."

"Then among the Cherokees a feud got started?"

"Yes. It continued from a very old pattern, going back into generations. It was primitive justice, always settled by the eye-for-an-eye theory—the blood feud. Then with the war the feud intensified—mainly on sectional lines and slavery—the North and South. The tribes had slaves, but not in proportion to the whites. They wanted to avoid war. But they were far from the Northern forces, and the annuities were stopped. The Confederacy made a treaty and promised annuities. Ross signed the treaty."

"But where did the Pins come in?"

"Before the war, those who opposed the treaty wore two crossed pins on their coats. So with the old hatreds revived, the war meant ruin to the Cherokees. Ross had a powerful hold over the fullbloods, and the Pins rode with the North and the treaty faction fought with Stand Watie. Among the Cherokees it was friend against friend, raiding and murder and house-burning. Stand Watie stripped the women and children of his enemies to give their rags to his own starved and naked. The Pins did also, yet many of their people and those of other tribes froze and died on the Kansas plains after the Creek Chief Opothleyahola was defeated."

"What about John Ross?"

Captain Jamison said slowly, "I don't know. He was both loved and hated. He disclaimed all knowledge of the treaty assassinations. His new home in the Territory was near Park Hill. His mansion in Georgia had been disposed of by state lottery, as was the other Cherokee property. Yet if he had prepared his people as the treaty faction did, and not waited to be marched out by force, thousands of Cherokees would not have died on the Trail of Tears."

The stone-walled cemetery was laid out in long rows of markers. It was deserted of all life except for a single black horse that stood near a clump of red haw bushes. Within the wall we stopped the wagon and tossed out our hoes and shovels. Captain Jamison led us to three new graves. In some places the earth was sunken and uneven, in others it was rough and high.

"Get these first," he said. "Drag in the loose dirt and mound it so the ground will settle evenly."

"How did these soldiers die?" I said.

"One drowned in the Neosho and one was shot by a whiskey runner. The one at the end was an old litter case—tuberculosis."

"I bet you've got a lot of good friends here," Scut said.

"More here than elsewhere," Captain Jamison said. "The war dead. The clear rivers you saw at Three Forks and Cabin Creek swept away the dead men and horses of both sides." He turned and slouched off among the markers.

"That man hates to leave Fort Gibson," Scut said. "One of those felons we marched around with told me he's part Indian."

"Your brain's full of horse feathers," I said.

When we got the litter case mounded, Ham said, "Let's take this drowned one next."

When we finished him, Scut said, "Where did Captain Jamison go? I guess he's all right, wandering around out here."

"The last time I saw him he was close to that black horse," Ham said. "Let's look."

A thicket of sprangly green thorn writhed at the edge of the red haw trees. As we reached it, the horse moved a fore hoof. Scut stopped as if he'd hit a stone wall. "Look there," he whispered.

Beyond the thicket, on a gentle slope near a grave set apart from the others, Captain Jamison sat beside Sergeant Nematode. They'd done quite a bit of work about the grave, for it was neat and clean and slicked up as well as those we had done. Scut muttered, "We'd better get out of here."

When we finished the third grave, Captain Jamison came back. He marked the location of the new mounds on a chart and we got the small markers from the wagon. "It ain't our affair," I said, "but we saw you on the slope with Sergeant Nematode. Whose grave was that?"

"His wife's."

Scut said, "You mean a real woman married that monkey?"

"A very beautiful girl," Captain Jamison said. "He had a furlough for the wedding and brought her here from Fort Smith. She was to go back on the next steamboat. On their first evening at the Fort, Sergeant Nematode fired the cannon at parade. She stood beside him."

"Well," Ham said, "what happened?"

"The cannon exploded. She was killed instantly. It was a tragedy to everyone."

"Then why did he stay in the Army?"

Captain Jamison looked at Ham coldly. He said harshly, "Sergeant Nematode is a soldier. There was nothing else he wanted to do but be an army man."

From below the landing near the Fort Gibson ferry a steamboat whistled. The captain turned his head. "She's a day early. We'd better get back to the base."

Chapter 5

THE VESSEL on which we are to make our first voyage looks more like a flat-fronted scow than a steamboat. It is like a low riding plank tossed into the water, four or five times longer than it is wide, with twin smokestacks standing side by side across the bow like match sticks.

They are tall stacks and directly behind and between stands the pilothouse, which is set upon the fore part of a long superstructure of windowed cabins which extends back almost to the paddle wheel of this critter. Beneath the cabin row is space for cargo to be shoved for protection against the weather.

There is enough deck room on the sides of this layout for us to walk around the steamboat and look down into the water. Most of these sand-river steamers don't draw more than two feet anyway, and often draw less. Since it is the custom for the boilers of these boats to blow up frequently from between here and Pittsburgh and New Orleans, there isn't a lifeboat on her.

Her, I say. She is the *Maizie Trout.* The name is painted on the front of the pilothouse, on either side of it, and across the back—the *Maizie Trout.* And yes, it is painted lower down on the rear of the superstructure above the paddle wheel, so she can be read farther away from behind whenever she passes another steamer.

In other words, in case you have missed it by now, this steamboat's name is the *Maizie Trout.* She carries a couple of long narrow platforms which rest on deck before the smoke-stacks to be slid out to a river bank or a landing to be used as gangplanks.

On either side of the *Maizie Trout* at the bow is a derrick. These are used in low water to set pilings to work the boat across dry sandbars. With block and tackle the steamboat is pulled upon the bar and the pilings are set again. The boat is edged forward until it reaches water. The procedure works like an insect putting its long legs out and moving its body to catch up. It is called "grasshoppering." But if the route of the *Maizie Trout* is blocked by a water-covered bar, she backs up and chews a channel through it with her paddle wheel. Then she turns around and lights out for the races.

That morning, getting ready to go down to Fort Smith, Scut and I are the first soldiers to board this vessel. We crossed the gangplank with the boxed post records on our shoulders. Then with Ham we helped carry the litter cases aboard. Only a dozen soldiers stood near the ferry, and a few others remained outside the gate of the almost deserted Fort.

Captain Jamison came on board and the gangplanks were pulled in. The whistles blew. The paddle wheel churned and we swung into the current and set out down the Neosho, back to the Three Forks country and the Texas Road and the covered wagons. Captain Jamison and Sergeant Nematode stood at the stern, watching the Fort fade beyond the trees.

We cowhands shinnied up on top of the cabins to have a

last look. The *Maizie Trout* would follow the Neosho to Three Forks, then swing south into the Arkansas. When the river curved to swing onward to Fort Smith, the Cherokee land would be to the north, the Choctaw Nation to the south. The Neosho lay in the glittering morning light like a blue ribbon, and beyond the banks in autumn-colored flares the overcup oak and cottonwood slid by. At slough-like places canebrakes crowded into the water and, as we passed, disturbed waterfowl rose and flew southward in a rush and roar of soaring wings.

Captain Jamison stood beside us. "How'd you get up here?" I said.

"Through the pilothouse."

"That ain't the way we came," Scut said. "We climbed up the sides. We didn't want to tangle with more authority."

"Let's bring some of the litter cases up," the captain said, "so they can take the sun. They've been shut in too long."

After we helped carry the litters of the sick through the pilothouse and went back inside with Captain Jamison to watch the river as it rolled onward, we noticed the unperturbed man who controlled our destiny. He stood behind a high-mounted wheel which had a dozen or more spoke handles extending from it. But this particular individual was unique. He was plumb barefooted, and his eyes were set straight ahead. He wore a wide-brimmed straw hat, and a pair of butternut overalls which stopped halfway below his knees. He was as thin as a hickory rail and a good seven feet tall.

"Where'd they find that?" Scut said.

"He's an Arkansas farm boy," Captain Jamison said. "Captain Keeter told me that he came to the landing at Van Buren, across the river from Fort Smith, where the river loops. He told Captain Keeter that he knew the Arkansas like a book. The captain wasn't feeling well that day, so he let the boy take the *Maizie Trout* upstream to Fort Smith. He did fine. After that he tried him to Skullyville. When he got the *Maizie Trout* over the falls at Webber's place in low water, Captain

Keeter made up his mind. He hired him, and the captain hasn't touched the wheel since."

"What's his name?"

"Jessup. He can walk a steamboat over a bar by conversation. He knows his business."

"He's like us," Scut said. "We know our business. It's cows. We're worth more feeding beef to the nation than being kept in the Army or hung by the neck until dead."

We were ker-plunking pretty well down the Neosho, and finally we came to Three Forks. Where the Arkansas came in from faraway Kansas to curve south, the river course was almost a straight line west for a mile or so, and in the distance we saw the flatboats and scaffolding moving up and all the activity where the railroad bridge was being built by the Katy.

But nearer still was the ferry which carried the traffic of the Texas Road. It moved slowly back and forth across the Arkansas, with a congestion of covered wagons on the north bank between the Verdigris and the Neosho. In the mingling waters of the rivers, Jessup swung the steamboat southward. The channel deepened.

"Boy, we're really traveling," Ham said. "We must be making six or seven miles an hour. Look at those trees slide by."

The wooded banks passed behind and we came to an open prairie. On it stood widely spaced patches of persimmon trees. This Arkansas pilot turns to grin. When he speaks, he's got a good drawl in his voice, like a slow-moving buzz saw cutting a walnut log. "It's going to be a hard year on folks if those persimmons don't make. I remember one year up at Pea Ridge . . ." And then he was off on some long-winded yarn about a poor crop year in that Ozark Arkansas country when all the people who lived there guarded the persimmon trees with shotguns to keep rambunctious razorback hogs away.

"Who won that battle?" Scut says.

"'Bout even, I'd say. We got some and so did the hogs. But it was a genuine tussle."

"Well, you had the hogs there," Scut said. "And the shotguns. Why didn't you shoot and eat hog meat?"

"Drat if I know," Jessup said. "We just started out to guard persimmons."

"Is he pulling our leg?" Ham whispers.

"Not till it's as long as his," I said. "Let's go see that wounded lighthorse."

We go out through the back door. The sick soldiers rest on blankets, most of them pretty silent, watching the trees glide by. The wounded lighthorse is as thin as a skeleton. The old Cherokee sits cross-legged beside him. The river had looped east, but now it swung back like an old rope tossed to the ground to run more southerly.

"There's one thing about it," Ham said. "You don't have to be drunk to ride the Arkansas, but it would help."

While the pupil-shrunken eyes of his son looked up, the Cherokee said, "Many years ago soldiers fight bad men on old whiskey road from Fort Smith. Below Webber's Falls is still big whiskey depot at mouth of Illinois. Many Cherokee wagons go there. Soldiers once search steamboats, too. Whiskey, horse thieves. All bad. Now my boy shot. Things no better now than ever. Always trouble. Always killing."

"Where are we now?" Scut said.

The Cherokee said, "About south of Fort Gibson."

"You mean we're no farther east than when we started?"

"Crazy river up here," the Indian said.

As the *Maizie Trout* clunked onward, we passed log cabins and big frame houses set among plowed fields. Cows grazed in open places and among the trees. The burned ruins of other cabins and houses swung by.

"The war," the Cherokee said. "Always the war. The whole country ruined. White man fight, it is good. Indian fight, it is bad. Outlaws from Missouri and Kansas raid Cherokee land when Yankee soldiers are gone. Steal cows and kill Indians. Then bad men at agencies and army officers steal Indian cows —hundreds of thousands. Bad men sell Indian cows to government to feed him again, and Indian end up with own cow meat. Officers and many Indian agents get rich. Why Indian always poor? Why his cabin always burned?"

In the afternoon a line of foaming riffles spread across the river. The steamboat picked up speed. It began to toss. "Hey!" Scut yelled. "What are we having—a storm at sea?"

"This called Devil's Race Ground," the Cherokee said. "Pretty soon now we come to Webber's Falls."

We went back to the pilothouse to see how Jessup took the threatening situation. He was standing at the wheel scratching the calf of one leg with the nail of a big toe. "Listen," I said. "Are we going to mire up in those flint rocks?"

Jessup took a brown twist from his overalls pocket and bit off a chew with his tobacco tooth. He settled it in his cheek. The trees on the bank sped by like arrows. "It ain't flint rock ahead," Jessup says. "If you want to see flint rock, you'll have to go to the Flint Hills. Now, one time in Arkansas . . ."

We took another plunge.

"Hey!" Scut yelled. "Look where you're going. Look out! There's a rock standing up."

"Tain't time to swing her." Jessup watched a blue heron fly up from the far bank.

"Why don't you slow this outfit?" Ham said. "Can't it go backwards? We're racing head-on to glory."

"She's like the wing of a bird." Jessup's lean jaws worked. "I'll sail her right over."

When we bore down just about where the riffle was meanest, Jessup gives a yank at that spoke handle which he has been balancing with one index finger, and the bow of the *Maizie Trout* seems to leap into the air and turn off anti-godlin. Just when her tail was where her nose had been, Jessup scratches the calf of the other leg with a toe nail and gives an opposite yank to the spindle.

The *Maizie Trout* straightens in line with the river and flies right over the churning water. With Jessup's toe still scratching a calf, that job of piloting was a work of pure genius if ever we saw one.

"You start in at an angle," Jessup explained. "You sense the current and beware the yonder side. That big rock back there ain't placed right. If I'd swung the other way, we'd a been reefed like a broken egg."

"You scrambled me," Ham said. "I won't ever be normal."

"Hey!" Scut said. "Did you ever ride a horse?"

"I truly don't fancy horses," Jessup said, his eyes on the river. "Horses are too dangerous. Once I got kicked in the head by a plow mule."

Later that afternoon we made it down to the falls on the river, dropping the reins of the *Maizie Trout* at the landing at Webber's place. We'd conquered the last straight stretch of the Arkansas without trouble, but the wounded lighthorse had become worse. He was in delirium and we moved him down to a cabin. Sergeant Nematode left the landing and walked into the settlement to seek a doctor.

He had hardly gone before six big Negroes, some bare-chested and others in bright-colored turbans and sashes, began to move bales of cotton up the gangplanks to the deck of the *Maizie Trout.* Before the war they had been slaves of the Cherokees. We wanted to stretch our legs, but didn't know if we could get leave or not. We found Captain Jamison and the old Indian sitting beside the bed in the wounded man's cabin. A slight wind came through. As we entered, Captain Jamison stood up.

"Is he better yet?" I said.

"He's worse. Now that we've put up here, why don't you walk about the settlement?"

"We were going to ask, but we didn't want to leave you with this trouble."

"You can do nothing. Go ahead."

We left the *Maizie Trout.* Before the war there'd been a fair-sized settlement at the falls. But it had all been burned, and among new houses scattered foundation stones showed where larger homes once stood.

We met Sergeant Nematode as he walked back down the road from the few houses and a church and a store or two which were set on the slope.

"Did you find the doctor?" Scut said.

Sergeant Nematode frowned. "No. He went to help at a mission school for two days—mumps and measles. Everyone else went to a barbecue in the hills—part of an old tribal dance."

We walked back to the river with the sergeant. Captain Jamison stood alone on deck watching the chanting Negroes at their loading. "Did you find him?" he asked the sergeant. When he was told, he stared impassively at the far bank. Then he said to us, "You didn't go far."

"No, sir," I said.

He seemed to want to leave the *Maizie Trout,* so he led us toward the gangplank. "Let's walk," he said, and we went with him back up the road to the churchyard. There were big trees among the gravestones. We sat down on a stone settle.

"How old is this town?" Scut said.

"One of the Old Settlers came first," the captain said. "Walter Webber. He was one of the Arkansas Cherokees. The Old Settlers moved to Arkansas many years before the Trail of Tears—the old feuds. Webber had a store on the river. He was a chief."

"How come he left Arkansas?"

"After the last treaty the Old Settlers were moved, too. Webber built a store and a trading center here, and a salt works. He had a big house. He shipped his own whiskey to the falls. He said Indians were entitled to whiskey as well as the white man."

Ham said, "You mean he stood behind a grocery counter in Indian clothes?"

"He was part white. Many of the civilized Indians had white blood. It had gone on for hundreds of years, with the Spaniards, the French, the English, and the Scotch. John Ross was only one-eighth Indian. When he came west he tried to unite the Cherokees; it led to trouble with the Old Settlers and even more with the treaty faction. Some said that Ross considered himself a white man, even though he was the Cherokee chief."

"You mean Willard Law's girl isn't all Cherokee?" I asked.

"I'm afraid not." Captain Jamison added, "You may wonder why some of the Creeks and Choctaws are in the Cherokee land. On south, you'll find Cherokees in the lands of other tribes. The Chickasaws were afraid to claim all of their land west of the Choctaws because of the Plains tribes. The Seminoles, west of the Creeks, had the same problem. The tribes allow certain privileges to each other."

"This Skullyville," Ham said. "This landing we'll stop at before we reach Fort Smith. Who was this man Skully?"

"There was no Skully," Captain Jamison said. "The name came from a Choctaw word–iskulli–which means money. It meant the place where the Choctaws received their annuities. It had the agency and stores and schools."

"Good Lord," I said. "There's enough of this treaty stuff to make a man feeble-minded. Anyway, the tribes all got here."

"In the South, the object was to take their land for the settlers," Captain Jamison said. "The Choctaws were first to come. They were from Mississippi. In Georgia, the Cherokees were herded into stockades at the point of a bayonet. They were without clothes and food. Thousands died on the Trail of Tears. They and others reached here without guns or means to exist." Captain Jamison stood up, and his shoulders hunched off among the gravestones.

"What's nagging him?" Scut said. "I just asked how old this place was. He's worse than he was at the Fort Gibson cemetery."

We loafed about the stone church. When Captain Jamison came back from the markers, he said, "Let's go to the steamboat."

As we walked down the dusty road to the landing, Ham said, "How come this place got burned?"

"Stand Watie lost a battle here. The Union Army burned the settlement."

"Did you help?" Scut said.

Captain Jamison said, "Yes, I helped."

"What did John Ross do in the war?" Ham said.

"At first he signed the treaty with the Confederacy. Later, the Union took him to Washington and kept him there. Opothleyahola, the Creek chief, said he was like a snake ready to turn over. Stand Watie did remain to fight with his people. Many of the Old Settlers feared Ross and the hundreds of his bodyguard. They fled to Mexico. But Ross did want to unite the Cherokees."

It was late and along the darkening road the wind began to blow in quick gusts. When we reached the landing, Captain Jamison went aboard the *Maizie Trout*. We walked to the falls. The tumbling line of water which flowed over the black ledge stretched across the river, which was at low stage. Three small steamboats waited to go upstream. They were drawn up near the bank, one behind the other. An old white man with sunken cheeks tried to help the first steamboat in line over the falls by means of a long rope strung to a yoke of oxen which he attempted to drive along the bank.

The paddle wheel of the steamboat stirred up a mass of foam, but every time the oxen gained a yard against the current, they soon lost two. "Hey!" Scut yelled to the old man. "Don't you know how to herd a steamboat?"

The old codger eased up on the oxen and put a crooked hand to his ear. "You'll have to talk louder!"

"Can't you herd a steamboat?"

"Board of Health and Sam Slickum!" he yelled, chewing his gums. "I ain't a swearing man, but I was to make five dollars apiece on these boats! Will Tanby does this work, but he chased off to a barbecue!"

The captain of the steamboat called to Scut, "Can you get us over the falls?"

"Sure," Scut yelled. "How much?"

"It's ten dollars a boat. Get going! We want to get above the falls for an early start tomorrow."

We walked down to stand by the old man and the long-horned oxen.

"Are you a man to be trusted?" Scut asked.

"Board of Health!" He chews his gums back and forth. "I been trusted all my life. That's why I never got anywhere."

"You ain't made a penny today," Scut said. "Whose are those horses?"

Four of them—strong beasts—were tied to a hitch rack above the landing.

"Board of Health!" The lips chewed. "Bootleggers', I reckon, or outlaws. They mostly are."

"And you ain't a drinking man?"

"Board of Health, I ain't."

"Then we'll borrow those horses," Scut said. "They've got good ropes on the saddles. We're going to leave a five-dollar William tied to a pommel and give you a buck a boat for the use of these oxen—when we collect from those steamboat captains, that is."

The gums moved faster than the teeth of a wintertime squirrel shaving a hickory nut. "Board of Health! It's a fair deal."

After Big Bill Cookson's escapade, we were flat broke, so we got organized. We unhitched the bootleg horses and rode out on the solid rock of the falls and threw the ropes to the steamboat. The old man took up his place on the sandy bank with the oxen. Meanwhile, the crews of the *Maizie Trout* and the other steamers had gathered on the decks.

"What's the name of this sea-going craft?" Scut yelled to the captain. "You ain't as plain as the *Maizie Trout*."

"The *Jarvis Q. Jud*—from Ohio!"

"First time on this river?"

"And the last!"

We hooked to the right side of the *Jarvis Q* with a dolly welter about the pommels and even a rope tied to the pommel of the extra horse. "Don't move till I give the highball!" Scut called to the old man as we splashed out on the ledge. He yelled to the captain, "Get ready to full-speed the paddle wheel!"

Then while everyone watched, we sat on the ledge and waited.

"Board of Health!" the old man yelled from the bank. "I ain't making a buck standing still!"

"Hold your horses!" Scut called. He kept looking down river. "Stay put," he told us.

At last he waved an arm. The *Jarvis Q* put on full steam. Its paddle wheel clunked, tossing its wake. The old man whipped his oxen. "Give me a pull to the right!" Scut yelled to me and Ham. "Hit the grit!" A gust of wind snapped upriver.

We pulled all at once across the rock ledge. Unprepared for what happened, the Board of Health man and his oxen fell into the river. But the *Jarvis Q* lurched over the falls. At last, with the churning wheel holding it steady, we drew in our ropes. Scut rode over to collect.

"Ten dollars is high for this," the captain grumbled over the side.

Scut grinned. "It sure is. But we got you over the falls. And that old Board of Health man has a pistol pointed. You'd better pay."

"This whole country is full of outlaws." The captain reached for his wallet.

"Yes, sir. Everybody is either a law or an outlaw. Now go upriver and tie to a tree. You'll get that early start in the morning."

When we pulled the other two steamboats over the falls, we paid off the Board of Health committee and left a bill tied to a saddle pommel. "How'd you know when to yank those steamboats?" I asked Scut.

"I kept looking down the river. When the trees along the bank began to shake, I gave the high sign. The cross-pulling gave a little broadside and the wind did the job. Every inch counted."

We went up the gangplank of the *Maizie Trout*. "That was well done," Captain Jamison said.

"How's the lighthorse," I said.

"No better. But the cargo's loaded. Captain Keeter has decided to make a one-stop run to Fort Smith. If there's not a doctor left at the Fort, we'll get one from the town. We'll stop only at the Skullyville landing."

"You mean steam all night?"

"Jessup says we can make it if the boilers don't blow, and we're stacked with firewood. We'll stop tomorrow at Skullyville for more wood and cargo, then run for Fort Smith. Jessup says the rest is up to what happens."

This happy pilot turns around and grins from where he sits at the bow with his feet dangling in the water. "Listen," I say. "Can you really make it at night?"

"I might can, if I don't hit a bullfrog."

About the darkening landing the lighted lanterns began to glow. In the yellow circles the bare chests of the idle Negroes glisten. On board the *Maizie Trout* two larger lanterns have been swung from long poles which extend from the pilothouse, and others swing from poles on the sides of the bow. Jessup sits, centered in the flickering light like an ancient idol. "Shove off!" Captain Keeter calls. He turns to talk to Captain Jamison.

This pilot didn't move from his foot washing. "Ain't you ready?" I asked.

"No use for me to hurry," Jessup said. "Let 'em get me a good steam. When I head downriver, I'll ride me a catamount." Two impatient blasts come from the stacks. This philosopher in butternuts says, "Did you ever see a scissor-tail chasing a crow? I did onct. Did you ever see a hop toad watching a fly? Well, this old toad comes up to the fly and he . . . Say, did you ever hear of a mile-or-more bird? He buries his head in a gravel shoal and makes a queer call. It sounds for a mile or more. Up on White River, that is."

Those on-again whistles become frantic. "Let 'em blow," this boy says. "They won't slow my speed." He gets to his feet and shambles up to the pilothouse.

The river was wide and sandy but now that night had come,

for the first time it seemed deep. It wasn't just a river any more—it was a winding blue racer ready to suck us down or slam us with a flick of its tail into a sandbank. We put out in a nightmare of Jessup's grins and whistle-tooting.

"Hey!" Scut yelled in the pilothouse. "Don't you want more light in front of this critter?"

"It don't make me no difference!" Now that Jessup was well underway, he turned the steamboat loose. The *Maizie Trout* shook from stem to stern. When we started from the falls, we were in a straight stretch of river—black as pitch save for the shimmering lights on the water and the stars. About four or five miles later, Jessup says, "Feel that air?"

"What air?" Ham says.

"That air. That cool air."

"I thought you were talking funny."

"It's off the mouth of the Illinois. We're making fair time. But we've got miles ahead."

"If it ain't an inch," I said, "it suits me in this night."

"What are those fires over there?" Ham asked.

"Whiskey runners," Jessup said. "That's their depot on the bank of the Illinois. There's another blaze springing up. Pretty soon the Cherokee wagons will drive in."

We went out the back door of the pilothouse to stand on the cabin deck. Overhead, the bright sparks from the twin whistles streamed.

The old Cherokee stood brooding, watching the distant campfires. "My son dying and I go to Washington to talk of Comanches. Maybe they better off than we. They ride, they see sun come up. They free."

We passed the mouth of the big Canadian. The glimmer of lanterns marked the path on the river.

Next day we put up at the Skullyville landing. The old Choctaw capital was several miles back from the south side of the Arkansas, but the landing was packed with Choctaws and Cherokees and whites and Negroes, who hurried on horseback or ran on foot among yelping dogs and scattering turkeys to see the steamboat. Loaded with cotton bales and adding more by the minute, the *Maizie Trout* settled and seeped steam and shook. This Arkansas boy walks on the cabin deck, chewing coffee beans and watching a flight of geese high overhead.

"The sun came up pretty this morning," he said. "But I miss the home mountains. Ain't nothing prettier than a line of razorbacks crossing a ridge in a red sunup."

During the day the river had rolled southeastwardly, at last making a wide loop as it neared Skullyville. When we put out for Fort Smith again, we followed the other arm of the loop back north. In the pilothouse I asked Jessup, "Will we make it by sundown?"

"If *Maizie* don't bust her belly band," he said cheerfully. "But she's been panting a trifle."

"The fireman is so weak from throwing wood in the furnace he can't stand up," Ham said. "When he gets to New Orleans, he says he's signing on for a voyage to Liverpool."

"He's a weakling," Jessup says. "It takes a good man for the Arkansas. I wouldn't trade for it." He squints. "Do you know how a nighthawk holds to a limb? It sits lengthwise."

"I've been told that," I said.

Later, while the *Maizie Trout* sped on, Captain Jamison pointed to the brown bluffs above the mouth of the Poteau River. "Old Fort Coffee used to be there. From the bluffs, the course of the river can be seen for miles. The Army stopped steamboats which carried liquor into the Territory."

When the sun sank beyond the wide black river bottoms and the Indian lands, the *Maizie Trout* pulled into Fort Smith, low in the water and steam popping from every joint. There were several landings, and long rows of shanties and houses were set back from the bank. An old cobblestone road led upward to the high town. On Belle Point stood the stone and brick buildings of the Fort.

As soon as the *Maizie Trout* pulled in, Captain Jamison sent a soldier up the cobblestones, and when the man returned we loaded the litter cases into army ambulances. Then we left the steamboat to walk to the Fort with our gear. We were halfway up the cobblestones with Sergeant Nematode when an explosion occurred. By the blast, it could have been only a steamboat.

We turned to look back. In the landing lights, the *Maizie Trout* rode as steady as a fishing cork.

"It must have been another one," Ham said.

Chapter 6

THIS NEW PLACE we woke up in next morning was almost as deserted as Fort Gibson, but it was an older fort. It had been abandoned before, but this time was the last go-round. The buildings were of stone or brick—the powder magazine and barracks, the officers' quarters, an ivy-covered commissary, and the quartermaster's building. And like any other fort, it had a guardhouse, which was our first acquaintance.

Sergeant Nematode led us there. "The captain says this is a formality. Tomorrow he'll put you in the soldiers' barracks."

"Man, after that river ride," Scut said, "I don't want even a cot. I can sleep forever right on that cold stone floor."

Before we knew it, that danged wake-up bugle blasted the atmosphere of the point. It seemed four of them blew in our ears at once.

After we ate, we put on those mashed-frontwards forage caps to be marched to headquarters. "Hey!" Scut says as we step out in a stride smart and clean. "We march like old veterans. Ain't nobody here as good as we are. We're getting some place."

We are led to a big building and to a table where Captain Jamison and a Fort Smith captain and two lieutenants sit. They constitute a second board of assassination. However, in view of these misfitting uniforms we wear, the new officers seem to be grinning.

This Fort Smith captain doesn't give us "At ease" like Captain Jamison, so we stand and answer questions with our backs poker straight. The upshot is that we are still to be held for investigation. "You'll be remanded to me," Captain Jamison said when those so-called gentlemen-by-act-of-Congress stand up.

We come out on the steps and look around at the level marching area which is surrounded by high stone walls. We couldn't leave if we wanted to. "We'll go to the commissary," Captain Jamison said. "It's being used as a hospital."

This was the two-story native stone building which was covered with the ivy and pocked by big rectangular windows. We go up the steep steps on the low side of the slope and through a heavy blacksmith-hinged door. The wide slab floor is laid of hand-cut stone blocks, worn smooth by use. A wide fireplace near the door is big enough to roast a steer in. The stairs to the second story are at the opposite end of the building. We follow Captain Jamison.

The sick from the *Maizie Trout* are kept upstairs, lined out in cots, as well as the Fort Smith sick. The old Cherokee sits by a cot which is placed beneath a window. The air is full of the smells of all kinds of medicine and chloroform, and a lye-soap scrubbing odor rises from the floor. An Army hospital steward in white clothes and a black-bearded doctor stand beside the wounded lighthorse. The doctor wears a dark blue suit with a heavy gold watch chain with an elk's tooth suspended between his vest pockets.

"Well?" Captain Jamison says.

The doctor motions him to move to where we stand. He follows the captain. "I'm afraid it's too late. It's a matter of time. You did all that was possible at Fort Gibson."

The captain's brown eyes seemed to flinch.

"I was here after you left last night," the doctor said. "I'll return at noon. Can you make the old man sleep?"

"No."

"He won't take a sedative," the doctor said.

We went down the stairs, and outside Captain Jamison said, "Let's go to the town."

We left the commissary building and the Fort and walked a short distance to the old garrison road which in past times had been cut through the heavy trees. Now it had become the town's main street. On a rise at the far end of the avenue stood a tall-steepled church; at the lower end were the river landings.

We looked up the wide sweep. "This is as nice a street as I ever saw," Ham said. "It ain't all false fronts. It's got some real stone and brick buildings. They don't run too far, but they all look good."

"From the river to the church," Captain Jamison said. "The whole street leads to it. A Catholic academy is there."

Scut said, "What do dressed-up people do when it rains—when the dirt street is muddy?"

"They lay planks from corner to corner," Captain Jamison said. Strangely, he laughed.

"We've got twenty-two dollars to spend," Ham said. "The result of our steamboating. Let's go to a confectionery."

While we were drinking a double-sized sarsaparilla at a cool wire-legged table, I said, "What's that big mountain down the river—the one we saw yesterday from the *Maizie Trout?*"

"Mount Vista," the captain said. "It's across the river from Van Buren. I've fished in a creek beneath it. From the summit you can see Sugar Loaf and other mountains in the Choctaw Nation."

"It juts out like it means business. Like it wants somebody to crack it on the chin."

"It's at the junction of the creek and the river," Captain Jamison said. He stared at a sloppily dressed soldier who stood at a counter. "By the way, here are three tickets to the opera house. A famous singer is in town tonight. The program will be upstairs in this building. The best people of Fort Smith will be here."

"You mean real caterwauling?" Scut asked.

"Some call it that, but there'll be other acts. Do I have your word you'll return to the Fort?"

"You sure do," Ham said. "You've got our saddles."

We left the soda parlor and walked back toward the river on the other side of the avenue. From Third Street we went on down the cobblestones. Between Third and the river were the houses and shacks we had seen from the landing.

"While you're out tonight," Captain Jamison said, "don't come to this part of town. It will be full of Territory outlaws. Some places are safe, but not all. Once it was lively and colorful along the old bank—bright-dressed Osages and other Indians and the wandering French with their pirogues and canoes. The Negro slaves worked at the wharves, and trappers and traders and the forty-niners came through, and the soldiers and explorers rested here."

Captain Jamison turned off the cobblestones to stop at a shotgun shack on First Street. He knocked at the door. An old gray-haired man opened it and stuck his head out. "Tom, is my package ready?"

"Just a minute, Captain." The man limped away to return with a square wooden box. "It's pretty heavy, sir."

We walked back up the cobblestones. As we reached Third Street again, the captain said, "That man was an old soldier."

"There's that church up there," Ham said.

That night we liked the opera fine, especially the part where we squirted some bird shot which we'd picked up at the armorer's at this fat crimson-clad female singer.

Being good cowhands, we got in our best work when she walked off after each song before coming back to take a bow. She moved off stage in little hunches. She had a high quavery voice and had hopped around while this enthusiastic flute in the orchestra tried to keep up with her singing in what was called a classic duet.

Captain Jamison had got us the best reserved seats in the house, among some elegant culture-talking ladies and black-suited gentlemen. Later on, one man in the back of the audience got up and shot a trained pig that wouldn't act with his revolver. In the excitement, the local idiot fell out of the balcony, and the meeting adjourned. The best people sat with us, but women from below Third Street with their ostrich feathers had to sit upstairs. When everyone left the performance, we put on our knee-length army frock coats and followed.

Next morning we were given three stiff brushes and soap by Sergeant Nematode and told to scrub the stone blocks of the commissary floor. "This ain't personal," he said. "It's just part of the army. It don't like for a man to lose his training."

At last Captain Jamison came down the stairs. "Are you finished?"

Sergeant Nematode said, "They're finished, Captain."

Captain Jamison motioned for us to follow. We went outside the door and stood on the worn steps above two long-nosed cannons set in the brown grass. Behind them were two piles of cannonballs stacked like pyramids.

Captain Jamison said, "The Cherokee lighthorse doesn't want to die within the Fort. I've got a tent for him on the river."

"You want us to help take him there?" I said.

"If you will."

"I don't get this," Scut said. "You don't have to let us decide. All you've got to do is give the order."

"That's true for now, but as soon as the officers meet tomorrow, you'll be free men."

"What do you mean?" I said.

"We've just had a rider with dispatches from Fort Gibson. The deserters were found at Chetopa. You had nothing to do with the Army horses. The men even had the Army saddles and rifles on other horses they had stolen. I want to ask something of you—will you stay on until the lighthorse dies?"

"If you want," I said. "But what can we do? I can't look that tired old Cherokee in the eye."

"You can do more than you think. Let me know later. I have a litter upstairs, so if you'll get an ambulance and bring three mounts, we'll move the lighthorse."

When we came back to the commissary, we moved the lighthorse down the stairs, trying to keep him level, and only his eyes were living. We loaded him into the ambulance. The Cherokee sat in the seat beside Scut. The rest of us mounted up.

"Hey, Captain!" Scut called. "Where do I drive?"

The captain said, "We'll take the road toward the old fort. I'll lead you." He got ahead and we followed.

"Is that the log fort they got mixed up on?" Ham said.

"What do you know about that?"

"They built it too far west and then had to move back to Arkansas."

"Yes," the captain said. "How does it feel to be free again?"

"It ain't bad," Scut answered. "That soldiering wasn't bad, either. But I almost hate to give up this uniform. I'm proud I served my country."

We turned off the road and went through a lane which was bordered with painted sumac and yellow willows. We stopped near the river bank. A hundred yards upstream stood a log cabin with smoke rising from a clay chimney. Near by a tent had been pitched beneath some cottonwood trees.

Scut stopped the ambulance and we removed the litter. We

placed the lighthorse on the ground inside the tent. I said to Captain Jamison, "Why didn't you bring a cot?"

"He doesn't want a cot. He wants the ground. He wants to see the sun."

"Will you bring the doctor?"

"No. He is beyond help."

"Who will stay with him?"

"A friend in the log cabin. The Cherokee and I will be here."

"Do you want us to stay?"

"No."

Next morning we were given a team of mules and a wagon and told by Sergeant Nematode to chop a load of wood for the Fort. We drove up Garrison Avenue to pass the church and angle off along Little Rock Road. A wagon train of half-covered ardent spirits bossed by a heavy set red-whiskered man moved toward town. He didn't care at all that his bottles showed in the wagons. We stopped the team among some heavy oak and nut-covered hickory trees on the side of a small branch and took out the axes.

The open slope to the branch was covered with dried-up May apple vines with their brown fruit. A few dry-leafed persimmon trees stood among the rock ledges above a wide pool in the water, its banks covered with crawdad castles. Near by was a smoky camp fire—more bootleggers. The red-whiskered man rode back to start one more wagon after the others.

"If he gets to the Territory," Scut said, "he'll make a fortune."

"He'll end up at the mouth of the Illinois," I said. "Or elsewhere."

"You know," Ham said while he worked, "hitting the same spot with an axe makes a man think."

Scut watched a spreading adder twist across the ground. "You ought to think. You ain't hit the same place twice."

"Anyway, this is one mixed-up world," Ham said. "Look at

us. Look at all the people we've run onto. Almost everyone had a worry."

"We set out to see the Nations," I said. "And the river brought us right between the Cherokee and the Choctaw land. That much is certain."

"We did get away from Highpockets," Scut said.

By noon the wagon was ricked high and we started back to the Fort. We passed the church and a couple of hundred yards down the avenue we stopped at Texas Corner, by the wide plaza. Hundreds of covered wagons were pulled up while emigrants stood about and talked and got organized in groups which would move south toward old Fort Towson in the Choctaw Nation or west to North Fork Town among the Creeks. A number of shanty-style eating places were clustered about the plaza, and since we figured we were free men by now, we went into the best looking one to get away from army grub and spend our money.

When we came out, Ham got pale—and not from what he had eaten. "Good Lord!" he said. "Look!" Not fifty feet away, standing as tall as ever, stood Kurbstone. He wore a black slouch hat and his conductor's suit. We ducked back inside the door.

"What's he doing here?" I said. "Putting a whiskey train together or looking for us?"

"It's us," Ham said. "I saw him while we ate, but I never got a straight look at him. He was poking around the back of every wagon out there like he was trying to find Leviticus. He wandered all over the plaza."

"There's more to that goat than we know," Scut said.

Kurbstone must have decided to give up, for he moved to a hitch rack and mounted a bay horse. He left Texas Corner and trotted down the avenue toward the river.

"Do we want to follow him?" Scut said.

"No," I said. "Let's cut over and go in the Fort at one of the other gates."

It was about nine o'clock that night. During our morning's absence from the Fort, we had been declared free men by the investigating board. Now we could go on to North Fork Town. We were about to hit the hay in the barracks when Captain Jamison entered. The few soldiers who were still at the base stopped playing cards or shooting dice and yelled, "Ten-hut!"

"At ease," Captain Jamison said. He hunched to our cots, but by his expressionless face we couldn't tell what he was thinking. He said in a low voice, "The lighthorse died tonight. Get dressed. I'll be outside." We'd looked for the man to die, but now that it happened we were jolted and weren't ready for it.

As soon as we dressed, we left the barracks. The captain stood on the steps. Scut said, "When was it, Captain?"

"An hour ago. I need your help. Will you come?"

"Yes, sir," I said.

"We'll go by my quarters," he said.

We waited while he went up the steps of the officers' barracks. He soon returned with the box the old man on First Street had given him. We walked across the parade ground and went out a gate in the wall where a lone sentry stood. Four horses were waiting. We mounted up. "Are you ready?" Captain Jamison said.

"Yes, sir."

We circled left of the Fort and struck out on the same trail we had followed yesterday. We expected some word as we rode, but the captain didn't speak. At last we turned into the black lane to the indistinct cabin. "Ain't we going to the tent?" Ham asked.

"No," Captain Jamison said.

In the yard we climbed down. An old dog trotted up and sat motionless by the horses, his tail thumping the ground. Captain Jamison led us inside the cabin. It had a dirt floor, but there was a table, and upon it a still, straight figure lay wrapped in the tenting. In one corner of the cabin a gaunt, sallow-faced man with a crutch under his arm stood beside an iron cookstove.

The captain placed his box beside the litter. "Where are they?" he said.

The man hobbled to a pile of sacks. He pulled them aside, revealing a stack of fringed deerskin Indian jackets. Captain Jamison picked them up. "Take your caps and coats off," he told us.

Before we could change, he had slipped a jacket over the old Cherokee's head and put one on himself. "Carry the box," he told me. "Be careful. It's heavy." The old Indian moved and they grasped the handles of the litter and moved through the door.

Captain Jamison led the way to the river. The Cherokee stumbled. "Can't I carry that end?" Scut said.

"No," Captain Jamison said.

They stopped at the bank and put the litter down. The captain waded in at the water's edge and dragged a canoe to shore. He and the Cherokee laid the litter in the canoe. Captain Jamison shoved two other canoes from the bank.

"Can you paddle?" he asked us.

"We'll be poor hands," Scut said. "We've pushed a rowboat, but that's it."

"Do your best. Do you still have my box?"

"Yes, sir," I said.

He fastened the canoe of the lighthorse behind his own, and we shoved off into the river. He and Scut and Ham were in one, the Cherokee and I in the other. The going wasn't bad, but I couldn't handle the paddle. Neither could Scut and Ham.

"The canoe will trick you," the Cherokee spoke behind me. "But the paddle is a fish. It will find its own way into the water. But what use is there for a paddle now? The night is black, and much has ended."

We moved down the river toward Fort Smith again. The lights of a few steamboats which were moored to the banks glimmered in long paths across the water. Two rowboats crossed ahead of us. "Whiskey," the Cherokee muttered. "Always they carry whiskey." We swung away from the town and the landing lights, moving nearer the farther bank. From a shack at the water's edge came shouts and fiddle music.

Captain Jamison said, "Already they move into the Territory."

The lights of the town and the landings slid behind. We cut back into the channel, and once again the blackness became the sound of paddles. The river looped. Above us, the indistinct bulk of a mountain broke. I called in a low voice, "Is that Mount Vista?"

"Yes," Captain Jamison said. "Do you have my box?"

"Yes, sir."

Had it been two hours or three since we left the cabin with the dead lighthorse? It had not been that long, yet it seemed so, for the river flowed endlessly. But now we felt the impulse of a sudden current. The captain held up his hand, then swerved his canoe and swung into a creek. It was wide and tree-bordered, but with its rapid flow it seemed deeper than the river. Captain Jamison stopped beside the right bank. We clutched for the overhanging bushes to hold steady.

"Catch your breath," Captain Jamison told us. "We'll wait." It wasn't breath we needed, but something to stop the ache between our shoulder blades.

At last he spoke to the Cherokee. "Old man, do you wish to speak? Do you wish to pray to your gods?"

The Cherokee said, "What words do we have when the frosts come? What words can stay the passing birds? What is the sorrow of a chief when he sees his son dead? Why was I not chosen to go before him?"

"You have spoken," Captain Jamison said. "And it is well that he go to his fathers. There will be the winds of the sky and the thoughts of the waters to bring him peace. He has fought long and well."

The Cherokee said, "Why should we wait? What more can we do?"

"Give me the box," the captain said.

He opened it with a tool he took from his belt. A clanking sound broke the silence. He pulled the canoe of the lighthorse to his own. While Scut and Ham held it close, he fastened two heavy iron balls with their chains and manacles about the litter. Then deftly he overturned the canoe.

"Ay–eee," the Cherokee cried. "Ay–eee." He clutched the branches of a bush and pulled himself upward. For a moment he stood on the bank, then he turned. As he ran, all sound faded upward.

Next morning we climbed the mountain. The chief sat in a rocky crypt beneath the summit. The blue-green creek lay below, but he gazed westward to the distant hills of the Territory and the Cherokee land.

We climbed the ledge to stand above him, where a few gnarled cedars twisted from the rock. Southward rose the bulk of Sugar Loaf and all the other mountains. And from where we had come in the night the river circled the far and unseen Fort and looped below to glide and curve onward toward the Mississippi.

Scut said, "You must like that old man."

"He is my father," Captain Jamison said. "We are of the Old Settlers. Once this was our land."

We are bouncing over a rocky road in this stagecoach, through the hills of the Canadian River to North Fork Town.

We rattle across the creeks on log bridges or mire in axle-deep mud, or bounce to the ceiling and come down again. A stage stop for fresh break-away horses is every fifteen or twenty miles. You get a basket of fried chicken for the trip and try to find your mouth. A stage line is a thought-up concocted scheme to keep the whole human race in misery.

Captain Jamison had bought our tickets and advanced us money for wrongful detention by the army and for labor faithfully executed in closing out two forts. We sat high in the saddle, if we could ever find horses for saddles. We were wearing our old cowhand clothes and boots again, after signing a final paper which said that all items which had been held in trust for us by the Army had been lawfully returned.

"I am coming from Fort Smith," a pretty young woman beside Scut says. She wears a pert blue bonnet. "I am a college graduate. I am coming West to study the Indian culture."

Where else could she come from? She'd got on the stage at the same time we did, with passengers getting on and off all night, and now with daylight breaking among the shaggy hills, she began to talk. Just then we hit a submerged rock which stuck up about two feet high in an unbridged creek bed, and she bounced to the top of the coach. She came back down and said, "When I was in college, I found the study of wild Indians to be an interesting subject."

We'd been jolting all night at breakneck speed with this filly, but she wasn't anything in our book—us being that nice, reserved type of cowhand that people read about.

"Do you know any Indians?" she says, getting off Scut's lap.

"No, ma'am," he says. "And especially not wild ones."

We hit another rock. "Do you know," she says, coming down again, "that they have a Great Spirit, just as we do?"

"Where are you from?" Ham says.

"From the East—from Pemberton-on-the-Holyoke," she says.

"I ain't heard of that town."

"Oh, it's a college on the river," she says. "How droll you are! Mr. Pemberton is a philanthropist. We have a houseboat for outings."

"We're from east of the last cotton gin on the Brazos," Scut says. "If you'll keep your head inside the window, you won't get it knocked off by a tree branch."

"Oh, I just love you," she says. "I am Miss Lockwood."

"Scut, Ham, and Scrape," Scut says.

Miss Lockwood hadn't said a word all night since leaving Fort Smith, being very prim and maybe afraid of her honor or losing it, but once she got wound up, she couldn't stop. "What are those things you are sitting on?" she asks, while those six stagecoach horses are breathing fire. "I can't see all of them."

"These things are called wore-out saddles and brush jackets," Scut says. "Put down on these seats like this, they make riding easier. We keep our spurs dug in."

"Oh," she says, holding her bonnet one-handed and coming down to land this time on Ham. "I do so love the West."

"What I want to know," I said, "is what in tarnation you like about it?"

"Oh, it's the freedom," she says, bouncing up and down. "You have no worries. You're just under God's open sky."

"You sure hit it then," I said.

"Didn't you say your stop was Beale's City?" Scut said. "This next stage stand is it."

"What about my bags?" She dusts the ceiling again and comes down with perfect aplomb on top of everybody.

"I reckon they're still tied on top," Scut says. "If the top's on."

We jolt over another rocky creek. Miss Lockwood bounces from me to Ham and back again. The stage driver blows his horn and we come to a stop on a hill. Miss Lockwood sticks her head out the window. "Why, this can't be Beale's City. It's only a log-cabin stage stop with one lantern still burning."

"It's Beale's City," I said. "It's on Beale's road. If he says it's a city, it is. Out here we don't argue with a man."

"Oh!" she says. "And where are all the wild Indians, and that quaint little house like they have in Arkansas?"

"Since leaving Fort Smith," Scut says, "I've been wondering when you'd ask about that quaint house. These wild Indians are still sleeping from plowing the east eighty yesterday. You'll find the outhouse right behind the cabin."

It is an hour after sunup—red and orange and streaky—and we are still jolting along when this holdup occurs.

The big man with the black mask across his eyes has chopped a few trees to fall across the road. When the driver stopped, we sat in the stage, waiting. "All right!" this benefactor of the human race says. "Step down!" He motions with his pistol.

The droopy-mustached driver and the shotgun rider have already stepped down. "Howdy, Bill," the driver says. "I brought you some customers. No mail, no nothing—just them. You got a chew?"

We step down from the stage. Big Bill Cookson recognizes us and gives a good horselaugh. "Well, you never learn. This time it's a pleasure." Once more we drop our guns to the ground and shell out.

The driver caught the tobacco plug Bill tossed him. He set his favorite tooth in it. "Have you seen the Starr boys, Bill?"

"I saw Old Tom and his boys the other night," Bill says. "Still feuding with their brother Cherokees. This buck Negro Blue Gum and his gang are acting up. I aim to take a reasonable view of things, but to me there's nothing as low as a horse thief."

"Well, that is one point of view," the driver says. He meditates a moment. "Bill, why don't you mend your ways? Go to Arkansas or Texas and run for Congress. You've got a full honest face."

"I aim to keep it so," Bill says. "I don't deceive my constituents." He catches the plug from the driver and rides into the trees. He looks back and waves. "See you next time, boys!"

Once more we climb aboard that egg-scrambler and tail out. We go up a hill and around a hill and across a prairie. Ham says, "When we get to North Fork Town, it won't do any good to go to the livery stable. We can't pay the horses out. Maybe we'd better look Leviticus up first."

"I'd forgot all about that goat," Scut said.

At the next stage stop a Cherokee and two Creeks climbed aboard. We moved our saddles over to make room. The driver changed fire snorters again and took off with the usual lurch. "Hey!" Scut says agreeably to our neighbors. "We've still got some Arkansas fried chicken. How about having some?"

"No, thank you," one of the Creeks said. He was a medium-size man dressed in a bowler hat and dark suit.

We swung nearer the South Canadian again, on the road to the ferry. "Going to North Fork Town?" Scut says.

They all nodded.

"We're Scut and Ham and Scrape," Scut says.

"My name is Collier," the Creek said. "This is Mr. Adair and this is Mr. McAfee."

"Where do you live, Mr. Collier? That big house we saw near the stage stop?"

"Yes."

"Is North Fork Town a good place?"

"Once it was very good. Back in the days of the forty-niners and the Denver gold rush the California Trail crossed the Texas Road there. It came from Fort Smith. The town was small, but there was business for everyone. It was a meeting place for the Creeks. But it was burned during the war, after the Battle of Honey Springs."

"It should be good for a few more days." Mr. McAfee laughed. "We Creeks hold a council there. We even brought Mr. Adair from Tahlequah to it."

The stage was whirling over a good stretch of road. We crossed the South Fork at the ferry and turned into the wide Texas Road. I asked Mr. Adair, "Do you know Willard Law?"

His face brightened. "He's a good friend."

"Ours, too. We helped him brand cows."

Ham said, "We're looking for a little lady named Mrs. Treadways. Do you know where she lives?"

Mr. Collier said, "Minnie Treadways?"

"Yes, sir."

"She lives about a mile this side of town, back in the trees. We'll pass the lane to her house."

"Wonder if this driver will let us get out there? If we went to town, we'd just have to walk back. We've got business with her."

"I'm sure he'll stop," Mr. Collier said.

Chapter 7

WHEN WE WALKED up the lane, this nice little old lady was standing in a sunbonnet in front of a cottage. She stood behind a picket fence and held a milk bucket in her hand. Two rows of late autumn flowers bordered the walk, and an apple tree heavy with red fruit stood in the yard.

"Good evening," Scut said at the gate.

"Good evening," she said. She had a shrewd face and she wore eyeglasses. She was as frail as a painted porcelain figurine, and we couldn't keep from liking her.

"I bet you don't know us," I said. "But you're Mrs. Treadways."

"Yes, I'm Mrs. Treadways." She looked at our saddles. "Land sakes!" she cried, surprised. "I do know you. You are the Texas boys. You came for the goat. But where are your horses?"

"In town at the livery stable."

She couldn't figure that one out. "But why didn't you ride them?"

"We're flat broke," Ham said. Then he told her how we left Chetopa and how we'd just got out of the Army.

"You poor things. And you don't have any money at all?"

"We did," I said. "But Bill Cookson held the stage up. This is the second time we've helped him."

"I declare, he's just like an overgrown child. I don't know what's to be done with that boy."

"We'll take the goat, if he did you any good. We'll go off and sleep in the trees somewhere."

"No," Mrs. Treadways said. "You can sleep in the shed. I won't have you put out like this."

"That's nice of you," Scut said, "but can't we do some work?"

"I'll help with the milking," I said. "But I never milked a nanny."

We went through the gate and around the side of the cottage to the shed and left the saddles before it. Mrs. Treadways led us across a branch to a pen where Leviticus and two nannies stood under some walnut trees. On down the branch was another pen of nannies. Leviticus had been at work on the green husks of the walnuts, for his whole mouth was stained yellow. He looked up from the ground and came to the fence wagging his stained whiskers as if he really was glad to see us. He looked like what was left over from an old man after too much chewing tobacco.

Mrs. Treadways placed the bucket beside a three-legged milking stool. "Come, Nannybelle," she said. She led a nanny from the pen. Then she put some hay and black-eyed pea vines in a tub which rested on two logs and sat down on the stool. "Now, Nannybelle." She began to tap her right foot on the ground.

"That's the most intent look I ever saw on a nanny's face," Scut said.

Mrs. Treadways began to sing:

> "Yes—we'll—gath—er—at—the—ri—ver,
> The—beau—ti—ful—the—beau—ti—ful—ri—ver . . ."

Every time a note sounded, her hands came down on Nannybelle's teats.

"I'll be jiggered," Ham said.

That Nannybelle was the most concentrated she animal in the Territory. With each note, a spurt of milk beat in the bucket. When two notes were close together, two spurts sounded. The way she raised a fore foot now and then, you'd have thought Nannybelle did all the work, and not Mrs. Treadways.

She put Nannybelle back in the pen and led Idabelle out. She began to pat her foot again:

> "Tramp—tramp—tramp—the—boys—are—march—ing,
> Cheer—up—com—rades—they—will—come . . ."

This nanny is just as concentrated as the first. "I never saw the beat of this," Scut said. "Looks like this one is waltzing."

"Are we ready to hit the crib?" Ham asked. "After that stage ride all I do is ache."

"You poor lambs," Mrs. Treadways said. "You shan't go to bed without supper."

Ham carried the milk and we went into the cottage with her. It was a single big room with a lean-to kitchen built out from one corner. A big four-poster bed stood on one side against the wall, a dining table was in the middle, and a tall foot-pedal Estey organ stood on the opposite side. On the sides of the front mirror, the organ had cut-out places where ornaments and pictures were placed. A triple line of knobby diapasons and other musical terms covered the front above the black and white keyboard. Near the door was a chest of drawers with another mirror set above it on the wall. On the opposite side of the door, about head high, the antlers of an elk's head stuck out for a hat rack. The elk had a wide mouth and blue glass eyes.

"Doggone," said Scut, "this is cozy."

We hung our hats on the antlers and followed Mrs. Treadways to the kitchen. It was warm and smelly in the lean-to with fresh light bread baking in an iron cookstove, a pot of rice boiling on top, and the deep sizzle and heady smell of spareribs cooking. Mrs. Treadways set the milk bucket on a table and fluttered back to the chest of drawers. She took out a white tablecloth and doilies. "Land sakes, I'm so excited to have company I tremble." She remembered she still wore her bonnet. She took it off and hung it on the antlers.

Then she saw blood on Scut's head. "Mercy me! Boy, you're bleeding."

"I got stove up on that bouncing stage," Scut said. "I can't make it stop."

Mrs. Treadways opened a drawer of the chest. She took out a big medicine kit which half filled it. The rest of the drawer was lined with bottles. She had more medicine and bandages than the Army. She got Scut's head plastered up and then, since we'd come in unexpected, she hurried to the kitchen to fry sowbelly to go with the spareribs.

Scut snickered. "What if she played 'Oh, Susannah!' for those nannies?"

Ham sat down on the turn-around stool before the organ and pumped the pedals. After a few mouse squeaks and one deep rumble from the opposite end of the keyboard he quit. He stood up and took a small teapot from one side of the organ. He lifted the lid and turned the pot sideways. A roll of bills fell out. One was loose. It hadn't been there long, for when it fell upon the keyboard, it curled open and half spread out. A face with a set of penciled-in whiskers looked up.

"Hey," Scut whispered. "I put whiskers on him at Booger Red's. It's like the one the old Cherokee had. That's more money Bill Cookson took from me at Willard Law's."

"Do you think she hides Bill?" I said.

"I don't know," Scut said slowly. "I sure don't know."

When we sat down to eat, Ham and I hung our pistol belts on the antlers, but Scut didn't. Mrs. Treadways' shrewd eyes looked at him as sharp as pin tacks, but she didn't say anything. When we drank the supper down with goat's milk, we helped do the dishes and got ready to leave for the shed.

"Oh, no!" said Mrs. Treadways. "We must sing first."

So we go to the organ and stand behind Mrs. Treadways, meanwhile watching the mysterious teapot while she sits on the stool and pumps the pedals and plays. We covered about every sacred piece in the song book that night and then go to the shed and take our saddles inside. We find a lantern and light it. Mrs. Treadways had lent us some blankets, and there was a pile of straw on the floor. It showed it had been slept on. There was a heavy plank to bar the door from within and we slid it in place. Then we hunkered back against the walls and looked at each other.

"What do we do now?" Ham said.

"Maybe she got that bill at a store in North Fork Town, just as we got it at Booger Red's," I said.

"Too many bills were in that teapot," Scut said.

"We're not sure about anything. She took us in, and she hasn't charged for keeping the goat."

"We were broke and she knew it. And as for the goat, we haven't left yet."

"Maybe she's waiting for us to make big money," Ham said.

"That's a laugh," I said. "But with Bill Cookson around, I know one thing—we're sitting guard tonight. I won't sleep till I know what this is all about."

After we watched the milking of the nannies next morning and ate breakfast, we left our saddles at Mrs. Treadways' and walked in to North Fork Town. We reached the Texas Road, which had made a sharp bend, and caught a ride in a jolting covered wagon. The road was as wide and crowded as ever, and near town it was twice as rutty. Scores of wagons were drawn up in the trees, where tired families rested.

"I sure hate to hit this place flat broke," Scut said. "I counted on having a good time."

"We're not broke," Ham said. "But we'll have to watch pennies. I said after Bill Cookson held us up the first time if I got more money, I was hiding part of it. I stuck a ten-dollar bill in my boot."

"Is it still there?"

"I don't know. I ain't had them off since I left Fort Smith."

"Then take it off," I said.

"You boys do it. I'm relaxing."

Ham leaned back in the wagon and we got the boot off, and stuck inside on the sole was the bill. "It's half rotten," Scut said, "but I guess it will spend."

The first thing we did in North Fork Town was go to the livery stable. We saw what looked like the boss and went to him. "We had some cowhands leave three horses here—Turkey Foot brand," I said.

"I almost sold those horses yesterday," the Creek owner said. "I thought you gave them up."

"Not us," Scut said. "What's against 'em?"

"I checked up yesterday—twenty-seven dollars for board and keep."

"Where are they?"

He led us out to the pole corral. "They look pretty good," I said.

"Do you want them now?"

"No. You've taken good care of them. We've got business in town. We'll get them later. We'll recommend your place to all our boys."

When we got away, Ham said, "What do we do now?"

I said, "Let's walk around and see the town."

Like Webber's Falls, it was building back after the war. Only a few hundred people lived in the village, but it was still busy, since it had the schools and the councils, and the Creeks always came in from the hills to trade. There was the regular cemetery and the soldiers' cemetery, and the three-story academy.

We walked back to a bench in front of the stage stand and sat watching the covered wagons and horses pass on to Texas. A crew of railroad men came in on a stage—surveyors, graders, and stump blowers. "Where are we going to get a job?" Scut says. "I feel dismal."

We try the railroad crew. There isn't a chance. "I don't even feel like spending that ten dollars," Ham said.

"We'd better save it," I said.

"We can't eat on Mrs. Treadways all our lives," Scut said.

"Buy a wild turkey from that Indian."

"She's got a yard full of turkeys."

"Then buy a nanny goat. Buy a sheep. Buy anything, but just take it back when we go. Tell her somebody gave it to us."

We went home with a couple of prairie chickens. After we milked and ate and had psalm singing, we went to bed. "I looked in that teapot tonight," Scut said by the lantern flame. "She'd moved the money."

"Maybe she don't trust us," Ham said.

Next day we found a brass brooch at a trader's store. It cost five dollars. We took it out to Mrs. Treadways about milking time. We found her beside the pen. "We got a job today," Scut said. "We brought you a present. Try it on."

She pinned the brooch to her dress top. "You nice boys," she said. A woman's call came from the gate. "I'll be back in a minute," Mrs. Treadways said.

We were pretty well hidden from the front yard by some heavy lilac bushes, so the visitor didn't see us. She was fairly good-looking, but horse-faced, with a hard-set mouth. She sat a fast-looking horse sidesaddle by the gate.

"Who was that woman?" I asked after psalm-singing time.

"That was Belle Reed," Mrs. Treadways said. "Jim Reed's wife—from Missouri and Texas—a fine girl. She makes the best candy." She went to the kitchen and came back with a tablet-written recipe. "This is Belle's own recipe for Sugar Candy. She wrote it out for me. Six cups white sugar, one cup vinegar, one cup water, teaspoon of butter, put in last, with one teaspoon soda dissolved in hot water. Boil without stirring one-half hour. Flavor to suit taste. And here's her recipe for Cream Candy."

"Hey! Let's make some," Scut said.

We boys did the mixing on the Sugar Candy and watched the pot boil. After our sweet tooth was satisfied, we went to the shed. "Who is this Belle Reed?" Scut said as he lit the lantern. "I've heard that name in the Territory, but I've heard too many names to remember it."

"That's the old girl Bill Cookson said he might hide with," Ham said. "She hangs out on the Canadian. She knows Cole Younger and Jesse James and all those outlaws. Some say she's in with Blue Gum. Somebody said if she didn't stop running around with the Starr boys, that when she got rid of Jim Reed, she was going to be known as Belle Starr."

"That's a pick," I said. "Which one is she taking?"

"That information ain't released yet. Some say it's Sam. She likes young men."

We heard horses gallop up to the yard. "Douse that lantern," Scut said.

We get up from the straw and look out this two-foot-by-two window. The dark shapes of a number of horses stand in front of the fence. Two or three men carry another man through the gate. Two other riders are still mounted. One seems to be sitting sidesaddle.

"That's Belle Reed," I said.

"We've hit the jackpot," Scut says, "if it don't hit us."

"What will we do?" Ham says.

"We're sitting up all night," I say. "With these pea-shooters ready."

"I wondered about that medicine chest," Scut said.

Next morning a murky sky lay over North Fork Town. It wasn't raining, but the solid clouds hung low, and the air was so wet you could reach up a hand and squeeze water out of it.

We had talked to Mrs. Treadways at sunup. The strange horses had left at midnight. "We ain't hungry this morning," we said at the gate. "We'll leave early and try for a job in town."

"What if I don't see you again?" Mrs. Treadways said. "Some friends have asked me to visit them in the hills." She looked just as frail and sweet as the first time we saw her.

Scut said, "The main thing is—how much do we owe you for keeping the goat?"

"Nothing. I was glad to do it."

"Well, if we get a job," I said, "maybe we won't see you again. We can leave our saddles today, I reckon?"

"Of course."

The first man we met in North Fork Town was Mr. Collier. The council meeting was set for tonight, but we got him out of a crowd of Creeks to sit with us on a whittled-up bench before the stage stand.

"What do you think of Mrs. Treadways?" I said.

"Mrs. Treadways?" He took his hat off and held it on his knees. "Why, she's a very respectable woman."

"That's what we think, but things are funny." We told him about last night.

Mr. Collier took a cigar from his pocket. He put it in his teeth still holding the hat with one hand, but he didn't light it. At last he nodded. "That's odd. I don't know that I've ever had any reason to think differently about Mrs. Treadways. Yet, now that you mention it in this way, many things occur to me. If I wanted to pass quick judgment, I could say you were right."

"Or wrong," I said.

"Or wrong," Mr. Collier agreed.

"We don't know what to do. It's nothing off our hides, but after what happened last night we're between a rock and a hard place. We didn't know who to tell."

"If it was the Starr gang, don't worry. The Creek lighthorse would like to know."

"You don't think we're wrong in telling you?"

"No. You may save lives and property."

When he left, we were at the nadir of disgrace. We were broke, our saddles at one place, and we couldn't pay out the horses. We couldn't even go to see them or sit on the top rail of the corral. If we went to the livery stable, the man would want to know why we didn't take the horses out. We walked that flat settlement over for work, in and out among people and horses, from one end to the other.

We were so desperate we decided not to go back to Mrs. Treadways'. About an hour to sundown a troop of soldiers bound for Fort Sill rode in and camped in the trees beyond the road. We walked over, hoping to find even that old army Chouteau cook to talk to. But this was a different outfit.

The town began to fill up with Creeks from the hills and prairies for the council meeting. Another railroad crew and a company of soldiers came in. We sat on a bench before an undertaker's shop.

"Hey!" Scut said. "I've got an idea. There's a dance tonight down the road. If we can rent a wagon to carry people, maybe we'll get rich."

"It's worth trying," I said. "Anything is worth trying."

A bareheaded, fairly young man in a dark suit stood beside us under a sign which said "Stanley Hightower, Undertaker." He showed Creek blood. He said, "If you want to take people to the dance, perhaps I can help you."

At that moment Leviticus walked into town.

"How come he got here?" I said. "Did that woman turn him loose?"

"I don't know," Ham said. "But I wish I was a goat and twice as happy." Just as if he knew where we sat, Leviticus came straight to us. "Oh, Lord," Ham said. "He's like a bale of cotton around our necks."

While we were rubbing this affectionate goat, the Creek said again, "Maybe I can help you."

"You'd be the only one that could," I said. "What is it?"

"I'm Stanley Hightower. I don't have anything lined up for

tonight." At the edge of the walk a black horse-hitched hearse stood.

"What do you mean, lined up?" Ham said.

"No business. For two dollars I'll rent my hearse."

"What about this goat?" Scut said. "Can we take him?"

"If you rent the hearse, it's yours till sunup."

"How much money we got?" I asked. We scraped up our money—two dollars and twenty-four cents. "We'll take it."

A shattering crash sounded, followed by a tinkle of falling glass. We turned toward the funeral parlor. Leviticus stood facing a jagged hole in the window.

"I was watching him," Stanley Hightower said. "He saw his reflection. He thought he was another goat."

"Well, we'll owe you for that," I said.

When the crowd left, we got the goat into the back of the hearse and shoved him forward. Stanley Hightower said, "You might go out to Angie Brokaw's. It's the yellow house down by the blacksmith's—this side of the wheelwright's. She's going to the dance, and you might pick up two bits."

"Is she a Creek?" Scut said.

"She's almost white. She's an old maid who likes to get out once in awhile. She's one-eighth Creek."

Some of the interested bystanders had put out word to the townspeople and railroaders that there would be transportation to the shindig. A man in a plug hat came up. "Are you the boys who take fares to the dance?"

"We sure are," Ham said.

"Where's your wagon?"

"This is it." Ham pointed.

"This hearse?"

"Sure. You look sick. What's wrong?"

The man said, "I'll walk."

Two other fares came up and left. We got in the seat and drove toward the blacksmith's and to Angie Brokaw's house, getting more curious glances by the minute, with Leviticus sticking his head out the back, than three zombies would in a church house. When we stopped at the gate, Scut said, "Who's it?"

"Shucks," Ham said. "I'll go."

Angie Brokaw had a plank house with a wide front porch and a fence. Ham walked through the gate and knocked at the door. A woman in a bustle and long-feathered hat came out. A drawn-out "b-a-a-a" came from the back of the hearse. The woman gave one look and ran down the street.

Ham came back. "That's the craziest woman I ever saw."

"We ain't getting rich on you," I said. "What did you tell her?"

"Nothing. I just said 'Lady, it's time to go. We came for you.' Then the instant she saw the hearse that goat gave his call. Let's tie the Old Scratch up front."

It was dark now, but we lit the front and back lamps on the hearse and drove through the ruts around North Fork Town. Creeks for the council and Cherokees moved about. More soldiers of a Fort Sill wagon train came in. People from the last stage stood on the walk before the stand, under a swinging lantern. Cowhands from a bedded-down Texas herd yelped into town.

"No wonder they call these Indians civilized," Scut said. "We haven't got a fare yet. Stanley Hightower really fixed us."

We stopped once more before the funeral home and climbed down. Three carriages filled with Creek schoolgirls passed, chaperoned by a preacher and his wife from the academy. Under their cloaks the girls were dressed in white middy blouses and dark skirts.

"What are they for?" I said.

"They're putting on a program at the council house," Stanley Hightower said.

Two other carriages drove by. They were filled with girls.

"Who are they?"

"Cherokee girls. They're from the school at Tahlequah. There's a speaking contest tonight."

We started the horses again, stopping to light one of the oil lamps which had blown out. Then, in disgust with all our bad luck and having wasted two dollars, we cupped our hands to our mouths and yelled "Free rides!" But even that didn't help. "We've got the hearse for all night," I said. "Let's watch the dance."

It was to be held about half a mile beyond town on the Texas Road. We drove out among a crowd of people walking or on horseback or in wagons and carriages. Another covey of cowhands galloped in, their dust rising in the light of the hearse lamps.

We pulled off the road and turned into the trees at a low log building. It was wide and spacious and surrounded on all four sides by an arbor-type outward roof supported by sturdy oak poles. Fires and pitch flares burned among the trees, lighting up the horses and wagons. As we stopped the team, a small man stepped out of the shadows.

He had a hung-down mustache and tobacco stains at his mouth corners. "I'm the U. S. marshal. Who did you come for?"

"Nobody," I said. "We're just looking."

"Then hang around. Maybe you'll do business later."

"Who're you after?" Ham said.

"Big Bill Cookson." The marshal grinned. "We ain't crossed trails in a week or two."

"You just hope you don't," Ham said. "What's your name?"

"Olinger. From Fort Smith."

"We've seen that town. But you better hope you don't meet another marshal. I heard that when you run out of outlaws around here, some of you shoot each other."

When the marshal left, Scut said, "Look over there."

Beyond the edge of the oaks, away from the wavering light of the flares, black-bearded bootleggers did their chores. They reached into brush piles or into their boot tops for a bottle. Some took a tin cup from their coat pockets and sold by the drink. Railroad men, soldiers, Indians, cowhands, and a few sullen half-breed women gathered about them.

"This dance will be well fortified," Scut said.

Ham said, "If all this country ever gets to be a state, the people ought to build a monument to the old-time 'legger and his boot. He did as much to open the country as anyone. They ought to put a mile-high monument right beside the state house."

Emigrants began to arrive at the dance from the covered-wagon camps. It was a chance to shake a leg and relax from the long travel. Inside the dance house jerky fiddles and banjos tuned up. Under the entrance arbor Olinger slouched by the door.

"Had we better let that goat graze?" Scut said.

"He's quiet right now," I said. "Let's leave well enough alone."

"Look who's coming," Scut said. "Where've we seen that before?"

A surrey pulled into the light and the driver helped a woman down. She was young and slender and blond-headed and pretty, and painted up and dressed like a million gold eagles. She wore a fur stole, and her fingers sparkled with rings and glass diamonds.

"Good Lord!" Ham said. "That's Betty Blye. We've seen her at every dance hall in Abilene and Newton. What's she doing here?"

"I've got a hunch," I said. "She's been sweet on Bill Cookson. I bet something brought her down here to meet him."

Betty Blye went through the door. "Then Bill had better hurry," Ham said, "the way those cowhands followed her inside. Listen to their coon hollering."

"Maybe Bill won't come tonight because of Olinger. He left the door and went right in after her."

When Olinger came out again, I went over to him. "What's Betty Blye doing here?"

"She says she came to reform Bill Cookson." Olinger spat and grinned. "She's looking for a goat."

"A goat?"

"Old Man Wallum's down in Texas goat—that cow and mohair and race horse king. He paid a thousand dollars for that goat up North. He had some of his boys meet the Katy at Chouteau, but it turned up missing."

"Who got it?"

"The conductor says it was a bunch of kids. Old Wallum has put up a five-thousand-dollar reward. He's even got John D. Rockefeller and all those other railroad officials on the griddle. If he don't get the goat back, he's threatened to buy the railroad. The Katy fired the conductor, got him a horse, and told him if he wants his job back, to start looking. Betty Blye wants Bill to get the reward so they can marry and start an honest life together."

"Bill Cookson would eat that goat for orneriness," I said.

I went back to Scut and Ham. But I didn't feel cheerful. On top of everything else, now we had Old Man Wallum and John D. Rockefeller after us, and soon they would be helped by Big Bill Cookson. We had to get out of the Creek country.

About midnight the man who had worn the plug hat in North Fork Town shoved his face up to the seat. "How about a ride back to town?"

"Sure," Ham said. "Six bits. Payable right now." When the man staggered away, Ham grinned. "With all that red-eye, everybody's going to love this hearse. But if they ride now, they pay for it."

I left again to talk to Olinger. When I came back, a crowd had gathered at the hearse. It looked like business after all. "Man, we hit the jackpot," Ham said. "We just rented this hearse for ten dollars a load. They're singing 'Nearer My God to Thee' and laying each other out in the back."

"I hear them. But we've got trouble. We've got to get out of town." I told them what Olinger had said about Kurbstone. I hadn't told them before, hoping still to get money to pay out our horses. "We ain't got a chance," I said. "If Kurbstone catches us and swears we stole this goat, which the old skunk would, Wallum will put us in jail for life. That railroad will crack down, and we're dead."

"Maybe we'd better ride in the back," Scut said, "and let those folks drive. I knew that goat meant something."

"If we get out of here without making a ruckus, Olinger won't know we've got it until it's too late."

We got the hearse turned around, with everybody in the back in an uproar, and jolted back to North Fork Town. "We've got another load paid for," Scut said. "And more sleeping in the trees. Think we ought to go back?"

"We need money now worse than ever. As soon as this bunch is unloaded, let's leave the goat with Stanley Hightower and come back for the others."

We drove to the undertaker's and left our fares. We went inside, but no one was there. Only a single lamp burned on the front desk. But we went back to the hearse and dragged Leviticus out. We shoved him into the office. "I'll close these blinds and keep him inside," Scut said. "You boys go for the other fares."

On the way back to the dance house the wind blew out the lamp again, and we stopped to turn the wick up and light it once more. "Ham, these civilized tribes have their own courts. Can they try outsiders?"

"While the lawyers argue those fine points," Ham said, "I'm catching a fast horse."

When we got our third batch of hilarity unloaded in front of the rooming house, a cowhand galloped up to the hearse. He peered hard into the seat. "Do you boys want to make a few bucks?"

"Not now," I said. "We've got to get this hearse across the street to Stanley Hightower."

"Twenty bucks," the cowhand said. "We want a sick man brought to town."

"Where's your camp?"

"Three miles down the road. The herd's off to the right."

"I don't know."

Ham nudged me. "Boy, we've got it rolling. We've got the hearse till sunup."

"It's pretty dark," I told the cowhand. "We ought to have more light. I don't want to lose this hearse in a mud hole."

"I'll be back." The cowhand whirled his horse. He galloped off toward the stage stand.

Chapter 8

YOU MIGHT THINK that no more catastrophe could happen that night, but it did.

With Ham holding two lanterns borrowed by the cowhand from the stage stand, we started down the dark road. Why did we want to save old Wallum's goat, anyway? Every minute around that thing only involved us deeper and deeper.

At last we followed the cowhand off the gusty road. Under the wide stars we came to a grassy prairie which was as flat and as merciless as a stove lid. A fire burned near a chuckwagon, and we stopped the hearse. Once the horses and the thumping of the wheels were still, we could hear far-off cowhands crooning as they circled the bedded herd on night guard, just making constant sounds to keep any sudden noise from starting a stampede. I'd have given a million dollars to be out there in the quiet night. As we climbed down from the hearse, other cowhands got up from the fire.

One slouched, grinning. "You want that sick man?"

"As soon as we get twenty dollars."

"Here's your twenty." He stuck out two gold pieces. "I'll show you." The cowhand went to the fire and pointed into the face of a sleeping man, big and broad-faced, his chest heaving and his nostrils snorting like a mountain lion.

"Oh, Lordy," I said. "It's Big Bill Cookson."

"He's not sick," Ham said, "he's drunk."

The cowhand grunted. "Well, when he wakes up, he will be sick—and a lot sicker, too, if that marshal catches him before he can draw a gun. Bill tried to see a girl at the dance, but came out here because of Olinger. He had his saddle pockets full of bootleg and drank the bottles empty so he'd have something to carry branch water in. Bill helped us drive burnt Choctaw cows to Baxter Springs last year, and to tell the truth, we don't have much use for Olinger. He's not lily white himself."

Ham whispered, "He won't come to till daylight. Let's take him. I'll sit ready to tie his hands if he wakes."

"Where do you want us to go?" I said.

"Take him to Stanley Hightower. Bill can sleep it off in the back of the parlor and be out of the way till he's sober. Olinger won't look for him there. Tell Stanley we'll bring Bill's horse and settle things when we come through town in the morning."

"I still don't know," I said. I wanted to get free of North Fork Town and head out quick for the Chic and Choc country.

"Listen," the cowhand said. "You've both got guns. If he wakes, one of you buffalo him. We'd take him in, but what if Olinger found us driving a hearse or saw us ride with a man thrown over a horse at this time of night?"

"All right, we'll take him."

So, on the way back to North Fork Town, here we are, driving Bill Cookson, a man who would be on our trail with Kurbstone as soon as he met Betty Blye.

After a while I stopped the horses. I took a lantern and

climbed down and went to the back of the hearse. From over the still body of Bill Cookson, Ham watched, his eyes gleaming in the light. I swung up and held the lantern above the outlaw's face, then sat in the far side of the hearse opposite Ham. With all that happened in the last two years, this was the blackest night of my life.

I said, "If anybody ever deserved killing, this skunk does."

"I reckon," Ham said. "But we can't do it."

"That's what I wanted to be sure about. That's why I came back here, just to look at him. Listen to him snore. A man can get shoved so deep in a corner for so long, he doesn't remember how to think. It wasn't all to see the Territory that made me go to Chetopa. I was afraid to go home with this one ear. I wanted to put it off as long as I could."

"I know," Ham said. "Me and Scut talked about it."

"What good has Bill Cookson done humanity?"

Ham said, "I've been sitting here wondering whether to reach in his pockets and take back some money for what he stole from us. I ain't done it yet, for that would make us no better than he is. But we could get rid of him. We could leave him here on the road."

"And we'd have twenty crooked dollars."

"Then you'd better stop talking crazy," Ham said. "It ain't in you to kill him."

When we got back to North Fork Town and stopped at Stanley Hightower's, I went to the back of the hearse again and looked in on Ham. "How is he?"

"He ain't wiggled. Even when you fell in the ruts."

"Those chug holes opened and grabbed two wheels."

"Let's see Stanley," Ham said.

"And leave Bill Cookson here?"

"Sure. If anybody looks and sees this snoring corpse, they won't tarry."

Scut was sitting comfortable inside the undertaker's office in a rocking chair, with the goat chewing a green funeral ribbon. "Ain't Stanley here?" I said.

"I haven't seen him. I've been rocking for two hours."

"Have you looked in the back of this place?"

"What would he be doing there? I ain't heard a sound from the back."

"Maybe not, but let's go see. We've got to leave town quick. We've got Bill Cookson outside."

Scut stood up. "Is that who you went for? Is he dead?"

"No, he ain't dead, just dead drunk. We got orders from a bunch of cowhands to leave him here."

"What next?" Scut groaned.

We opened the door to the back. A dimly burning lamp shone from a wall fixture. Three shapes lay stretched out under long blankets on three narrow tables. "If Stanley's here," Ham said, "there ain't no way to tell him from the rest unless we uncover somebody."

One blanket moved and Stanley Hightower sat up.

"You scared the wadding out of me," Ham said. "Is that a tie you're wearing, or have you got the black tongue?"

Stanley got to his feet and moved toward us, yawning. "How'd you make out?"

"Mighty well," I said. "But we sure earned it. We've got Big Bill Cookson in the hearse—passed out."

"Why do you tell me?"

"That 3-X brand sent him in. They said for you to lay him out till morning. They'll settle up then."

"Well, let's go get him."

We stopped at the door, watching until the street was clear, then we dragged Bill Cookson inside and laid him on a table. He was moaning and groaning, but what he said to himself didn't make sense to anyone. Stanley half-covered him with a blanket.

"What's that picture?" Ham pointed to a charcoal sketch beneath the green wall lamp.

"That?" Stanley said. "Oh, it's a sample of the work I do."

It was an old man with a benign expression under his closed eyes. Stanley rummaged through a stack of drawings on a desk. He pulled one out. "Here's what he looked like. He's sour—mouth all pulled down. Well, that wasn't his nature at all. He was the most pleasant man I ever talked to. False teeth made him look that way. I just padded him."

"I hope you don't get hold of me," Scut said.

Stanley studied Ham. "You'd make a fine corpse. You've got good lines."

I picked up the picture of a girl, her face in repose. "Who is this?"

"The daughter of a Creek chief," Stanley said. "The most beautiful girl I ever saw. Once I was in love with her. She died of tuberculosis, as many Indians do. They die of that, or cholera, or smallpox. Sometimes it's malaria."

"She really looked like that?" Ham said.

"Yes," Stanley said. "Come over here." He led us to one of the tables and pulled a blanket back. "Now, see this man's face? It will never come out right. It's too coarse. It's got a nose like a turnip. I do my best, but I can't help everybody."

"Where'd you learn this business?" Scut asked.

"In Scotland—Edinburgh—where I went to medical school. For a while I thought I'd be a doctor."

"How come a Creek Indian going to Scotland to school?"

"There's Scotch blood in the Creeks, just as there is in the other tribes. Some of us go back to visit old relatives. They look strange over there sometimes, wearing those kilts."

"I reckon," Ham said. "But if you're a doctor, how did you get into undertaking?"

"I'm an artist. The cemeteries are full of my work. A doctor is a practitioner. The last thing to be done for a person is to lay him away. My best work lasts forever, the doctor's dies."

"Do you do much business?" I said.

"I did at Fort Smith. But I wanted to come home. I haven't done too well in North Fork Town. Settlers die on the road, cowhands get shot up, outlaws get killed—always someone, the babes in arm and the sick and halt, but very few can pay. Soon I'll move on."

It was getting pretty creepy in that place, with Stanley talking and Bill Cookson mumbling to himself. "We owe you two dollars," I said. "But we did pretty well, so we'll make it five."

Stanley shook his head. "Just two."

"Well, here's an extra five for the window. We've got to be going."

"Come back to see me." Stanley was gazing with rapt interest at the picture under the lamp.

"So long," Ham said.

Before opening the front door to let the goat out, Scut pulled the blind aside. Under the street lantern swinging in the wind before the bare-fronted rooming house, Betty Blye stepped down from her surrey. "She's going inside," Scut said. "Boy, we've got to get out of this place."

The tall figure of a man moved from the shadow of the hearse and crossed the street toward the rooming house. It passed beneath the lantern to follow Betty Blye inside. It was Kurbstone.

"Here's our money," I told the boys. "Hurry. I'll take the goat out the back way. Go down to the livery stable and pay our horses out. I'll meet you at the dance hall. Then we'll go by Mrs. Treadways' and get the saddles. I sure want to be out of here before daylight."

A few hours after we left North Fork Town, we saw the sun come up over the Canadian. It looked mean and brassy, as if it would be something to conjure with; one of those hot autumn days which leaps suddenly upon the Territory.

When Scut and I got our saddles, with Ham keeping the goat at the mouth of the lane, Mrs. Treadways' place was deserted. Not wanting to be seen on the road or the South Fork crossing, we turned into the trees and swung east toward Hi-Early Mountain. We crossed the North Fork above the junction, now having only the one wide river to the south. The only thing was, we were headed away from the Texas Road again and didn't know when we'd get back to it.

"Hey!" Scut said. "How does an owl hoot?"

"How do I know?" Ham said.

"You'd better learn," Scut said. "We're sure on that trail."

There were some big bundles of hills all about, and brown rocky bluffs covered with every color of bright leaf you could think of, and after some rough going we came to a half-green swale with a spring in it. We got off our horses to caucus.

Scut said, hunkering, "This is the first time since leaving Chetopa that I've felt human, having my own horse between my legs. The first time I saw Kurbstone walking on that train, it swayed so much I thought he was drunk. When I walked, I thought I was drunk. Then I looked for the steamboat to blow up, and I got banged on the head in the stage. This Territory transportation just ain't made for a man used to the hurricane deck of a cow pony."

After the goat and the horses drank at the spring, we sprawled to do some thinking. "We can't go north," I said. "Every place from here to Kansas will be looking for us. And from now on it's not safe to go south."

"We could leave Leviticus," Scut said.

"Maybe. But even if Wallum was lucky enough to get the goat back, he'd still be after us and we'd be stuck anyway. What that conductor swears to on a witness stand will be done to save his own hide, not ours."

"Scrape, what's got into you about this?" Ham said.

"I don't know. I ain't figured it out myself. But it's about the biggest thing in my life. It's tied us up with something that's more than a goat—it's people."

"You've got to make a start," Ham said.

"It's always easy to sit at the tail gate of a wagon and tell where the driver went. But the thing is, the other man did the driving. Maybe I don't have what the driver had. Slick Pilifer would know what to do, but I don't. I'll do something, but I've got to figure the road before I take the lines."

"Well, we'll sit steady," Scut said.

"I'd like to hide out a while—have time to think it over. If I can get out of the Territory and cross Red River, I'll have kinfolks in every county in Texas to hide with till I give Wallum this goat."

"Is that it?" Scut said.

"It's just maybe."

"You've no reason to like Wallum," Ham said.

"I wasn't thinking of Wallum. When we leave here, let's hunt a hiding place."

An outburst of sobbing came from the trees. It was so unexpected it frightened us more than it did the horses. We crept toward the direction of the sound, and a woman lay in the fallen leaves near a red-berried haw tree where a fidgity side-saddled black mare stood. The woman heard us and sat up, fear in her eyes.

It was Miss Lockwood, from Pemberton-on-the-Holyoke. Her face and arms were scratched, and her skirt was torn. "Oh!" she cried, standing to run toward us. "How glad I am to see you!"

"How did you get here?" Scut said.

"I can't ever tell! It's horrible. There was shooting and I ran."

"If somebody is after you," I said, "you'd better talk fast. We're not too safe ourselves. How long have you been here?"

"At least an hour. The horse threw me into the trees. I was too afraid to move."

"Come to the spring and wash up. Then tell us what happened."

She got herself in hand sooner than we expected and began to speak in a steady voice. She wasn't at all the chatterbox she'd been on the stage. Maybe in spite of all her palaver and ideas of do-gooding, she had been just a frightened young woman and getting more and more that way the deeper into the Territory she came. Then when she had got started with all the talk on the long ride, she couldn't stop.

"Did the shooting happen in Beale's City?" Ham asked.

She was cleaned up now and calm. We all stood together.

"No. It was back in the hills. The day I arrived, Mr. Beale drove me with my luggage to the cabin of an old Indian and his wife. He was a church official of some sort. Mr. Beale had decided that their home would be a good place for me to begin. They knew all the young Indians I could work with. But on the very first night some robbers came. They took the man's church money from a cupboard and abused his wife."

"What did they look like?" Scut said. "Who were they?"

"Five men. An old, tall dark man and four younger men. And someone was on a horse outside the door. I just knew she was a woman. Two nights later they came back again. They said that more money was in the cabin, that it was hidden under the dirt floor. They forced the Indian to dig it up. As they left, the Indian's wife fired a pistol at them. The robbers fired and when his wife fell, the old Indian picked up the pistol. He wounded two of them, then he was killed."

"You mean they both died?" I said.

"Yes."

"And the outlaws didn't harm you?"

"I don't know why, but they didn't try to—not then. I did what I could for the old people and next morning I sent a boy from another cabin to get Mr. Beale. He came and helped bury them. He said he had heard that one of the robbers had been taken away to have his wound treated. Yesterday I learned that the other one was hurt too badly to be moved and would have help brought to him from North Fork Town."

"Did Beale tell you who this wild bunch was?" Ham asked.

"I think he knew, but he wouldn't tell."

"You mean you stayed in that cabin alone?" Scut said.

"The old people had no relatives, and I decided to use it until the property was disposed of. But last night everything was different. They had brought someone from North Fork Town to help the badly hurt man. Then they came to kill me."

"What do you mean?" Scut said. "They came on a shooting spree to get a woman?"

"Yes. They had heard of what I'd done for the old people, and that I intended to stay. Perhaps, too, they were afraid I would testify against them. They brought an awful Negro with them—Blue Gum."

"What happened?" I said. "How did you get away?"

For the first time her voice shook. "I still don't know. They called for me to come outside the cabin. Blue Gum stood by the door, I heard them call him that. And in the distance a woman had got off her horse. She moved off with a man to talk. The tall old man with the whip told me to walk into the trees. Then I don't know what happened. I was screaming, and I ran until I came to the woman's horse. Somehow I was on it and racing away. I'd learned to ride at Pemberton, but never like that. Even with all the pistol shooting, I heard a woman swearing."

"Lady," Scut said, "do you know what you've done?"

"Only that I've raced the horse all night. I was lost, of course—on mountains and in deep creeks, and I gave up. Then at the river the horse seemed to know where to go. We forded it, and here I am."

"You fooled Old Tom Starr's gang," I said. "And you stole a mare from the best horse thief of all—Belle Reed. We saw her and that mare just a few nights ago in North Fork Town."

"Well," Scut said wearily, "where do we go now?"

"I hope I haven't caused you trouble," Miss Lockwood said.

"You haven't. We ain't been caught yet."

"Do you know what I wish?" Miss Lockwood said. "I wish we had some of the fried chicken we had on the stage."

"So do we," I said. "Maybe you'd better lead up Belle's mare—since you know her best. We'll break out some fresh fish hooks from our saddle pockets and hunt a deep branch."

We had our gear and our blankets and tarps with us that night for the first time in ages, and under the heavy stars it felt like home on the range again. A fire would have been nice, but it was one thing we dispensed with. We camped in a thicket.

Scut sprawled, leaning back on his elbows. "I've looked at that old Big Dipper a lot of times, but never like this. I think Slick Pilifer is about the smartest man on earth. But he made one mistake—letting us come on this trip."

"It ain't all bad," Ham said. "We're finding our personality."

Miss Lockwood sat near a single tree. "I'm beginning to find mine, too."

"What do you mean?" I said.

"In college I thought only of myself. But now I think of people—the poor old Indian and his wife, and how the thing they worked for most was what caused their deaths. I've even thought of the stage driver. Mr. Beale told me how the man tried to reform Bill Cookson."

"Bill's reformed now, if he's woke up," Scut said. "Or deformed from all the red-eye he had last night. We saw him."

"What I mean is," Miss Lockwood said, "I think one can get in—shall I say a rut, so to speak? I had many thoughts at Pemberton, but they were all in-grown, only about myself. Here they are about the people."

"You mean that at first you really came here for yourself, and not the people?" I asked.

"Yes. I see it now. I came for myself. Do you know what it meant to stand by and see an old couple shot down?"

"We've seen a few cowhands turn up their toes and sprout daisies," Ham said.

"I haven't learned anything," Miss Lockwood said. "But I want to stay and try."

"I knew an old philosopher up on the Brazos," Scut said, rising with his spurs rattling. "He opined that when the words got as heavy as the going, it was time to hit the hay."

If we'd had any sense when we tore out from North Fork Town, we'd have bought some coffee with our leftover cash, since the eating places were opening. But still and all, being cowhands, we brewed up a passable drink from acorns and some parched corn we found in Belle Reed's saddle pockets. It's not the taste of things on the trail that counts; it's the custom.

We had a few rancid strips of sowbelly and about a cup of corn meal in the bottom of Ham's saddle pockets, so with some catfish we caught in the branch we had a royal breakfast. We mounted up and set out slowly that morning, avoiding every dim lamp post along the way, heading for a clump of distant hills and following Leviticus, who turned out to be a pretty good lead steer. At times the going was rough and rocky, but not knowing where outlaws hung out, one way to us was as good as any.

By about noon we'd fought our way around the side of a rough mountain, and we came to a deep canyon which ran between it and another. We stopped to consider the situation. Before we got a word out of our mouths, we heard a gobbling sound above us.

"Doggone," Ham said. "If somebody wouldn't hear pistol shooting, I'd get that turkey."

"I'm going up there anyway," Scut said. "Maybe I can hit it with a rock." He got off his horse.

This gobbling continued and got madder and louder than ever, until we thought the old bird was getting ready to fly straight down from his hiding place to land on top of us.

Now, it is still the custom of some of these civilized Indians to set up a big turkey-gobbling in the brush when they spot their mortal enemy and wish to seek revenge or kill him. It is one of those things which puts terror in the adversary, and it means that unless he has a faster horse and a truer pistol than the gobbler, he is lost. It is a sort of battle cry.

So when Scut slides down the grade in a little while, with all the gobbling ceased, Ham and I are not surprised at what he says—when at last he can talk for laughing.

"That Cherokee Indian up there has been having woman trouble. His wife gets so mean to him that when he can't stand it any more, he leaves the cabin about once a week. He just goes out in the brush and gobbles. He sits up there getting madder and madder and making a racket like all get-out until all of sudden he feels quiet and peaceful inside. He ain't killed anybody, and he goes back and lives with his wife for another week. He says come on up the mountain and he'll sell us some food."

Miss Lockwood is laughing. "Oh, how they would like that at Pemberton." She caught herself. "I mustn't say that again."

The horses pick their way up the mountain, and soon we come to what is half a dugout and half a cabin set in the slope and rocks and trees. Around and above it and in and out of the brush appears to be a field which is run in lines of dirt-heaped semicircles, like terraces.

"He don't know farming," Scut said. "My old man always said to run furrows uphill so it would be easier walking down."

We stopped the horses in the yard. It held the usual ash hopper to make lye for hominy, barking dogs, and a big grinding wheel. The Indian and his wife were there, she dressed like most farm white women and he in a deerskin jacket and white man's britches. Dark-faced children stood around the woman, clutching her skirts. "Well, we got here!" Scut sang out. He turned and looked about him. "Hey! Look down there!"

Far off and below was the Canadian, its broad stretches winding in a loop about an area of fairly level and treeless land. Ham said, "Look at that big mountain across the river and all the wide land."

"It's beautiful!" Miss Lockwood cried.

"What can we buy from you?" Scut asked the Cherokee.

But a change had come over the Indian. His face was tight with fear, and so was his wife's. Yet he said, "You can have bacon, cow, yams, squash, pumpkin. Corn meal, coffee, salt, sugar."

"Load us up with all of it."

The Indian did. We filled our saddlebags and he filled two tow sacks with food and another with ears of corn for the horses. We slung the sacks across our saddles. The children still stood not moving. Scut was on the ground when we mounted. He said, "How much do we owe you?"

"Nothing," the Indian said. "We want nothing."

"Nothing?" Ham called down.

"No. You take it all—free."

"Listen," I said. "We didn't come up here to beat you out of anything. We want to pay for it. How much do we owe you?"

"Nothing."

Then I knew why. They were all staring at Miss Lockwood, even the children. But then I knew, just as I caught Scut's eyes, that they were not staring at her but at her horse—Belle Reed's mare.

"Scut, climb up. We'll see that you get money," I told the Indian. "But it won't be so it will hurt you."

As we picked our way down the mountain, Ham said, "It looks like we hopped into the frying pan."

"And get ready to hop into the fire," I said. "It's not over yet."

We camped close to the canyon, which had a full stream of water jolting over the rocks. It was a nice spot you could pass all your life in, and that was just about what we would do, pass it and leave it behind forever.

Next morning when Miss Lockwood woke up, she looked about surprised. Maybe she had heard the noises, as we had. "Good morning," she said.

A ring of four horsemen surrounded us—four horsemen and a woman.

"Good morning," Miss Lockwood said again.

Chapter 9

WHEN THEY led us to the flat land we had seen from the mountain, they called it "the Bend," and now and then "Younger's Bend," where the river looped.

A few sacks of food might fill your belly, but not the wonder of surprise. Belle Reed, slant-mouthd and cruel, rode before us. The broad-shouldered man beside her was Jim, her husband. She wore a felt hat slanted to one side, with weather-beaten and sun-stained embroidered flowers on the brim.

We knew it now, but too late—the big ridge across the canyon was Hi-Early Mountain. We had come straight to the Belle Reed country without knowing it. The other mountains stood across the river. Somewhere between them must have been the ford where Miss Lockwood had crossed the Canadian.

The men who rode with us were somber and silent. No one

sang a happy hymn on this march. The creek bent to the southeast, and then we turned abruptly to the level land. When we reached it, it wasn't as level as it had appeared to be from the mountain. There was a gentle slope, with the river hidden from view, but we climbed higher. At last after a few acres, it leveled. Then we moved across it.

The mountains across the river stood clear and bold, especially the big one, and through the half-leafless trees on our side, the water glinted.

"Scrape," Scut said, "it's just a matter of principle with me. But I'd rather be hung by a law than an outlaw."

Belle Reed turned her face. "Who is an outlaw? You have my horse."

"Nobody is, ma'am," Scut said. "I was just admiring the scenery."

I'd heard it said that as a girl Belle Reed was a Confederate spy during the war in Missouri, before she ended up bad in Texas, but I think about all she did was run or ride across a field one day like any frightened girl and yell, "The Yankees are coming!" But I wasn't quarreling with any part of that history now.

But give her time—for when she married into the Starr clan, an old Indian was to tell Tom Starr that she was like a snake, and would poison anything she came in contact with. And she did everything possible to fulfill his words. She stuck to her own business, and she was the best in the West, especially in the Territory. She became Belle Starr after she married Sam in a certain way.

Before and after Sam was shot and killed, when a husband or sweetheart dropped off in one odd death or another, always in violence, she took the next. Right now she chased back and forth between Texas and Missouri. But at the present moment she was looking at the mountain across the river as if expecting some sign.

A flash of light shot from the peak, and another, as from an army heliograph, as if someone hidden there had waited for us to appear before flashing a signal. Jim pulled his horse toward Belle and they talked together in low voices.

"Do you think this is the Starr bunch?" Ham muttered.

"No," I said. "Old Tom isn't here. Two of these men are pure white, one is Indian, and Jim Reed is white. The gang has split up for some reason, so maybe the Starrs stuck to the timber."

We stopped and dismounted at the edge of some trees where the level land dropped toward the river. "I never saw a better hide-out," Scut said. "Not for it to be in the open. If they keep watch from the mountains, they know everything."

"You can bet they keep watch," Ham said. "And if they need it, they've got running room in all directions. They must know this country like a book."

A lean-to covered by a tarpaulin stood among the trees, a half-room of logs at the back. "You think she stays here all the time?" Scut said.

"She probably stays in some of these hill cabins," I said. "The Starrs, too. That's probably why they wanted to get rid of Miss Lockwood."

So far, there had been an unspoken truce between the two women. Miss Lockwood had not spoken—neither had Belle Reed. You would have thought some sort of battle was about to start, but neither knew where to begin. The horse Belle rode was a good one, but not as good as the stolen mare. Yet Belle Reed had not so much as glanced at the animal, either at the camp where we had been surprised, or here.

An old proverb says "Never reveal your cards to a woman," and Belle and Miss Lockwood, standing and looking at each other, took it seriously. Then Belle Reed said, "Come inside." And Miss Lockwood followed her to two straight-back chairs which stood beneath the lean-to.

With his back against a tree, the dark Indian sat holding a rifle. The two whites hunkered by a pile of stone which served as a fireplace. Jim Reed slouched over to stand by Wallum's goat. "Where'd you get this?" he said.

"It's one we're taking to Texas," I said.

"Are you boys from Texas?"

"You know mighty well we are.'"

Jim Reed laughed. He scratched his backside. "Well, stop bragging about it. I'm from Texas, too, a long ways from it, and from Missouri. I aim to stay that way."

"That's our conclusion about us," Scut said. "We haven't seen Texas for so long, it may be off the map. Hey, we haven't had breakfast. How about us cooking up chuck from those tow sacks?"

Jim Reed said, "You wouldn't want to get your pistols, would you?"

Ham said, "My belly's so weak I couldn't pull a trigger."

"We've done some riding ourselves." Jim went to the sack and dumped the contents on the ground, but picked up the pistols he had put in the sacks earlier.

"You're a man after my own heart," Scut said.

"I'm after everybody's heart."

"You've got a pretty wife," Ham said. "You sure watch over her."

That was a joke. It was Belle Reed who did the watching. She had those men tied so tight to her finger they hardly moved. Scarcely a minute passed without one of them looking at her like a weather-beaten slave in bondage—where she sat in the lean-to with Miss Lockwood.

Miss Lockwood came to the fire. "Just think! As a girl Mrs. Reed learned to play the piano in Missouri. And she knew Jesse James. When Mr. Cole Younger went to Texas, she became his sweetheart. Isn't that wonderful?"

It sure was—watching that brooding specter sitting in the lean-to with a long-holstered pistol at her waist. We were getting along pretty well with Jim Reed and making ready to begin the cooking, when Belle got up and told him to wash the skillets and scrub them with sand.

The dark image with his back to the tree hadn't moved. What surprised us about the gang of outlaws was that there was so little talking among them. Now Belle had become indifferent even toward Miss Lockwood. She sat in her chair and ate from a tin plate, silent and grim, while Miss Lockwood ate with us by the fire. Belle took no enjoyment in eating; she was like a mechanical figure which sat and every so often raised a fork to its mouth.

"Hey!" Scut yelled. "We made some candy from one of your recipes!"

"From mine?"

"We sure did."

"Where did you get it?"

"We stayed at Mrs. Treadways' in North Fork Town."

"How well do you know her?" Belle said sharply.

"Not too well," I said. "She kept this goat for us. We were just passing through."

"How did you meet Miss Lockwood?"

We told her that. Afterward she got up and walked about the fire, not looking at us or at Miss Lockwood. "I told her everything I knew about you," Miss Lockwood whispered. "She knew it soon after we got here."

"You're dealing with a smart woman," I said. "She doesn't even trust herself."

"She's worried," Miss Lockwood said.

As the morning droned on, and since we had no plans for the future, it seemed that the gang was determined to do nothing but sit in camp all day. Belle Reed went to her lodging. Soon she snored as loud as a buzz saw. The rest of us stretched out in the sun and dozed. Only that unblinking man by the tree stayed awake.

After a while he got up and came to the fire to kick Jim Reed on the hip. "Get up," he said. "They're coming." Jim got up and called Belle.

Three people on horseback rode from the dappled light of the trees—two men and Mrs. Treadways. Their horses were still wet from fording the river. At the camp Mrs. Treadways looked down at us and smiled. "Well, mercy me. We do meet again."

Belle Reed stood watching her. It seemed that Mrs. Treadways had spoken first to us, rather than break the woman's awesome silence. It was as if her keen mind had earlier decided that she would force Belle Reed to speak first.

"Hey! You're wearing that little brooch." Scut helped Mrs. Treadways from her horse. "We didn't expect to see you here."

Belle Reed moved impatiently. She said in a harsh voice, "How is he?"

Mrs. Treadways said, "He died in the night."

"Why didn't you save him?"

"Ask your Maker," Mrs. Treadways snapped. The sharp look we had seen in her eyes the night Scut kept his pistol on was there again as she looked from us to Leviticus. "Why are you here?" Before we could answer, she pinpointed Miss Lockwood. "Yes, I've heard of you." She asked me, "Are you together?"

"We met up by accident. And then we got captured."

"When did you leave North Fork Town?" she asked sweetly.

"A couple of mornings ago."

Then she snapped the bull whip. "When you left, did you know Bill Cookson was dead—killed where you left him?"

"What did you say?" Belle Reed rasped. Her face was purple with rage.

"Killed?" I said. "He was alive and snoring the last we saw. How'd you know about him?" Ham's worried face was on me.

The shrewd look was in her blue eyes. "That doesn't matter. Did you kill him because he robbed you?"

"Listen," said Ham. "This is the craziest stuff I ever heard. And since you seem to know all about it anyway, we ain't got a thing to hide."

Mrs. Treadways said to me, "You were the last to leave him."

"You bet I was. I went out the back door of Stanley's place

with the goat because people we didn't want to see were at the rooming house. Stanley was stretching out on a cot and I asked if he wanted to bolt the door. He said no, that he had to get up soon, anyway. I left and went into the alley."

"Why didn't you want to see the other people?"

"That doesn't have a thing to do with this. And when we went out to that herd, we didn't even know Bill Cookson was there."

Belle Reed said, "How was he killed?"

"He was stabbed in the heart—stretched out on a table. Stanley Hightower is held for murder. It's ridiculous. There's no better boy than Stanley." Her eyes were still boring mine.

"Stanley didn't do that," I said. "It's not in him to do a thing like that."

"Then, who did?" Mrs. Treadways said. "You say you didn't. You say Stanley didn't."

"Hey!" Scut asked me. "When you went out the door, did you see anybody around?"

"I don't know. It was black as pitch. I waited inside a spell to let you boys get to the livery stable, so we'd all end up at the dance house about the same time. But yes—I remember somebody was at the alley corner—just a shadow. But the whole town had been full of people. I didn't pay any attention to it."

"I wonder," said Ham, "if someone who wanted to kill Bill Cookson knew he was inside?"

"Now, that's smart," Scut said. "How'd he kill him if he didn't know where he was?"

"I haven't got it all figured yet," Ham said. Suddenly he got quiet.

When we had a chance, we got as far away from the others as we could. "Listen," Ham said. "I shut up quick because even while I was talking, I really got the answer. Scrape, the crazy way you talked in that hearse I thought at first you killed Bill Cookson. But what if someone knew he might try to get Old Man Wallum's reward money? What would he do if he was a crook? He'd put Bill out of the way."

"You mean Kurbstone?" I said.

"Sure. He was there."

"I'm so mixed up I can't see straight," Scut said. "But if Betty Blye talked to Kurbstone in the rooming house, she didn't even know Bill was in the parlor."

"No, but she could have told him she and Bill were out to get the money."

"It gets pretty tight," Scut said. "Somebody who knew about everything—us and Bill and the money—told Kurbstone where Bill was hidden."

"Olinger," I said.

"Why?"

"Maybe he and Kurbstone are in on some whiskey deal. Maybe Olinger was just friendly. He wanted Bill out of the way, but he'd be afraid to do it like this. With a pistol he could hide behind the law, but maybe he didn't want the showdown after all."

"You wouldn't find a federal marshal in on whiskey," Scut said.

"Out of that corrupt Fort Smith court? I heard a dozen people there say they're trying to get rid of that crooked judge and get a good hanging one."

"How would Olinger know we had the goat?"

"He ain't blind. He probably found out from some of those revelers we brought to town. Or maybe he didn't know."

"Maybe he was in the trees still looking for Bill and saw us go to the cow camp," Ham said. "He could have watched us unload, and he could have stood at Stanley's back window."

"If Kurbstone saw you leave with the goat, why didn't he take it then?" Scut said.

"He wanted to get the big game out of the way first. Then he'd get us when it suited him. Maybe Bill was in his hair, anyway."

"Well, we sure solved this case," Ham said. "There's no use to call the Pinkerton Agency."

"What are we going to do?" Scut said.

"About what?" I said.

"Stanley Hightower."

"There's nothing we can do. If he's held in jail, we couldn't get him out, even if we got away from this gang."

"He sure treated us square," Scut said. "But now we bring everything down on him. When Kurbstone and Olinger tie him in with us and the goat, he won't have a chance. Kurbstone would swear to anything, just as he would with us."

"I've got a funny hunch," Ham said. "Old Lady Treadways was sure riled up about Stanley."

We walked over to Belle Reed. "We want to go to North Fork Town to see Stanley Hightower," I said. "Maybe we can do something to get him freed."

"Why should I help free him?"

"Because I say so," Mrs. Treadways snapped.

Belle Reed laughed harshly. "You?" She acted as if she had been struck in the face. "Why do you want him freed? Have you forgot Bill Cookson?"

"No. But I know Stanley Hightower. Unless they go, I've spent my last night in your hills."

She was a sassy thing, no matter what her calling was.

"Can we use your house?" I asked.

"No." Her blue eyes burned into ours, one to the other. "It is watched by the lighthorse. And now they want you."

"Where are those nannies?" Scut said.

"A neighbor is keeping them."

"Well, I just wondered," Scut said lamely.

"I guess it's time to go," I told Belle Reed. I went to Miss Lockwood. "You'll be safe. Don't worry about Belle. Right now Mrs. Treadways bosses her. Just sit tight for a few days. And watch the goat for us."

"Will you bring Mr. Hightower back?"

"We'll do our best."

We saddled up and rode back toward North Fork Town.

The jail of the crossroads settlement stood on a side street. It was a stone building with barred windows, and at night it looked like a square, squat hump of adobe. From the windows slim paths of yellow light slanted. We had waited to come into town after dark along a tree-bordered creek, and our horses had been left at the blackest hitch rack. We stood watching the jail, trying to get our bearings.

"If that was some cow-town jail," Ham said, pulling his hat lower, "we could rope it and turn it over."

"And kill Stanley when it caved in," I said. "First, we've got to figure this out. Too many people know about us and Leviticus. He's not a goat any more. He's a public character."

"Go on," Scut said. "Don't state the problem and stop."

"I stated it. You and Ham take it from there. Let the Brain start it."

"We'd better work at night," Ham said. "And keep out of the way of the lighthorse."

After a caucus we decided we'd better let Stanley in on things first, so Ham went to the jail, since he looked more like a Creek than Scut or I. We backed up against a stone wall. In about thirty minutes Ham came back. "Let's get out of town."

We didn't talk until the horses cut back toward the creek. Then we got off and sat. "Stanley agrees with us," Ham said. "He hasn't got a chance. It's funny about Bill Cookson—everybody liked him. They like Stanley, too, but they think Bill got a raw deal."

"Stanley hasn't had his turn," I said. "Did you tell him we came to help?"

Ham nodded. "He'll try to think of something. He says to come back tomorrow night."

"Could you talk to him alone?"

"Sure. There's just one guard. He sits at the far end of the hall. Stanley's cell is halfway to the front door. The guard took my pistol and locked me in with him."

"That's what we can do," Scut said. "Next time, change clothes and you stay inside. That's how those dime novels do."

"Are you crazy? Anyway, Stanley has had a lot of callers. Mr. Collier was there."

"What does he think?" I said.

"He told Stanley that nothing in this case meets the eye. It's all a frame-up. Kurbstone is still in town, and so is Olinger. Stanley said that when he was ready to drive his hearse here from Fort Smith, Olinger met him on Garrison Avenue and wanted him to haul a load of liquor."

"That fits. Where is Betty Blye?"

"She's still here. Maybe we could use her. Maybe she could get the guard interested."

"She's pretty smart," Scut said. "But maybe she's cooking up her own game. Do you think Kurbstone watches her?"

"Sure."

"Life is simpler for an honest man," Scut said.

When Ham came from the jail next evening, Scut and I were backed against the same wall. He said, "Let's wait. Stanley says if the light in his cell goes out in ten minutes, he wants us to do something."

"What?" I said.

"It's too long to tell now. Let's wait for the light. We can talk in the woods."

It had been a lonesome mess, hiding out this way with so much on our minds, but there was no help for it. Mrs. Treadways' cottage had seemed to be deserted, but three of us together couldn't take a chance on an ambush by the lighthorse. We couldn't take a chance by day in town, either. We skulked along the road by day and hid by night, save for this one trip to town by the back way after dark, and even then we were among the camps of the covered wagons.

"It's out," Ham said, as the center light faded. "Let's ride."

Back in camp, when we had the horses hobbled and talked things over, Scut and I learned Stanley's scheme. He'd been having bad appendicitis and cramp colic pains since last night. No matter what the guard did for him, it got worse, and especially after he ate. "He won't be of any use that way," Scut said.

"That's just the point," Ham said. "He's not sick. He's just leading up to something. The guard comes into the cell each time to help him. That's what he tried again after I left, to test the guard."

"Oh, so that's it."

"Tomorrow he wants us to ride out to see a man named Amon Tilby. This fellow keeps some money for him. He wants us to get it, a good horse packed to the gills, and cram a jacket and a hat in the saddle pockets. We're to keep this horse in camp, but come to town tomorrow night as usual."

Tilby lived in a big two-story house on the North Fork. He was portly and impressive. He had a face like a moon, and about as many dogs and children in the yard as a sky on a dark night has stars. He was standing in the yard and his black hair flowed over his shoulders. As we nodded and got off our horses, he said, "What can I do for you?"

"Nothing," Ham said, and then spoke some outlandish Indian word.

Tilby looked at him queerly, then said, "Where did you learn that? It's an old name in our family."

"I learned it sitting in jail last night. Stanley Hightower taught it to me."

A hard expression came to Tilby's round face. "Who are you?"

"Scut and Ham and Scrape," Scut said. "We're friends of Stanley's, and he sent us here today. Your name is Tilby."

Tilby nodded.

"We want Stanley's money, a full-packed horse ready to ride, and a few other things," Ham said. "Now, what about this?" He sounded off with another Indian word.

"Very well," Tilby said. "And this?" He sounded off with something halfway between a word and a gobble.

"That's what Stanley said you'd say. He said it would have an -iski in the first part. And every time I practiced this one in the cell, I got my tongue twisted." Ham let out with another word.

Tilby said, "I haven't been allowed to see him. I'm a relative—they think I could kill him to save him from disgrace, or do anything. I do have the best lawyers for him, but I doubt if they can help."

Ham told Tilby, "He said to keep him posted down the Texas Road, by that first name I gave you."

"I will."

Tilby led us to a corral as big as the best in Texas, some distance behind the house. We picked out a large bay that seemed able to pound the miles. An armed Creek horseman wearing moccasins circled the corral. While Scut roped the horse, I asked, "Why do you have a guard?"

"Did you ever hear of Blue Gum? He's been a frequent visitor among the Creeks. He's one reason we have so many lighthorse out."

"We've heard of him."

When the bay was saddled and packed, Tilby said, "If I knew what you planned and when, I would like to be there. But for me to be seen in North Fork Town would be the worst thing for Stanley. Collier can do more than I can." He gave Ham a deerskin bag which pulled him to his knees. Tilby laughed. "It's all gold. Tell Stanley I matched every gold piece of his with one of my own." When we were ready to ride down the lane, he said, "How will you do it?"

"It's Stanley's show," I said. "You know as much as we do."

"Something has changed him," Tilby said. "He sounds like a Creek again."

"He's all right," Scut said. "Up till now he just couldn't find his way out of something."

When Ham came back from the jail in the rain in his slicker, he was laughing. "That's the craziest one Indian I ever saw in my life. He says to be ready tomorrow night. He wants a bottle of ipecac and a pack of makings and that jacket and hat stuck through the window. He says we can drop the hat and the jacket in with the makings, but to slide the ipecac down on a string."

"You mean that's all we do?" I said.

"Yes. Except to have that loaded horse right here where we stand—with ours."

"Boy!" Scut said. "He must plan to float out that window."

As we rode out to camp, Ham said, "Somebody's got to come in tomorrow to buy that stuff. Everything's closed now, but so far we've made it fine. It had better be me."

"Our hero," Scut said.

But when Ham came back to camp an hour before sundown next day, he was worried. He got out of his saddle and slumped like an old man. "I got what Stanley wanted, after trying every little place there was. But that town is full of lighthorse and that's not the worst."

"Ain't anything worse than lighthorse for tonight," I said.

"Oh, yes," Ham groaned. "Maybe you don't remember the day a red-whiskered whiskey-train driver passed us while we were chopping wood on Little Rock Road. Well, he got here today. He and Kurbstone and Olinger were sitting on the top corral rail at the wagon yard, talking things over. Then they got their drivers and looked the town over. I bet we've been spotted."

"Let's cook up some chuck," I said. "We've got a busy evening and a long night's run ahead."

"I forgot to tell you," Ham said. "The lighthorse captain found three full whiskey kegs in Stanley Hightower's hearse."

"And him in jail?" Scut said. "Well, it will take the pressure off somebody."

"Let's cook up some chuck," I said.

It was a clear night—no moon, but almost too many stars for our business, there in the shadow of the wall. We wished it had been darker, what with all the Creek lighthorse patrolling the town, but we dismounted at the same place, looking up and down the street.

"It's about time," Ham said.

"Who goes?" I said.

"Not me," Ham said. "I'm too short. I couldn't reach the window."

"Scrape," Scut said, "there ain't an inch in height between us. Me and you come out together. But standing in a saddle makes my feet tired. We've elected you."

I turned to my horse. "If somebody comes along, get in a scuffle to attract attention. Keep them away from the jail. This won't be easy."

With sacking tied to my horse's feet, I rode down the street and at the corner turned into the next street until I was behind the jail, then cut straight across a vacant lot toward the light of Stanley's cell. I stopped beneath the window and got the hat and jacket out of the saddle pockets and stood up in the saddle. I looked down through the bars. On the cot below, Stanley Hightower slept, his face to the wall. But his shoes were off, which was the sign.

I dropped the jacket and hat. Stanley's head turned and he looked at the window. The makings and matches were in the jacket. I took the bottle of ipecac with the tied-on string from my pocket and slid it over the barred sill. It went down easy, not making a sound when it touched the floor.

Stanley was moving about the cell in his sock-feet. He had shoved the jacket and hat beneath the cot, and now he raised the bottle of ipecac to his lips. I got down into the saddle and rode the same way back to Scut and Ham and untied the sacking. "Are you ready?" I said.

"Yes," Ham said. "We're ready, but we don't know for what."

Two shadowy lighthorse turned the corner by the jail. They rode our way. The lanterns of the jail front revealed them clearly. "Good Lord," Scut said. "It's happening."

"Get down and look at that bay's hooves," I said. "Lift them up, quick."

The lighthorse plodded nearer and stopped. One called, "Any trouble?"

"Got a stone in a hoof. Our pal's gone to the livery stable to see if we can put up. How's the hay?"

"If you are as tired as you look, it won't trouble you."

"Thanks," I said.

They rode on, but still we waited—the stars bright, the night long. Time stopped and whittled a stick on the hitch rack. "This is the longest night of my life," Ham said.

We waited and watched the jail. Then a man sauntered out to stand in the lantern light. He wore a slouch hat pulled over his eyes. He looked up and down the street, in no hurry at all to move on, reaching into his jacket pocket.

He took out some makings and rolled a cigarette and lit it, head down, the match flare hidden in his cupped hands. He crossed the street and turned at the corner to come our way. Then he lurched against the side of a store, vomiting, the sound seeming to rattle the night, the dropped cigarette tossing a shower of sparks from the walk.

"It's Stanley," Ham said.

The man shoved himself away from the wall and came on. "Where is my horse?"

"This is yours," I said.

He mounted, clinging to the pommel. Then he vomited over the side again. When he straightened, he said, "Let's ride. Slow."

We rode past the jail and toward the undertaking parlor and the stage stand. As we passed the lantern of the rooming house, a single lighthorse rode by. "Hello, Bob," Stanley said.

"Hello, Stanley."

So that was that.

At the edge of North Fork Town we struck out at a good lope. Then by morning, after a slow night, we returned to Hi-Early.

Chapter 10

IF, AS SCUT had hinted at Tilby's, Stanley Hightower needed to be awakened from a deep sleep or something, the days in jail had done their work. He no longer dreamed—he was alive. The old Creek blood came forth. After the constant retching from the ipecac had ceased, he had ridden steadily and silently, but with morning his face was pale. Yet a harder, more confident expression sat upon his features.

"You sure beat yourself around a stump," Scut said.

The mountain of the gobbler loomed blue. Ham said, "You left a trail only a coyote could follow."

"Only a coyote would follow it. I didn't want to hurt the jailer, but it was the only way. He'd always helped me, so when I began to vomit, he thought I was dying."

We knew we were watched from the moment we saw Hi-Early, but it didn't matter. We rode through the rocky brown cuts and up the slope to the Bend. From the north ducks and geese were flying over, yelling their taunt to the world.

"I haven't heard that sound in years," Stanley said, glancing skyward. "At least not in the open."

"It's the only place to hear it," Scut said.

When we reached the lean-to, only Miss Lockwood was there. We introduced Stanley and she said, "I understand you are a doctor."

"I was."

"Mrs. Treadways said you saved her life. When you came home from Fort Smith, you sat over her day and night to save her from fever. She told me more; that you gave her all your medical equipment."

"It was no use to me. Mrs. Treadways had been a nurse in Kansas City."

"She told me so, and that she had stolen the hospital money. She came to the Territory and married a Creek."

"And a few months later," Stanley said, "he was found murdered in the woods. But the lighthorse could prove nothing against her. Did she tell you that?"

"Yes. She said there was nothing for her now but to help people, no matter who they were."

"She's not a bad woman," Stanley said. He went beyond the lean-to and began to heave.

"Is he ill?" Miss Lockwood's face showed lines of strain.

"He drank a bottle of ipecac," I said.

She whispered, "It is habitual?"

"I hope not. But it got him out of jail."

At noon Belle Reed and Mrs. Treadways rode up from the river, the silent men behind them. There was never in the West a camp so completely dominated by women. They ruled the universe as far as the eye could see, especially the one in the embroidered hat.

"Hello, Stanley," Mrs. Treadways said.

"Hello, Minnie." He helped her from the horse.

"Hey!" Scut said to Belle Reed. "Ham bought you some sugar and stuff yesterday. Let's whip up some candy."

She didn't crack a smile, but went straight to her lean-to.

In the afternoon we rode from the Bend, southward toward the Canadian. Belle Reed, like a brooding vulture, stood upon the hill in her hat and long skirt and watched us go. We forded the river and soon were beyond the mountain.

"Where do you want to go?" Stanley asked us.

"We haven't had time to think," I said. "We didn't believe Belle Reed would let us leave like this."

"It was Mrs. Treadways," Miss Lockwood said. "And she persuaded Belle to let me keep the mare."

"Shall we stick together?" Stanley said.

"I don't know why not," I said. "Since we're all looked for by somebody. But I don't think we'd better get near the Texas Road for a few days."

"If we get deeper into the Choctaw country, we'll have the Sans Bois Mountains to hide in. We'd have caves for protection, but also more outlaws. Robber's Cave is a big hide-out."

We crossed the Fort Smith road we had ridden over by stage and continued south. "We could cut southwest to McAlester or Perryville," Stanley said. "They are on the Texas Road. We'd have hills and mountains and prairie and could strike the road there."

So, on an open space, we swung our horses and settled down to a steady jog. "Do you know this Choctaw country?" I asked Stanley.

"Yes. I used to hunt here with Choctaw friends. I know the main lines of the hills and creeks and mountains, so we won't have trouble that way."

"I wish I could have seen the old North Fork Town."

"I liked it," Stanley said. "And it could be amusing, especially when the forty-niners and the people of the Denver gold rush came through. Many moved up the Arkansas from the Mississippi by steamboat through Little Rock and at Fort

Smith they bought their outfits. But when they reached North Fork Town, they sold or gave away wagons, cargo, tools, everything. They'd learned to depend on one thing—the Western pony—and to travel light. Many Creeks and traders became rich on the windfall. Now the road from Fort Smith to Fort Sill comes through the town. But its best days are gone."

"It looked good to me."

"The war hurt."

"Won't the railroad help?"

"The railroad will be the death blow. The Katy will miss North Fork Town. The people already plan to move the store buildings to the terminus, a few miles south and west. They may call it Eufaula, from one of our old towns in the South."

"I hate to see that."

"So do I. North Fork Town will be no more, but thank God, they won't take the dead. I remember a long-ago council meeting, when we gathered to hear the old chief Opothleyahola speak. He mentioned our lost land in Georgia and Alabama. He said that once a large island stood at the mouth of the Chattahoochee, but in time it had been almost washed away, even as the white people have washed away the Indian. He said that before long the island would all be gone, and we could almost shoot an arrow over the little country we now possess, yet the whites want to rob us of a portion of this. Each passing year has proved his words."

"You know what I think? For a long time you've been dying with one way of life. You've got to think of another. There's not a smarter or better trained man in the Territory than you, but you have to take up undertaking. Why?"

"I don't know. Something pulled me into it."

"Were you in the war?"

"No. I didn't want to see the war—Creek against Creek—Nation against Nation. That's when I went to Scotland."

"So when you came back, you really wanted to bury the dead—your whole race, especially the Creeks."

Stanley Hightower looked off the trail. "You might call it that."

"You didn't act like a sick Indian last night."

"What do you mean?" he said, turning his head back.

"That island really got small. What are you going to do?"

"The railroad will sound the knell of the Territory. The whites will overflow us. I had my profession. I was to bury it."

I was pretty disgusted with Stanley, so I dropped back to ride beside Ham. He said, "With your luck, you're a fine one to give him a lecture."

"I'm the very one," I said. "One ear and all."

But the land led on—the prairies, the wooded hills, the flowing streams, the deer and loping coyotes. Our leather squeaked, there was the plod of the horses, their hooves dull-sounding or splashing the glittering creeks or ringing clear and sharp in stony beds.

After an hour, Stanley stopped suddenly. For some time we had been sided from the trees by a small group of riders, but now they changed course to ride forward across the prairie to intercept us. One was a Negro.

"Who are they?" I said.

"In the Territory, who knows?" Stanley said. "It could be a wandering band of outlaws, or even Blue Gum's gang. Well, we won't waste time on this." Without warning, he drew his rifle from its boot and placed four quick shots near the riders. They stopped to watch us, then turned and rode into the trees. We went on.

All afternoon Miss Lockwood had ridden silently. Stanley moved his horse beside her. "Will you stay in the Territory?"

"At least for a while. Everything I brought is lost, and I've no money. I have to stay."

"Hey!" Scut said. "It's getting late. Let's hunt a camping place."

As we neared another line of trees, a number of mottled milk cows appeared, plodding toward a stone-chimneyed log cabin and the calf pens. "Where are we going?" Ham said.

"To see a friend of mine," Stanley said. "Miss Lockwood will stay with the family tonight."

"Who is this friend?"

"Thomas Moseby—a Choctaw. I hunted with him."

The cabin was double—that is, it had an open space or dogtrot between the two sections. Low log sleeping sheds were built to one side, perhaps to bed the five assorted children who were approaching the cows. In the yard a man stood with his wife, pointing to a newly cleared field, the piles of old brush still burning. He wore rough work clothes, she a long calico dress.

In the dogtrot stood an ash hopper and knee-high mortars hollowed from tree trunks for making hominy, and heavy hickory pestles and clay pots. When we stopped the horses beside a watering trough, Stanley dismounted. "Tom!" he called.

The Indian turned with his wife. He was dark and swarthy —a fullblood—half lost in the smoke swirling about him. He walked toward us, but as he recognized Stanley an odd look, almost immediately obscured, came to his black eyes. Then it seemed almost as if he would hestitate or stop walking, but after his indecision he came on.

"How are you?" Stanley moved forward, extending his hand. "And your family?"

"They are well. But why do you come at this time?"

"To bring some friends. To stay with you tonight. I will tell you more tomorrow."

"If you have anything to tell me, it must be tonight. Tomorrow I leave for Red Oak. The day of my execution is near."

"What?"

"My execution. When I saw you, I thought you had come to go with me."

"My Lord," Stanley groaned. "What happened?"

"I was drunk. I killed a man."

"You were tried fairly in the courts?"

"It was a fair trial." Tom Moseby spoke without emotion, his eyes without expression. "I asked for a stay of execution until I laid my crop by and cleared one extra field." He turned and looked at the patches of plowed land among the trees and to another where shocked corn stood, and at the log outbuildings and his few cattle and chickens. "It's not much for a man to leave, is it?"

"It is what value it has for you, and for your family. It could be very much. What punishment did you choose?"

"To be shot. And my choice of place—Red Oak. I was a boy there."

"How will you stand?"

"I will not stand. I will sit at the foot of my coffin and face the sheriff. I will ask for the red mark over my heart."

"You will die a brave man."

"Yes."

"Will your family go?"

"We will all leave at daylight in the wagon. I have asked but one brother to go, to drive it back. I want no one else from here with me."

"Would you want me?"

"No."

"Then I will leave." Stanley mounted his horse. He looked down. "Good-by, Tom Moseby."

We rode back to the prairie and followed the line of trees toward a growth of willow and cottonwood which stood beside a creek. "It is brutal," Miss Lockwood said. "Horrible."

"It is the law," Stanley said.

"No man should have such an execution. It is inhuman."

"It is inhuman to you because you are fully white, and because Tom Moseby faces Choctaw justice. You say it is inhuman and brutal. I say it is merciful—far more than the mercy which is shown by your courts. When they pronounce a man guilty, he is degraded and imprisoned foully like a beast. He is led to the gallows, often in chains or manacles, to drop masked at a rope's end through a trap in the floor."

"Stop!"

"No. I will go on. No execution is good, but it is the law of your race and mine—the law we cherish. Until the law changes—or mankind—we bear it. Yet by Choctaw law, Tom Moseby has been a free man since the day he was sentenced. On only his promise to return for the day of execution he was allowed to live with his family, to gather his crops, and clear a field for the future. Is that not mercy to the condemned? When he is at Red Oak, his family may witness the execution, or even stay near him, or wait at some creek or behind a building. Then they can hold services at a church. Then they put his coffin in the wagon."

"I'm sorry," Miss Lockwood said.

At last we stopped the horses. It was getting dark, and after we ate and settled back by the fire to rest, we heard a weird chanting among the trees.

"Swing low, sweet chariot, comin' a for to carry me home—
Swing low, sweet chariot, comin' a for to carry me home."

The voice was deep and full as the last bass notes on Mrs. Treadways' organ. Stanley Hightower stood up. "That's Uncle Wallace, the old Negro."

"We've got that spiritual down in Texas, too," Scut said.

"The world will have it soon," Stanley said. "It's Uncle Wallace's song."

"You mean he wrote it?"

"Let's say he made it up—he and Aunt Minerva. He is an old Choctaw slave. Years ago they were hired out by their master to work with the missionaries at Spencer Academy."

"Since we have that song in Texas," Scut said, "I always thought some Texan wrote it."

A horse loomed in the trees. From above the saddle a black face looked down, the gnarled head grizzled in kinky white. "Hello, Uncle Wallace," Stanley said. "Get down. Come eat with us."

"Brother Stanley! It's been a long time. But no, I can't get down. I've got a preaching tonight. Did you come for Brother Tom's execution?"

"No. I learned of it after I got here."

"I was in the country and was sent for by the family. May the good Lord forgive us all. I loved Brother Tom. He was a good man. Brother Stanley, may the Lord bless you and your friends."

"Uncle Wallace, who will be at the preaching?"

"Only his kinfolks. He wants it that way. I'm the onliest preacher."

"Where will you preach?"

"We've fixed a little arbor under the trees. We've got some log seats, and one alone set up for Brother Tom and the family. I've got to go on for the praying, Brother Stanley. I'll see you in the Kingdom." He turned the horse and rode off.

I couldn't sleep that night for having the creeps. Maybe that Negro and his song did it, coming out of the trees that way. And while we all had trouble enough, a family sitting on a log in an arbor had trouble, too.

When we broke camp next morning and struck out, I rode beside Stanley. "I want to ask you something; how many of the Five Tribes had slaves?"

"They all did—some more than others, of course. Walter Webber up at the falls had several hundred, and a few of the Choctaws had over five hundred, more than the entire tribe owned when it moved West. At one time before the war, most of the slaves near the falls disappeared; they were trying to reach New Mexico. They didn't know where to go and were found starving on the salt flats of the Arkansas."

"Who owned most of them?"

"Cherokees with white blood—and the whiter the blood, the more slaves."

"You mean full bloods didn't have slaves?"

"Some did, but not many. Even among the whites of the South, the plantation owners possessed most of the slaves, not the common man. He was hard put to feed his own family. If he had any, they were almost like his own people."

"We had only a few in my part of Texas. Most slaves were down in the cotton-picking country. Until I got to the Territory, I didn't know Indians owned slaves."

Stanley said, "My family kept four. I remember my mother one night—how she sat up with Aunt Creasie while her own children coughed in bed—because Aunt Creasie's croup was worse than ours."

"There's a rancher in our country who moved from Louisiana after the war. He had been married there. A long time ago a slave from his family and one from his wife's family had got married. When the war ended, the slave boy was fifteen years old. One morning, after this Lousiana man reached Texas, he came out on his porch and found the boy sleeping there. He was free, but he had walked from Louisiana and hidden out all across Texas to get to that white family again. He'd run off from his own people."

"Did the rancher keep him?"

"No. After the boy got rested up, they had a long talk. The rancher gave him a horse and sent a cowhand with him back to Louisiana to be sure he got there safe, to join his family. Some of our best cowhands are Negroes. I reckon over a fourth of all the trail drivers are Negroes or Mexicans."

"There was some intermarriage among the Seminole and the Negroes," Stanley said, "more than with the other tribes, because of their close life together in the Florida swamps."

"Seminoles were good fighters."

"Yes. The other tribes submitted first to the treaties and marched on their Trail of Tears. The Seminoles fought to the bitter end."

"That's that Osceola I heard of."

"He was a great chief—one of the last free Indians. But he was deceived by the army and trapped. He rotted and died in prison."

"But what about these Negro outlaw gangs—those led by

men like Blue Gum? Are they still mad at the tribes about slavery?"

"Men of an outlaw nature—red, black, or white—would be mad about anything. Race isn't all that matters. Before and since the war a number of Negro towns have sprung up in the Territory, run by law abiding people. What did you think of Uncle Wallace? He is the other side of the picture."

"He's a believer."

"Yes," Stanley said. "But at first it wasn't easy for the Indian or even the Negro to accept the white man's religion. Many were punished, even lashed and beaten, because they listened to the missionaries. Some were accused of witchcraft. A few were even killed—here in the Territory."

We nooned and ate. Miss Lockwood said, "I've never ridden this long before. We've been gone from the Bend almost a day."

"Why don't you rest?" Stanley said. "Tom Moseby's cousin lives near by. I might get some information about the lighthorse."

While the rest loafed around after eating, Stanley rode off. When he came back, he said, "So far, so good."

"You mean not even the Choctaw lighthorse are out?" I said.

"Not for us. But even one is an army."

"Why?"

"In an emergency, a lighthorse can make the citizens join him. If they don't, they can be fined by the Nation. I wouldn't care too much if only the regular companies were riding, but too many others scout the hills for bootleggers and horse thieves."

"What if they arrest you?" Scut asked.

"That's it," Stanley said. "If I resisted, I could be shot. It would be legal. They cover everything. Once the boys at Spencer Academy ran away from school. The lighthorse were sent to bring them back. They also enforced the laws of the United States on order of the Indian agents."

"They ride high, wide and handsome?"

"No. They are under the same laws as anyone. If they fail to spill liquor when they capture it, they can be imprisoned or fined. If they are found drunk, they can be fined. They are appointed by the district chiefs."

"How do you Creeks get your officers?" Ham said.

"By walking away."

"How come?"

"The districts meet, then the candidates walk in different directions. It's an old custom. The people follow the man they wish to vote for. The count is made and the vote is final. It has been a fair election, for everyone has seen the outcome."

Miss Lockwood stood up from the sandstone ledge she sat on. "I think of poor Tom Moseby."

"Don't," Stanley said.

We were tired—not from riding, for it had not been hard since leaving the Bend, but we were ready to rest and not look for an outlaw or a lighthorse behind each tree.

Scut said, "We couldn't find a better place than this to camp. Why don't we shuck traveling and sit?"

The brown bluffs across the creek stuck straight up some sixty feet. Under big trees, they were moss-covered and old. They must have been there and worn down gradually since the beginning of time.

We concluded to stay. Old Wallum's goat waded the fast-flowing creek to stand above us, his horns high. Ham took his boots off and lay down and snored. Scut said to Stanley, "Does that Indian you visited have any hogs?"

"His yard is full of them."

"Did he have a fall garden?"

"Yes."

"Tell me how to get there. I know what I want to eat tonight."

When he rode off, Miss Lockwood said, "Look—the late sun comes through the trees like a yellow butterfly."

Stanley said, "A sun can be everything."

Someone else had known that—a Cherokee lighthorse dying beneath a tent flap on the Arkansas. And far to the west on the wide plains other tribes, the Comanche and the Kiowa, lived and rode in the sun, and their days never ended.

Miss Lockwood had gone back to her ledge. "Will you tell me about religion?" she asked Stanley.

"Whose?"

"The Five Tribes' religion. And yours."

"I know only my own. I cannot speak for the Tribes." He had taken off his jacket and hat. He leaned back against a bare sycamore, the ground about him covered with fallen seed balls.

"What is your belief?" Miss Lockwood asked.

Stanley stuck a hand into a streak of light. "I suppose it is but one thing—when I see it—the sun. I am not certain about things."

"What, for instance?"

"God. And when I say God, I mean the god of so many peoples. The god of the Indian, the white man, the god of the faraway islands in the Pacific. In my lifetime I cannot know all these gods."

"God is good," Miss Lockwood said.

"Is He? Whose god? Which god of all the religious tribes of the white race is best? Who knows? Sometimes I think that all the gods of your race are evil. I have seen the missionaries of all faiths come among us when our old people had their own gods. They have helped us; some have, yes. But they have confused the Indian, as they have themselves."

"What do you mean?"

"I have been in the cabins of the sick and dying—in the hills and the lost places. I have seen workers of all faiths come there. There would be first one and then the other faith. But did they stay together in that last hour to help the dying? No. As each other faith came to add another number to the saved souls in their Book, they left on sight of each other, their noses in the air. They would not even speak. Rather than all stay to help with wrappings and blankets over the sores of the dying, they left. They would not speak to each other. Which of these white gods was right?"

"I see," Miss Lockwood said. Her eyes were large, and while her nose was long and a little curved, her lips were fully molded. She was very intent.

"Don't misunderstand me," Stanley said. "I have no objection to any man's god. But should I say there should be some unanimity among yours?" He held out his hand again. "The sun is always warm. Once more, I like the sun. Have you heard of John Jumper, the Seminole preacher?"

"No."

"He was so confused about one verse in the Bible that he quit his church and joined another." Stanley laughed.

" 'Lo! The poor Indian
Whose untutored mind
Sees God in the Clouds
Or hears him in the wind.

"Have you heard of Samuel Worcester?"

"No," Miss Lockwood said.

"He was from Massachusetts. He became a missionary among the Cherokees in Georgia. In spite of the agitation to crush and remove the Cherokees, he stood by them. When the state legislature passed the law which required a license for those living among the Indians, he opposed it and was led to jail at the back of a wagon. Other missionaries feared the state, and returned to their homes. With the removal, Worcester came west with his Cherokees and opened the mission at Park Hill. He brought the old Cherokee printing press to the Territory in a buggy. The Cherokees never understood all his theology, but when he died they called him a man. They knew and loved him."

"Why do you tell me this?" Miss Lockwood asked.

"Because as we go southward, you will see white preachers

and their poorly clothed wives living in leaking log cabins, half-starved, or riding thirty or forty miles a day to help the sick and perhaps to die overnight themselves from fever or even snake bite. Why do so many Indians bear white names? Because the new names were taken from their white teachers. The Indian can undestand Worcester's type of religion. But many cannot understand why preachers or teachers organize secret clubs of blood vengeance, as among the Cherokees, or bring a trunk full of pistols to a boys' school of another Nation to favor the cause of abolition—or any cause."

"Did that happen?" Miss Lockwood said.

"Yes. The battle of religion in the Territory is hard. And when one faith with its converts will prevent another from starting a new school or church, not all Indians, especially fullbloods—like Tom Moseby—can understand this."

Scut rode back to the bluffs, grinning like Leviticus eating a nest of yellow jackets. "Hey! I got some side meat and spareribs. I got black-eyed peas, and we've got rice in the tow sacks. We're going to have some old hopping-john tonight, and hog meat. Pull out the skillets and boiling pots."

Ham sat up. "That's the nearest I've come to heaven all day."

Chapter 11

"HEY, SCRAPE!" Scut yelled. "Turn that one-eared weather vane and see if you hear what I do."

We sat our horses on a hill in deep timber, trying to catch some sound from the Texas Road. Stanley hadn't wanted to burst upon it too suddenly, so Scut and I were making a private scout. "Yep," I said. "That's an old covered wagon. It needs a greasing."

"Those things howl louder and with less effort than a wolf," Scut said. "Want to go on?"

"No use to. We've located the road. Let's high-tail to Stanley."

We found the rest of the outfit sitting on the ground, with Ham throwing his bowie knife at a tree. We'd made it this near the road in unhurried stages, since once we reached it, we couldn't go anywhere anyway.

"We could try a stretch or two at night," Stanley said as we poked sticks into a cooking fire, squatting to watch the coals build up. "We could hide and sleep by day. I'd like to follow the road to a friend west of Perryville to see if I've heard from Tilby."

Ham said, "I asked who that man Skully was. Maybe Perry is a Choctaw word."

"No," Stanley said. "Perryville was started over thirty years ago by James Perry, of a Choctaw and Chickasaw family. He built a stage stand and a trading post. The town was the seat of Tobucksky County, and had a Chickasaw school. But it's in ruins now, burned in the war."

"Why did they build a Chickasaw school among the Choctaws?"

"The two tribes have always been close. A citizen of one is a member of the other. One called his daughters Chickie and Chockie, after his own and his wife's people. The village of Chickiechockie was named for them."

An hour before dark we put out for the Texas Road. We thought we'd be fairly safe in night travel, since most of the big wagons would be pulled off into the trees so families could sleep, and other people and freighters should be camping somewhere about. That left only the lighthorse and outlaws to worry us, and Wallum's goat.

We'd rubbed Leviticus down with spots of red clay so he wouldn't show up too much, and if we heard horsemen from before or behind, we'd still have time to drive him into the brush. With the clay and his yellow goatee, he beat anything for looks that ever came from the pit.

We broke camp about sundown. It was still daylight when we came upon the covered wagon. What we couldn't understand was that it stood among the trees so alone, far from the road, in a small open spot without sight or sound of a human around, the ragged wagon sheet flapping in the wind and two worn-out mules standing close.

We stopped our horses. "Do you think we ought to ride up?" Scut said. "They don't even have a fire."

"I'm not sure we should," Stanley said. "It could be a whiskey wagon and have an outlaw watching from the brush. It could be here for a rendezvous. No traveler would camp this far from the road."

The longer we watched the wagon the more we became fascinated. It was like being charmed by a snake ready to strike. "There's something familiar about that wagon," Scut said.

"You just opened my mind," I said. "That's the wagon we helped get tar up above Chouteau. But how come it's just now getting here?"

"That must have been it we heard this morning," Scut said.

Knowing we'd be safe if the wagon was still owned by the folks we had met earlier, we left Miss Lockwood and rode up. We'd seen from the trees that no one was near the front wheels or about the seat, so we cut to the tail gate. When we looked inside, we saw the tired man and woman.

They sat on two boxes with their heads down, and between them at their feet was a pallet on which lay a blanket-wrapped bundle. The man heard us and raised his eyes. "Hello," Stanley said.

"Hey!" Scut said. "Remember us? We got you that tar. But how come you're just now getting here?"

The man stepped down from the back of the wagon. "We've had trouble." His face was gaunt and his hollow eyes were as deep set as the bottoms of two cups.

"What kind of trouble?" Ham said.

The man licked his fever-blistered lips. "Up at Three Forks the team bolted on the ferry and the wagon fell in the river. We lost the kingbolt and split the wagon tongue and broke one wheel. When we got hauled out and mended up, somebody stole one of the mules that night. The weather was as sticky as a bucket of new syrup, and as hot as a Saturday night in Jerusalem. Next day a hailstorm almost killed the other mule and tore up the rotten wagon sheet."

"Man, you did catch it," Scut said.

"That ain't all. We finally made it to North Fork Town with one mule, and the first night there we got him stole."

"You ought to write a book about trouble," I said.

"Then," the man said, "I worked three weeks in the woods, chopping crossties for those advance railroad men so to get money to buy those two beat-down animals there. We left North Fork Town just the other day with the boy sick, and tonight he's dying. We pulled off the road this morning to let it come in comfort."

"Where is the boy?" Stanley said. "How old is he?"

"He's five. That's him in the bundle."

"What's his sickness?"

"We thought at first it was cramp colic, but we believe it's more."

Stanley swung upward into the back of the wagon. He unfolded the dirty blanket from the boy's body. He looked at his face and his hands. He placed his fingers across the forehead. "He has a high fever." He took his pulse. "Help slide the pallet to the back," he told the man. "I need more light."

They let down the wide tail gate and eased the pallet crosswise along the back of the wagon bed. Stanley hopped to the ground and peered once more into the boy's face. "How long has he been sick?" Only now did we see the small grave which had been dug near the opposite side of the wagon.

The woman on the box stirred. "He took down in North Fork Town two days before we left. I told the man not to travel, but he says, 'Yes, old woman, we've got to get to Texas.' "

"Did the pain come suddenly?"

"It came in no time at all."

"What kind of pain? Was it severe and sharp?"

"It nigh drove him out of his mind."

"It could have been kidney or gall-stone colic. But I doubt it." Stanley unbuttoned the boy's shirt. His fingers barely touched the midsection, moving back and forth lightly.

Miss Lockwood had ridden up. She asked, "Is it appendicitis?"

"I think so. If it's renal colic, the pain will run to the scrotum or groin." His fingers kept moving. "He feels no pain here. He's never had gall stones?" he asked the woman. "I've never known it in a patient this young. If it is, it might be due to a congenital malformation."

"He ain't had stones that we know of," the woman said.

"Then I doubt if it's hepatic or renal." Stanley's fingers moved to the right side of the stomach. "Has he vomited?"

"He stopped vomiting," the man said.

At last Stanley straightened. "What is it?" Miss Lockwood said.

"Rigidity over the stomach muscle." He asked the woman, "Did the pain stop suddenly?"

"It must have, for he stopped crying from it. He just gets weaker."

"I think the pus has formed. It's appendicitis," he told Miss Lockwood.

"What can we do?"

"Nothing. I'm afraid it's too late." Stanley felt the boy's pulse again and walked from the wagon.

I followed him. "For an undertaker, you're a pretty good doctor."

"I will help bury him. We'll make camp here tonight."

"Right now I want to ask one thing. If you had your cutting instruments, what would you do?"

"I'd operate. Even that is risky now, but it's his only chance."

"Then get ready. Mrs. Treadways was afraid we might get hurt or shot, so before we left she gave us your bags and bandages. They're in the tow sacks. Now what do you want us to do?"

"First, we've got to place the wagon so I can work. The bed is too high. Then fill every pot or tub with water and boil it. It's getting darker, so get all the lanterns filled and lighted."

We went back to the wagon. Stanley told Miss Lockwood, "Mrs. Treadways gave the boys my instruments. Did you know it?"

"Yes."

"Why didn't you tell me?"

"I had no reason to. I never thought you'd use them."

"I'm going to operate," Stanley said.

"Can I help?"

"You'll have to. First, I'll tell you what to do. It will be bad, because I won't have all I need."

While Scut gathered our pots and pans and then a wash tub and some boilers from the wagon, Ham and I looked for a flat rock to drag in for Stanley to stand on. About a hundred feet from the wagon we yelled back, "Come over here!"

Stanley hurried to us. "What is it?"

"Look at this narrow branch. It's got a level bank and a rock bottom. If we pulled the wagon across and let the hind wheels stay in the water, the back end would come out just right. You could stand on the bank."

"Tell the man to hitch up." Stanley went back to Miss Lockwood.

When we were ready to move the wagon, Stanley told the man, "Drive slowly. We don't want to jolt the boy." The wagon started and he walked at the back with Miss Lockwood, holding the child in place. We passed in and out of the trees until the man eased the front wheels of the wagon across the branch. "Stop!" Stanley called. "Stop where you are."

Scut had built a fire on the bank. He stacked rocks about the flaring wood for the water-filled vessels to rest upon.

"Unhitch your team," Stanley told the man. "We don't want the wagon to be jerked while I'm working." He placed his bags on the wagon bed. "Do you have any sheets, pillow cases, shirts?" he asked the woman.

"We've got two sheets and some towels. The rest is on our backs."

"Are the sheets clean?"

"We stopped to wash yesterday. They ain't been used."

"Bring them." He said to Miss Lockwood, "Tear the sheets in strips and squares." He opened his bags, placing the instruments on a towel. He sorted them, muttering, "I don't have this—or that." He placed three bottles beside the towel. "These two are anesthesia."

"Where do you want these bandages and cotton?" I asked.

"Beside the towel. Now take the instruments and boil them. And wash your hands. Leave the towel folded, then when the boiling's done, unfold it and put the instruments on it. Take them out of the water with the forceps. Don't touch them."

"You mean those pliers-looking things?"

"Yes."

While the instruments boiled, Stanley took off his hat and jacket. He rolled up his shirt sleeves. As he talked with Miss Lockwood, he washed and rubbed his hands in alcohol.

He said to us, "We have only three lanterns. I want one to hang above from the back bow, and the others to be placed at either end of the boy." He glanced up to the curved bow. "Are you ready?" he asked Miss Lockwood. They prepared the abdomen. "Let's begin."

Stanley placed a gauze mask over the child's face. "The anesthetic, Miss Lockwood. Stand close," he told us.

The man and woman wandered into the trees.

Miss Lockwood dripped the anesthetic. Stanley pulled back the boy's eyelid. He took the pulse. He pinched the boy's shoulder, at first easy, then harder. "Scrape, take the bottle. A few drops at a time, when I tell you."

He placed the folded strips of white cloth about the stomach. Then as his hand moved, Miss Lockwood gasped. "Steady," he said.

It wasn't a man who worked now. It was only hands. The light from overhead struck the swiftly moving fingers. "Tie off. More cotton. Insert at the right—the left now—the bottom. Clamp. Scrape, where are the other boys?"

"Right beside you." From the Texas Road sounded a flurry of pistol shots.

"I need better light. Help them get in the wagon to hold the end lanterns high. Hurry. Give me the—no, I forgot. I don't have one. Miss Lockwood, hand me the instrument on the left. The light at the foot—higher, please."

As the shots and sounds from road ceased, Stanley said, "It's ruptured. Cotton. The blue bottle—pour it on the cotton. Quick. Scrape, give me more now—more—stop. Miss Lockwood, wipe my face and forehead. The blue bottle again. Pad now. Who stands at his feet? Ham? Hold the top lantern steady—the wind's harder. I get shadows. Hold your own higher."

It went on and on. At last the voice, the monotonous voice which had sounded always above the moving fingers, said, "Ready to sew. The drain, please. The curved needle and catgut."

Stanley stepped back from the wagon. "Clean him up," he told Miss Lockwood. "Then use the alcohol. I'll help in a moment."

"His people have coffee boiling," Scut said. "Do you want some?"

"Yes."

Stanley Hightower walked under the trees. I followed him. "Wherever you might have done this before, you were never better than tonight."

When a woodchuck comes out of a hole, it's apt to blink before it sees daylight. It was that way with Stanley. He'd come to daylight, but he couldn't believe it.

We'd sat by the fire and watched the wagon all night and when sunup came, Stanley said, looking in at the boy, "He might make it. The big worry is infection and I tried to look after that. You'd better sleep," he told Miss Lockwood. "You can't hold your eyes open."

"Hadn't you?"

"No. I want to watch."

"What cure do you have for frozen muscles?" Ham said. "You nearly broke my arms last night."

In the afternoon the boy whispered, "I've been sick."

"You certainly have," Stanley said at the tail gate. "You put on about the best sick I ever saw. Look what a big wrapped-up stomach you've got. Don't touch it, though. It might pop."

The boy's eyes searched Stanley's face. "Who are you?"

"I am a doctor."

"I never saw a doctor before."

"Then take a good look. How would you like a few spoons of broth tomorrow? Not many—just two or three."

The boy nodded.

"You're not hungry now, are you?"

"A little bit."

"Well, we'll wait till tomorrow. The sun and wind will mend you." He lay down on the brown grass of the bank. In a few minutes he was asleep.

Miss Lockwood walked to the wagon. She looked refreshed. "Have you slept?" she asked us.

"Since we left Chetopa," Scut said, "if we had sleep, it would stultify us."

"Did the boy wake?"

"He wants a son-of-a-gun stew and beer cheese," Scut said.

We moved the swollen-wheeled wagon out of the branch and camped in the clearing for a week. Then Stanley said, "There's no more to be done here. Tomorrow we leave for Perryville."

Wallum's goat, whose shadow in our predicament had begun to loom larger than any hill he had stood upon since we left Chetopa, now assumed greater proportions as we entered the lower Territory.

With what news we had gathered over the past weeks, beyond all doubt Wallum had sent more riders up the road from Texas to scour the Territory. Yet Leviticus seemed indifferent to all our forebodings, and that night as we left the covered wagon and shoved our way from the brush to the Texas Road, to all appearances he had no thought of that or anything else.

We'd reach McAlester before we struck on to Perryville to meet Stanley's friend.

Stanley said, "Tonight at McAlester we'll cross the junction of one branch of the old California Trail. There'll be the usual number of outlaw camps in the woods, yet since we might meet these same gentlemen on the road, our best chance is to shove on."

"Which way did this part of the old Trail go?" I asked.

"On beyond Fort Arbuckle," Stanley said. "Through the Chickasaw country."

So with Leviticus daubed among his red spots with a few black patches from the scrapings of the tar bucket, we put out down the road in the blowing night.

"How old is McAlester?" Ham asked, riding near Stanley and Miss Lockwood.

"It's new," Stanley said. "It started last year. James McAlester, a white man, put up a tent trading store at the crossroads. He married a Chickasaw, which gave him Choctaw rights. Geologists say large deposits of coal are there. When the railroad comes, McAlester plans to begin large-scale mining operations."

Miss Lockwood said, "Mr. Pemberton thinks that oil is in the north, in the Cherokee and Osage country. He became a philanthropist through oil—in Pennsylvania. He employs many geologists."

It was rough going on the rutty road—the slow march of the horses, the night swirling with dark and heavy clouds. At times, as we swung left or right to make our way, even the bordering timber could hardly be seen. Suddenly Stanley stopped his horse. "It's too quiet," he said. "Let's edge toward the trees."

Whatever instinct had waked to warn him proved to be in time. We were barely off the road when a line of jogging horsemen appeared on our own path, going south. "Who are they?" Scut whispered.

"They could be soldiers, outlaws, or lighthorse," Stanley

muttered. "But whoever they are, they mean business. It's a determined outfit."

At last the riders were lost in the darkness. "Do you want to start?" I said.

"Yes," Stanley said. "At their gait, they'll soon be far ahead."

Fearing the riders, or others, we bypassed McAlester, swinging southeastward off the road to cross the California Trail before we looped back to the south. By sunup we were camped on a high hill. We'd spent a night of being on and off the road to stop and listen, winding among hills and watercourses or across flat prairie. At one time on the road the horses had walked directly into an approaching band of riders. With curses, the men swung into the trees on one side, and we on the other. We passed with the wide space between us, and each group went its way without interruption.

Stanley had said, "Well, it shows how the other half lives."

As we unsaddled on the hill, we looked about. The drop on our side of the crest was sheer. A flat valley stretched to a line of low foothills, the taller and wider summits rising boldly and far away. Toward the southeast the clumped tops of other mountains spread across the distance.

"Those are the Jack Fork Mountains," Stanley said. "The others are the foothills of the Sans Bois."

"Man!" said Scut. "And once we were northwest of the Sans Bois. Wonder if Belle Reed has any business there today?"

"If she's as hungry as I am, she'd better start eating," Ham said.

We followed Ham's advice and then, this time observing the old adage of a departed outlaw named Bill Cookson, we set watches for the day to sleep. When we were all awake again, Stanley glanced toward the southeast. "What do you think of the clouds?"

"They look pretty mean," I said. They piled upon the horizon above the Jack Fork country like a solid wall.

"Look!" Miss Lockwood cried. "What is that?"

A little-used road or trail came from the south, and upon it two wagons flanked by a number of horsemen had appeared. "What do you make of it?" I asked Stanley.

"I don't know yet," he said. He moved to the edge of the drop and nodded, as if to himself. "Yes, they could be. They're prison wagons."

"Prison wagons?"

He turned. "Yes. The federal marshals from Fort Smith come to round up criminals—white, black, and Indian. It's a rough job for one or two marshals to take six or a dozen outlaws back for trial; some are killed trying it. So they make up the prison trains. They hire extra deputies and empty the jails of the Nations or pick up suspicious characters or whiskey runners."

A dismal half-yellow light from the approaching storm covered the valley. "How do they keep them from escaping?" I said.

"They are chained and well guarded. At night a heavier chain is fastened among the trees. They are fastened to it and sleep on the ground."

"Good Lord," Ham said.

"The Territory has the meanest cutthroats in the Union," Stanley said. "To them, murder is a pastime. Until an honest federal judge sits at Fort Smith to control the country, it will continue this way."

"Could the guards be the riders who passed last night?"

"I doubt it. The deputies go out with the wagons. These have probably been to the Choctaw settlements to the southeast, or to Doaksville—the old treaty town."

"If you people will look where I'm looking," Scut said, "you'll see what I see."

The prison wagons had neared the base of the hill. Even as we turned to follow the direction of Scut's finger to look below, rifles cracked suddenly as hidden riders burst from the trees. "They are the ones we saw last night," Stanley cried. "It's an ambush. Get down!"

We fell flat on the summit, but even from the brush the view of the valley was clear. Each prison wagon was drawn by four big horses. Two or three beasts had fallen in the first burst of outlaw fire. Others screamed and struggled in fear to bolt. The outlaw volley had been aimed to stop the wagons.

The prisoners stood and faced each other from their wooden benches. They struggled. In one wagon, a yell of triumph sounded as all from one side moved like a long caterpillar over the back to leap upon the ground.

"They are all handcuffed," Stanley said. "But a heavy chain runs between their arms from the front of the wagon to the back. They tore the hasps loose."

But something stranger had happened. At the first outbreak of rifle fire, one of the wagon guards had turned his horse. He galloped off, passing across the outlaw course. "That skunk!" Scut said. "I bet he set this up."

From the harried guards burst their first crackle of rifle fire, One dismounted, standing to aim at the fleeing rider. He stood tall and straight, shooting almost leisurely, shot after shot. At last the rider fell from his horse. He staggered upward, and running badly bent, caught the animal. He mounted with difficulty and galloped off again. But more rifle fire came from the bushwhackers. They rode down on the officers, changing now to out-thrust pistols.

Three men had ridden after the escaping prisoners. A Negro, hulking huge and bold above the others, ran like a heavy-footed giant. He dodged toward the trees. But the tall man had called the officers to the far side of the wagons, using the standing prisoners as a shield while he opened a strong fire upon the bashwhackers.

"Oh, ho, Alamo!" Scut yelled. "He's not confused. He's cool as a cucumber."

"So is that outlaw he just shot," Ham said. "He hasn't moved since he shook hands with his saddle."

There was more activity in the wagons. Other prisoners fought among themselves, struggling to jerk free from their chains. Then as a burst of fire came from the bushwhackers, some screamed, falling before the ragged volley. As they fell, others threw themselves flat between the side boards. With the return fire of the wagon guards the bushwhackers fled, their horses galloping eastward.

"Scrape," Scut said, "that shows to go you. Look at the tall man. Always use your head."

The battle had lasted not more than five or ten minutes. Meanwhile, the tall rifleman had sent two more men in pursuit of the fugitives. Soon they and the three others returned, driving a trotting line of spent prisoners.

"When they broke free, I counted eight," Stanley said. "But only seven return."

The train was ready to be underway. The dead horses had been unhitched and dragged away from the wagons, and the fallen outlaws' mounts had been put in the traces.

Stanley said, "Those on the ground are beyond help." As the officers dragged four bodies to a wagon and stacked them among the prisoners on the wide bed, he said, "No, I can't help. I can't help at all." He twisted on the ground to look at Miss Lockwood.

She pushed herself up from the brush. "How do you like the far West?" Stanley asked her.

She stood to look out upon the valley. "I don't know," she said. "But the Negro who got away was Blue Gum. I can't ever forget him."

Chapter 12

HAM AND SCUT and I sat on the top rail of a corral behind a mansion. We were as out of place as three rats under the wrong pew in the wrong church. That building towered above us with six chimneys, like the White House in Washington, D.C. I guess the White House has six chimneys. If it doesn't, it ought to, to come up to this place—the home of Stanley's friend, west of Perryville.

"Scrape," Ham said, rubbing the sole of a boot on a lower rail, "I'm sick at heart."

After the battle in the McAlester valley, the rain had blown out of the Jack Fork Mountains. It was perhaps the queer yellow atmosphere which helped start it, and when the faint light was lost in sheets of blinding water, there wasn't anything anywhere to stop the thunderous downpour.

As we watched the yellow lightning slash nearer, while the

clouds marched across the distant hills before the deluge struck, Stanley said, "There's no use to think of travel tonight. We won't be high and dry anywhere, but here we'll be high. Every creek in the Choctaw Nation will swim."

So we battened down and lived with the bullfrogs who hopped up the hill to climb the highest trees to goop for air. When daylight came, the valley was a white sheet of water. Even yesterday's battle seemed far off and long ago. We stayed that day on the hill, and most of the next.

About midafternoon we put out again. "I've got to see Chandler," Stanley said.

"Is that the man at Perryville?" I said.

"Yes. He lives several miles out of town, but I'm afraid to cut across country because of the rises. We'll go back to the Texas Road. Chandler has a store near Perry's old stand."

So here we are on another night, our horses knee deep in mud, slogging the black road. Only now there are pools of light. Every few hundred yards the lanterns swing and shine. From the time of the big rain until now every wagon which had been on the road or tried to travel later had bogged down. No one slept alongside in the trees. The men cut poles from the woods, trying to prize the wagons out of the water-filled holes and ruts. What good that did no one could tell. If once they got out, they moved on a few yards to sink again.

"Look yonder." Ham pointed to one pool of brightness where a man stood with a lantern. "A woman's bonnet is floating in that hole. Pretty soon he'll tell us that his wagon and his whole family are underneath."

Stanley said, "That yarn goes back to the time Chicago was settled, and even beyond. It was told in Babylon or some place, maybe in China, thousands of years ago. People have always had roads and troubles. Also, a wry sense of humor."

Scut said, "I was told that story started when Houston was settled on the bayou. You sure tear down my faith in Texas. When I was a boy, I was told that those dogtrot cabins like Tom Moseby had were Texas cabins. I thought Texans invented them."

"They're all over the Territory. And they've been in the South and elsewhere for a few hundred years."

Scut said, "It's plain to see I've been skunked. Hey! I want to ask you—do people all over the country eat black-eyed peas and hog jowl on New Year's Day for luck?"

"Yes. In many places."

"Doggone! I guess if something ever does get to Texas, we take it and say we did it in the first place. I remember the day I was born. I looked up and said, 'Mama, what's that big bright thing in the sky?' She says, 'That's a sun, son. That's a Texas sun.'" Scut scratched his head. "It wasn't until I drove cows to Kansas that I knew they had one too. I thought we just lent them a chunk of ours."

We put up a hard fight on the boggy road, and before reaching Perryville we cut west through the night hills and splashed the booming creeks to reach Chandler's place. This was our first westward march off the road—the others had been to the east. "Does Chandler have a double cabin?" I asked.

"No, it's larger," Stanley said as we cut our way off the trail to go over an open rise. "We are almost there."

The tree growth began again. At last we came through the woods to a half-seen swath of lane almost as wide as the Texas Road. It was bordered by giant trees—or rather, at one time long ago the lane must have been cut through other trees. Enough dogs raced up, doing enough belling and baying to stock a hound-dog pound.

"We're here," Stanley said.

Then as we rode closer in the gloom, we saw the outline of a big white house. "Ain't you brought us to the wrong place?" I asked Stanley.

"No. This is Jeoff's place."

"Scrape," Scut whispered, "we're cowhands. We've got a home under the stars a million times bigger than this place, but this scares me to death."

"There's no help for it now. We're stuck."

As we came to the house, a black-clad Negro with a lantern

met us at a line of perpendicular hitching posts. He bowed. "Gentlemen, I heard the dogs. Do we have visitors tonight?"

"If you remember me," Stanley said.

"Yes, sir. I do remember you, even in the dark. You are Mr. Stanley Hightower. Get down, sir."

Stanley helped Miss Lockwood from her horse. "Will you look after the horses?" he asked the Negro.

"Yes, sir. As soon as I call William."

He went to the house and came back with another Negro. William asked Miss Lockwood, "Do you have luggage, ma'am?"

She laughed. "Not a bit. But will you take me in?"

"Yes, ma'am. Mr. Chandler will meet you at the door."

We were led up the path and over a wide porch with the roof supported by a bunch of straight-up, tree-top-high columns. At the door Mr. Jeoff Chandler met us. He was a short, stocky man. After all those civilized formalities of greeting and bowing and scraping were over, we were led upstairs to a bedroom by William. He was dressed all over in solid black and wore a black bow tie. This room is about twenty by thirty feet in all directions.

"Hey!" Scut said. "You don't expect us to sleep in that outfit?"

The bed was as big as Aunt Tillie's half acre and it had mile-high walnut posts sticking up at the corners, with a bunch of deep-colored fancy drapery strung from around the top to hide the bedclothes.

"Why, gentlemen," William said, "this is one of the best rooms in the house. Don't you like it?"

Ham said, "Ain't you got a plain old shed out back?"

"No, sir. That would be unheard of at Mr. Chandler's place."

After he left and we had stripped down to our long drawers and socks and shirts and got in that drapery-lined palace, a knock came at the door. Scut got up. "I started to bolt that outfit," he whispered, "but it wouldn't look right in an honest man's house."

The door opened cautiously, an inch at a time. William's head poked in. He came toward us with three long cloth contraptions which had puffy red balls as big as black walnuts on the ends, with a bunch of frizzled white stuff sticking from them. "Here are your nightcaps, gentlemen. Would you like a foot warmer?"

"You mean an old hot rock wrapped up?" Scut asked. He took a cap from William.

"Oh, no, sir. These warmers have the big burnished pan and the long handle. They came from England. They were made in Manchester."

"We'll skip it," Ham said. "We were made in Texas."

"Very well, gentlemen. Good night."

"When you come to bed, grandma," Ham told Scut, "leave your wooden leg by the marble table."

In the morning there came that knock. "Here comes William," I said.

"He's as bad as Wallum's goat," Ham said.

William came in with a silver tray which held a big silver coffeepot and cups and saucers and a silver sugar bowl and cream pitcher. He bowed. "Good morning, gentlemen. Here is your coffee. Will you have breakfast in bed?"

"Anywhere," Scut said. "But ain't there a table in this house?"

"Downstairs, sir," William said.

At breakfast in the big dining room there was so much silver run out beside the plates it was confusing. Scut said to William, "Hey! There ain't no use to dirty up all these things. Take this back except for one fork and a spoon. I've got my own knife."

Mr. and Mrs. Chandler had a daughter about the same age as Miss Lockwood, and they were gay and chattering away like two schoolgirls at a tea party. Miss Lockwood wore one of the daughter's fresh dresses. They sat and talked with Stanley.

So now we are sitting on the top rail, looking at the back side of the white mansion. Scut says, "This is terrible."

The house is about a hundred and fifty feet wide. On the front porch, which we can't see from the corral, are eight round columns spaced to hold up a top piazza which has a waist-high balustrade about it. Those trees we saw last night spread their branches above the tall brick chimneys and shingle roof. There are three big rooms with all their windows on either side of the wide front door, and directly above them on the second story the same pattern continues. The individual cast-iron hitch posts we saw all have ornamental horse heads on top, with iron rings in their noses to tie a real horse to.

"Maybe we'd better get out to Perryville," I said. "We can't live in this civilization. I'd rather be on the trail with a goat."

Scut said, "Scrape, I still don't figure you and Wallum."

"I'll give him the goat and call things even. All I want to do is get this goat to Wallum myself."

Stanley Hightower and Mr. Chandler walked to the corral. "Let's go to Perryville," Stanley said. "We'll pick up what news we can, and I want to send a letter to Amon Tilby. He'll answer direct to Mr. Chandler."

"Did you write Mr. Collier?" I said.

"No. He's doing enough. If the letter went astray, I wouldn't want him to be involved." Since he'd shaved and slicked up before breakfast, Stanley looked like a different man from the stubbled outfit we had ridden with for so long.

We set out at a fair jog from Mr. Chandler's mansion, which was north of Perryville Creek. The creek crossed the Texas Road and wound east to join Old Brushy. Along it were the cabins of Choctaw farmers and cattlemen. Children played on the banks. We stopped to look at some fat cattle and rode on to Perryville.

Before entering the old place, we paused on a rise to reconnoiter. The war-ruined town had only a few stone and log buildings left, and most people had moved to what would be the terminus when the Katy came through—McAlester. From where we sat we saw the almost deserted streets which held more disheartened turkeys and hogs than people. A few washings flapped from the clothes lines.

"What caused the battle here?" I asked Stanley.

"Perryville was a Confederate supply point," Stanley said. "General Cooper retreated here after the Battle of Honey Springs."

"We heard about Honey Springs at Fort Gibson," Scut said. "It was fought between Three Forks and North Fork Town."

"The Union won this one, too," Mr. Chandler said. "The Confederates fled, but first they salted the wells. Then General Blunt finished the route he started at Honey Springs and burned the town. Most of the Choctaws and Chickasaws stood for the Confederacy, so it brought the war home. We'll ride in," he told Stanley. "It looks quiet enough. I don't see the lighthorse."

When we reached the village a line of covered wagons moved through on the rutted road, and beyond the remaining houses a rain-drowned crew of Texans drove a herd northward. We stood backed against a white-washed store which had a few plowshares and grinding wheels displayed in front while Mr. Chandler went to the stage stand to post Stanley's letter and see if mail had come.

"How long will it take to hear from Tilby?" I said.

"Three or four days," Stanley said. "It depends on whether he has the information, or if he has to inquire."

"Look there," Ham said.

Five men sat on a log in the rubble between the livery stable and inn. They wore black suits or robes and hats, and some had their collars turned backwards. While they talked among themselves, every so often their hands went into the air.

Scut said, "Two of them are the priests of Chetopa."

"Another is a Mormon," Stanley said. "I've seen and heard of him. When the old Mormon colony settled in Texas, he was one who returned. He was a good wheelwright, and on his return through the Territory he married and set up shop in Cherokee land."

"Who are the other two?" I said.

"Protestants, I suppose."

"None of them has understood a word but Leviticus," Scut said.

The stage bounced and lurched into town, the driver blowing his horn. While the horses were being changed at the stand, three of the black-suited men including the Russian climbed inside the coach. The other two mounted their horses at the livery stable. Still talking, they fell in behind the stage. Then they and the stage horses were all off and out of town at breakneck speed, the robes flying, the stage bouncing and tilting, the two horses galloping behind, their tails out.

"Just looking the country over," Ham said.

When Mr. Chandler returned, he said to Stanley, "No mail, but there's trouble on the road from one end to the other. The Katy is having a hard time in the north."

"How?" Ham said. "We rode on that train."

"Partly due to the railroad's effort to get the Indian land along the right of way. The prize was up to twenty square miles of land for each mile of track laid—about three million acres. Then the Katy wanted a Fort Smith branch—another million. The Cherokee Nation maintained that Indian land was not in the public domain of the United States and was upheld. The Katy had planned to run the rails to Fort Gibson, but instead, they surveyed to Three Forks."

"We knew that," Scut said, "but what does it have to do with the trouble?"

"It's the same problem we've always had with emigrants," Mr. Chandler said. "Even before Texas became independent, the United States wanted the Mexican lands. Some emigrants on their way to cross Red River to the Texas colonies would drop off in the Territory if they found a spot to their liking. They'd squat and build cabins. With the coming of the Five

Tribes, they'd be moved on by soldiers, but many solved their problem by marrying into the Nations. Some felt free to set up their own law. The intermarried gangs which see the *advantage* of having a railroad near their land, or a town site, have blocked tracks, stopped trains, thrown switches, and fired at engineers. Trestles have been torn down. And as the rails drive deeper into the Territory, the real riffraff comes in—the adventurers of the brawling terminus. Oddly enough, other squatters don't want the railroad even close to their land."

Stanley said bitterly, "It will happen all through the Territory, until the rails reach Texas."

"We must have the railroad," Mr. Chandler said.

"I know—the big word. We call it progress."

"The line will cross the Arkansas in January," Mr. Chandler said.

"Have the Creek lighthorse been here?" Stanley asked.

Mr. Chandler nodded. "With our own."

"Where are they?"

"They rode south yesterday toward Limestone Gap."

Stanley pulled down his slouch hat. "We'd better leave." We mounted up. As we rode back through the trees he asked, "Was there any talk in McAlester of the prison-train raid?"

"Indeed there was," Chandler said dryly. "Your friend Olinger was in it."

"Wait! Was Olinger the one who rode away—the one who was shot?"

"Yes. And he was the deputy who planned the ambush with the outlaws. The lighthorse say something big is in the wind. That's another thing they're checking. A week ago Olinger and Blue Gum are supposed to have had a rendezvous at Boggy Depot. At least they were seen talking there. Then quite by accident Blue Gum was captured in the Jack Forks by Bench Buckley's men and put in the prison wagon."

"Buckley must have been the tall officer," Ham said.

Mr. Chandler nodded. "He was to meet another prison wagon from the west at McAlester and go to Fort Smith."

"Was Olinger caught?" I said.

"No. And Blue Gum hasn't been seen. He's undoubtedly free, since anyone at a cabin in the hills could strike his irons."

"I can't understand why Olinger and Blue Gum should be together," Stanley said.

"Neither could our lighthorse."

On the third day, while we waited with the hogs and turkeys behind the Perryville livery stable, Mr. Chandler walked to the stage stand. He returned with a letter from Amon Tilby. Stanley read it and looked up. "Tilby says that Kurbstone has married Betty Blye, and some time ago they were seen with Blue Gum and Olinger—before they met at Boggy."

"That's a tie-up," Scut said.

"But why?" said Stanley.

"It's not for any good," I said.

"There was a holdup on the Texas Road last night," Mr. Chandler said. "Choctaw Nation money."

"Blue Gum?"

Mr. Chandler nodded and swung his horse. "Yes. He's reported to be in the vicinity. Let's go home. I want to check some rifles."

"Has Olinger been found?"

"No."

Ham said, "I still wish we knew why that whole gang split and Olinger and Blue Gum were sent to Boggy Depot."

"One thing," Scut said, "is three Turkey Foot cowhands and a goat. And Stanley is their life insurance because he killed Bill Cookson."

"The way you look," I told Stanley, "you must have more bad news."

"I have. Mr. Collier was shot and killed getting off the stage near his home—bushwhacked."

Scut said, "They've got a net about us that won't break."

"We've got to get out of the Territory," Stanley said. "We'd better strike for the Kiamichis and go to Arkansas." He looked at me. "Here's your part of the news. Wallum's cowhands have been in North Fork Town."

"What do you think we ought to do?" I asked the boys.

"Scrape," Scut said, "Ham and I signed on to follow you to glory. If it's the mountains, we'll ride. If it's the road, we take it."

"That's mighty noble, since you don't know where to go either."

"Let's discuss it tonight," Mr. Chandler said.

"Look," Ham said, a strange expression on his face.

A medicine-show wagon had drawn up before the stage stand. It had a half-covered, half-open wagon bed. A large canvas sign hung across the front:

DR. AEGOSPOTAMI'S MEDICINAL TOURS—
GUARANTEED NEW PROCESS ELIXER
Gorgeous Gesticulating Girls—Wild African Cannibal
Rejuvenating Elixers Compounded Instantaneously

A tall, florid man in a long coat and top hat climbed down from the wagon seat to walk to the back. Just as he did, the banjo-playing Negro cannibal with a grass skirt and filed and painted red teeth came from behind the cover, followed by two lightly clad dancing girls and a brown Indian girl dressed in the same fashion. A brushy mustached, fox-faced man of medium height followed the entertainers.

Dr. Aegospotami stood in yellow boots, a turned-up black twister under his nose, snapping a riding whip in the dust while the banjo began to play. He spieled to the empty street. "Ladies and gents, come one, come all! Step up! Share the free entertainment by the original Turkish dancing girls and the native Indian maid. Share the elusive secret of Life, Hope, and Hereafter. Step up! Come one, come all!" The girls put their arms above their heads and began to dance.

"Well, what about it?" I asked Ham. "We've seen medicine shows in cowtowns. What's different here, except there ain't a hundred cowhands around?"

"Dr. Aegospotami is my old man," Ham said. "I saw him once in Seguin, and another time in Dallas. I've hit the jackpot."

Two Indians stopped to watch the show. They stood cracking pecans in their teeth. Dr. Aegospotami gave an irritated flick of the whip at the Negro, who began to beat the strings faster and louder. A booted white man with a woman in a faded sunbonnet stopped to watch, the man scratching his backside. A hog got beneath the wagon and stretched out.

"Do you want to go over?" Stanley asked Ham.

"No."

Dr. Aegospotami nodded to the mustached man, who moved back into the wagon. He climbed over the tail gate to pick up a gold trumpet from the wagon bed. He began to play loudly in time with the Negro. The mustached man came back, bare to the waist, wearing a short yellow dancing skirt. He put a box of blue medicine bottles on the wagon bed.

"Hey!" Scut said. "I saw him in Abilene. He's Senator Larnus P. Snaffle from Texas. He's got more irons in the fire than Kurbstone. He ain't a Senator yet, but he put up an office in Washington. He's working on the Texas legislature to elect him so he can put through a land grab in Congress when the Katy crosses the Red."

Dr. Aegospotami handed the trumpet to the cannibal. The girls still danced, even without the music. The cannibal put the trumpet down and ate a human finger which looked like a broken-jointed chicken wing, and the Indian girl left the dance to beat a tom-tom beside him. Dr. Aegospotami made another pitch. "Gents and ladies, for the one and only—allow me to introduce Senator Larnus P. Snaffle from the great state of Texas—a master of the Parisian arts of Terpsichore, a graduate cum Lordy of the foreign universities. He will present The Dance of the Goldfinch. Then I reveal the Eternal Secret."

An Indian came up. He was on the right track but carried the wrong load. He sat down against a wagon wheel and snored with the hog.

Senator Snaffle began to hop about the stage with the girls, his arms high. Dr. Aegospotami reached for the trumpet, but the yawning cannibal had misplaced it. He handed Dr. Aegospotami the banjo, and later joined in himself with the trumpet.

"What Senator Snaffle needs," Scut said, "is a stomp dance with these Civilized Tribes." He told Ham, "Your daddy won't sell any medicine to that audience."

"Let's go," Ham said.

As we neared the hitch posts before the mansion, Stanley said sharply, "Who's that?" A heavy set man well over six feet in height stood by his horse. He wore a wide-brimmed black hat. He was so tall that until we came closer we thought it was Bench Buckley.

"That's John Jumper, the Seminole preacher," Mr. Chandler said.

"Yes, I recognize him," Stanley said, "but I haven't seen him for years. I told Miss Lockwood about him."

When we stopped the horses, we saw John Jumper better. The dark hair which came down below his hat was tinged with gray. He had almost a Chinese look and wore large gold earrings, and the set of his heavy features was full and benevolent. A heavy gold watch chain hung across his chest.

Stanley and Mr. Chandler greeted him. As a Negro approached to tie his horse to a ring, John Jumper said, "No, Brother Samuel. I will do that." His giant frame was like an oak tree. "I am late, Brother Chandler. I was slowed by the rains."

Mr. Chandler said, "John, we've all been slowed. But we have the revival arbor set up. My people will be there tonight. Let's go to the house."

John Jumper took the saddle pockets from his horse and we followed him and Mr. Chandler to the porch. "Have you seen Uncle Wallace?" he asked Mr. Chandler.

"Stanley Hightower did. And he saw Tom Moseby before he died. Tom was a good husband and soldier. It is a sad business with him."

"There is a man," Stanley told us, as Jeoff Chandler and John Jumper walked on to the porch, "who led the Confederate Seminoles to war. He is a chief. He was made a major by the South. He saw his beaten people hide and live in the bottoms of the Washita like beasts, without fields or food or clothes. He is a great person."

We'd got up early that morning for the ride to Perryville, so after a good noon meal at the dining table we were ready to go sit at the corral again. Stanley said no. "With the lighthorse riding and Olinger and Blue Gum in the country, and Wallum's men, we can't take the chance. If we are seen, it will mean the end. Jeoff has put men out to warn us against the lighthorse, but we'll stay in the house. If lighthorse do come, we'll go upstairs."

"Hey!" Scut said. "Would it make Mr. Chandler mad if I brought in my saddle and slept on the floor? I get sunk so deep in that bed I suffocate."

That afternoon we stayed downstairs in the big front room until Miss Lockwood and Mr. Chandler's daughter began to beat out a duet on a square piano from St. Louis, so big it must have been hauled south by mule train. When they were flitting over the tinkling high notes like a pair of dizzy swallows chasing a bug in the wind, we went upstairs to the room.

"When that blond-headed Chandler girl gets wound up," Scut said, "she sure is expressive. She gets one wrist up in the air and lets it hang for five minutes like it was broken. A bug lit on a finger and went to sleep, and she didn't even know it till William got there."

We got so tired of sitting in upholstered chairs and wanting to see daylight in that interior coffin that we got up and walked down the wide hall. "Hey!" Scut said. "Here's a room we ain't been in yet."

The door was partly open, so we went in. The room was filled with comfortable chairs which we could see by the light of the half-drawn blinds, and bookcases stood about the walls.

"Good Lord, look there," Ham said. Mounted on a pedestal above the highest was a red-painted human skull.

"We came to the right place to be buried," Scut said. "Look at this." He took a long cane tube from the wall with darts and arrows fastened to it.

"That's a blow gun," I said. "That must go 'way back. Look at the big bows and spears. Here are some barbed fishing hooks."

"What's this outfit?" Ham took down a long hickory stick with a small hide basket at one end.

"That's for those ball games we heard about," Scut said. "The Choctaws and the other tribes laid out those big fields and caught the ball in that sack and ran each other ragged back and forth to those poles they set up at each end. If they didn't get where they were going, they beat the other side to pieces. Every town had a team."

"Here's a fishing net," I said, "made out of woven vines."

"Look at this." From a separate shelf, Ham picked up a paint-faded tom-tom. The top and bottom were hide-covered and tight, but there was something odd about the sides. They were slightly curved, and with his finger Ham found a battered hole and moved a chipped but still hanging fragment about. "Why, this old thing is made out of clay." He held the hole to the light. "It's got a wood frame inside, but it's made of clay."

Within the room a deep sigh sounded. While we had been looking at the weapons, the sun had shifted just enough to cast a brighter shaft through the blinds. It struck on something—a dark face—and a heavy featured old man raised his head and looked up from a chair. In the glare, his gold earrings glittered. It was John Jumper. He had been sleeping.

"We didn't mean to wake you," Ham said. "We were just looking."

"I come to look," John Jumper said. "Many times. What I see here I think about."

"We've been thinking too," Scut said. "Why is that skull up there?"

"It is very old. That is all I can tell you." A kindly light was in his eyes.

"How come you Seminoles were the last to give up to the white man?"

"Because we had less to give—only ourselves, only our freedom. We were the swamp people."

"You sure got a deal. You had a false treaty too, didn't you, just like the Creeks, just like almost everybody?"

"We are in this room," John Jumper said. "And tomorrow the sun rises—or sinks forever. Before I die, I will come again." His heavy face became even more kindly. The black bow tie under his run-around goatee looked somehow out of place. "But still, we will try to the last—before all the white man's strength. Once we had our land, our people—then we were brought here. The land we were promised has all been changed. It is dust. It is no longer ours, for now the government says, 'Give the land back to us again, that we may make homes for more Indians from the north and from the plains. You are forgot now, Seminole, and all our promises.' So there must be another treaty! There is but one way left for the Indian; when the heart is cleansed of bitterness, the eye can see."

"We'd hoped to visit your country," I said, "but we've been shoved too far off the trail."

"Yes," John Jumper said, "I knew that." He stood up and moved through the doorway, so huge he almost bent his head to pass through it.

"He comes from a whole family of chiefs," Ham said.

"But it's over," I said. "It's all over. And he knows it."

In the morning we put out toward the Texas Road. Last night while the shouts of John Jumper's revival rang from the arbor, we talked things over with Mr. Chandler. We decided once more, in spite of everything, to follow the road or at least to stay near it.

Jeoff Chandler said, "The important thing is for you to keep posted on what happens. In the Kiamichis, you can't, but I have friends along the road you can count on. Take it slow, be cautious, and I'll get a letter to you at Boggy Depot. Your name will be what you gave Tilby. Do you need money?"

"No," Stanley said.

After we left the mansion, we crossed Perryville Creek and struck south.

Chapter 13

THE TEXAS ROAD forked at Perryville, one branch driving on through Limestone Gap, the other swinging more to the west to circle and drop south to Boggy Depot, where once more it joined the other. Ahead lay the limestone ridges, and eastward the dim land of the green pine hills—the Jack Fork ranges and the unseen Kiamichis.

"I still think," Stanley told Miss Lockwood, "that you should have stayed with the Chandlers or taken the stage to St. Louis."

"No. If you can put up with me, I want to see it through. I wrote for money to be sent in care of Miss Chandler, and she can send it to Texas. Or I can get it from her when I return." She was in her old clothes again.

"Do you still mean to come back to the Territory?"

"Of course. I really think that everything has guided me for the best."

It was slow going, crossing or circling the hills, keeping away from the Road. Yet now and then from high places it was seen below stretched like a narrow path in the distance, where small white-topped wagons moved like crawling snails.

"It's wonderful," Miss Lockwood said, as we stopped on a ridge to watch.

"Yes," Stanley said. "It is—from a distance. It's movement. It is one people going somewhere, over the bones of another."

"You haven't talked that way in days."

Stanley said, "I realize how far it is to Texas. I also know that sick people are in the wagons. Most of them will get there. But some will be buried in the trees. It has been that always."

"I don't think I am a pioneer," Miss Lockwood said. "Yet in a way I must be. I have left all I know behind."

"If you end up in our Comanche country," Scut said, "you'll be a pioneer."

We camped that night beyond a break in the ridge which marked Limestone Gap. Stanley looked at the darkening creek and then at the hills. "We faced slow time today, but we made it."

Then before we could even move, we were ridden upon by four outlaws. They galloped upon us, pistols pointed, from two directions—upstream and down—as if they had watched us from some nearby hill and knew exactly what spot we'd pick to camp. They were led by a giant Negro, who shouted orders and sat a great red roan while the others dismounted.

Stanley looked at Miss Lockwood and told us, "Don't use your pistols. Drop them, or let the outlaws have them."

"It's Blue Gum," Miss Lockwood said. She spoke calmly, as if this could be no worse than what she had gone through at his hands before. The scar-faced Negro, a dirty rag wrapped around his neck, towered in the saddle, his dark eyes on Stanley.

"You're Stanley Hightower." He spoke in a flat, deep voice. When he said Hightower, it was almost as if he said "Hah-tah."

Stanley, enraged at being trapped, glared at Blue Gum. "What do you want?"

"Get yo' horses saddled. Pack yo' things. We got a long ride ahead."

"The woman, too?"

"Sho'. She be safe—this time—if you do what I say."

"How about putting our guns in the tow sacks? You carry the sacks."

"Don't try no foolishness."

So now we are riding east over the land beyond Limestone Gap, toward the lower end of the Jack Fork ranges. As night falls, we make our way between the rough bases of many concentric ridges, into narrow valleys surrounded by the dank air of tumbling creeks in their rocky beds. We wind higher and deeper into the pine-needle country.

Scut says, looking up through the tree tops to the best friend a cowhand ever had on a dark night—the endless white raft of stars overhead, "Still going east—maybe a little north. But we've put some miles behind us."

Blue Gum rode solitary before us. Another Negro and two whites brought up the rear. Miss Lockwood whispered to Stanley, "Do you know why yet?"

"No," he said in a low voice. "But they must want us to do something for them. And apart from holding us for ransom, I don't know what it could be. They haven't tried to rob or kill us, and if they wanted money, they would have taken it first."

Blue Gum growled back, "No talking, white folks."

"Hey!" Scut says. "How much do you weigh?"

"I weighs two-forty-five. And I'm all man."

"You sure are. You're the biggest hunk of stuff I ever saw. There ain't a bone edge or an ounce of fat on you."

"Shut yo' mouf, boy."

"You'd better shut up," I told Scut. "We've got along with him so far."

"I was feeling him out," Scut whispered. "I learned something—he can talk without getting ready to shoot."

"He's just in his own bailiwick."

"As much at home as we are on the Chisholm Trail," Ham said. "I wish we were there."

One thing certain, Blue Gum was nobody's fool. What proved it was that he was here now, leading us ever deeper from one pine-topped canyon to another, the black creeks clearly sounding in their downward rush. At last a gray light came among the fringed ridges and showed a foggy glimpse of sky overhead, only the largest stars remaining up there, and now and then even they were lost among the pine tops. It was almost sunup.

Blue Gum stopped his horse. "Go right up this trail first," he said. "One at a time."

We rode upward on a ragged path over fallen leaves and pine needles and upon flat sandstone ledges, the foggy air sharp and tangy as the tired horses climbed ever higher. In the half-light of daybreak the depth of a narrow valley was clearly seen, far below and deep and mist-covered.

"Look!" Miss Lockwood cried. "See where the creeks run together. It's like smoke rising."

Blue Gum called, "There's two trails up ahead. You take the left one."

We did, winding still higher among projecting ledges. Then a sheer wall brushed us on one side, almost shoving us outward. A broad width of sandstone appeared, its sides rimmed by tilted trees and boulders. It was a solid ledge, and bore signs of being lived on.

"Get off yo' horses," Blue Gum said from behind. We dismounted on the rock and saw the fire-blackened mouth of a cave. "Get yo' doctor bags and go in there."

Stanley motioned, and we took the bags from the horse. At the mouth of the cave, we bent to pass beneath an overhanging ledge and at once, as if in an instant's cut-off, the outside glare was gone. Foul air smote us. In the orange light of a broken lantern, half covered by a filthy blanket, Olinger lay on the rocky ground. He glared, his flitting eyes two hot marbles of hate. A dirty bandage was about his chest.

"You took long enough," he rasped to Stanley.

"Shut yo' mouf," Blue Gum said. "Now see what this man can do for you."

Stanley knelt beside Olinger. "Could I have more light?"

"Tukabatchee," Blue Gum said, "fetch me the big one."

A skeleton-like Creek moved from the shadows. He lit another lantern and placed it beside Olinger. Stanley removed the sticky bandage. He studied the wounds in the upper body, moving Olinger's shoulders to look at his back. He turned him again, then raised the lantern above his face. After a moment he put it down.

"I can't help you," he said.

"Why?" Olinger's crazed eyes danced.

"It's moist gangrene. You knew that. Look at the wounds—the color—the condition of the flesh. I can't help you now. The blood supply is blocked."

Blue Gum said, "You help him, white man, or you don't leave here."

"Very well, I don't leave."

"That girl don't leave."

"Very well. She doesn't leave. But you won't find a doctor in the West who can save him. By the way, how did you know I was a doctor?"

Blue Gum's cagey eyes were on Stanley. "I hear things."

"You heard it from him." Stanley nodded toward Olinger. "And others. And you probably heard that on the Texas Road I operated—a boy with appendicitis. Did you pull a holdup near Perryville?"

Blue Gum laughed. "Man, yo' head sho' go 'round. A man that smart—now, why can't you save this man?"

"The flesh has mortified."

"You come outside. The rest of you, too," Blue Gum told us. When he towered above the valley, he said, "How long he got to live?"

"One day. Two at most. Man, go look in his eyes. He's dead now."

"You keep him alive until he tell me something."

"If he doesn't want to talk, he's got you beat. There's nothing you or I can do."

"Then make it easy, so maybe he talk."

"All I can do is keep him cleansed with disinfectant. Later I can give him morphine."

"Then you go do that."

When Stanley came back from the cave, the sun was high above the mountain. Blue Gum waited on the ledge. He said, "Now work on me. You work on my neck. I got a real misery."

"What?"

"I got a carbuncle."

"Untie that rag and take your shirt down. Sit on that big rock."

"I been in bad shape," Blue Gum said. "I got the nosebleed, too."

"Bend your head a little. You haven't done any hard running lately—to get nosebleed?"

"Oh, I runs a little once in awhile." With his great head bent down, Blue Gum let out a wild cackle. "Not long ago I sho' run hard. That when ole Olinger got shot. Bench Buckley knock him right out of the saddle. That Bench a real man."

"I'll have to operate," Stanley said. "The carbuncle is green. It's ready to burst. There's dead tissue inside."

Blue Gum jerked his head upward. His eyes rolled. "You mean I rotten like him in there? You mean I going to die?"

"Not from this carbuncle. But I'll have to open it and remove the dead flesh. I'll burn it out with carbolic acid. It will hurt."

"I sho' don't want to die now. You burn it then. You burn it."

Stanley said, "I'll need my assistant—the nurse."

"Then get her. You get her quick."

"You haven't had diabetes, have you?" Stanley asked. "Carbuncles can be fatal with diabetes."

"Lawd, no. I ain't had it. I never heard of it. What else it do to me?"

"As I said, with carbuncles it might be fatal, or the other way around."

"Lawdy, you get that acid bottle. I stand anything."

Stanley nodded and we set up our hospital. Blue Gum said, "What's that boiling water for?"

"To sterilize my instruments. You wouldn't want appendicitis germs, would you?"

"Did you hear that bird?" Blue Gum said.

"No," Stanley said.

Blue Gum told his men, "You hold yo' pistols on him. You watch him good."

Stanley daubed a bottle-moistened piece of cotton on the carbuncle. "This will ease the pain a little. I'll have to cut deep—a crosscut. But even that won't hurt as much as the acid."

"Oh, Lawd!" Blue Gum told his men, "You boys bring me a stick." He put a scaley pine branch in his mouth and clenched his teeth. After the incision, the acid hit and the chips flew. Blue Gum leaped off the rock as if the Devil had put a blowtorch to his britches. When he had been worked on and sterilized and bandaged, he told his men, "Now you come get cured."

"Are they sick?" Stanley said, washing his hands in hot water.

"Something wrong with every one of those men."

The first outlaw sat on the rock. "What's your trouble?" Stanley said.

"I got ringworm."

"Where?"

The outlaw took off his hat. He was gaunt and sunken-cheeked and sallow. "You're eaten up," Stanley said. "Hand me the scissors," he told Miss Lockwood. "I'll cut some of his hair." While he was working, he said to Blue Gum, "I haven't felt well myself lately. All I think about is dying. Not a night goes by that I don't hear rain crows and hoot owls. Not one crow, but many—they call all night. It's a bad sign."

"It sho' is. Lawdy, I been hearing them things, too."

"You and I might die before Olinger."

"Don't talk like that. Don't talk like that."

"This is a beautiful case of *Tinea Capitis,*" Stanley said, working on the sallow outlaw.

"You done said that was ringworm," Blue Gum said.

"That's another name for it. Do you have any whiskey up here?"

"We plumb out of whiskey. Once in a while we get some Choc beer."

"You can use a mixture of alcohol and walnut hulls for ringworm, after letting it stand for several days. I'm out of alcohol, but maybe whiskey would do." He moved to a pot of water to wash his hands again. "If they had whiskey," he muttered to Miss Lockwood, "there could be trouble." He turned to the outlaw. "We'll use limewater for now. When you get to some Indian corn at a cabin, put the grains on a shovel and press with a hot flatiron. It will leave an oil when the corn burns. Rub the ringworm with the oil."

"I know another cure for ringworm," Ham said. "Find a woman who's going to have a baby, and she sticks her left-hand little finger in her mouth and rubs it on the ringworm. But it's got to be the left-hand little finger."

"Go down to the creek," Stanley said, "and find the woman. Then come back with one other thing—a big portion of faith."

When we finished doctoring the other outlaws, it was noon. For hours we'd hardly looked at the valley. But now we did, and it was vast and clear. We put up our cutting tools and built our separate fire to eat by. Stanley had told one outlaw to go to the creek and take a daily bath for a week. But instead, they all climbed into their saddles and rode down the valley on some other business, while Blue Gum remained alone to stare morosely from the ledge.

Miss Lockwood began to laugh. She became almost uncontrollable. "The bold bad bandits! I wonder what was wrong with Robin Hood. What ailment did he have?"

"He was no better," Stanley said. "It's the life they lead. No sanitation, riding long hours, poor diet. If Blue Gum's men found Indian corn, they'd eat it. They wouldn't try to cure ringworm."

"I've been meaning to ask you about that skull Mr. Chandler had," I said. "Why does he keep that thing?"

"It's a family heirloom. It's well over three hundred years old."

"Where did they get it?"

"His ancestors took it. When some of the early Spaniards visited a Choctaw village in Mississippi, they molested the women. At Chandler's house, you were looking into the eye sockets of a Spanish conquistador."

"He was well kept," Scut said.

"About John Jumper," Ham said. "I heard Blue Gum had been a Seminole slave. Is that true?"

"Yes. After the war he became a freedman and was granted his own land. He was quarrelsome, and lost his property by drink and gambling. He murdered several innocent Creeks because others had killed Seminoles during the war."

While he ate, Blue Gum came to the fire. "I'm sho' worried."

Stanley said, "Is your neck hurting?"

"I been hearing rain crows. I been hearing hoot owls. I been hearing birds I didn't know before."

Scut winked at Ham. "We ain't heard a hoot owl."

"We ain't heard a rain crow," Ham said.

Blue Gum said, "Doctor, ain't you heard a hoot owl?"

"No. I hear mine only at night. It's a bad sign when a daytime man hears a cry nobody else hears. It means bad luck."

"I know it," Blue Gum said. "I sho' do know it."

"I'm going to stretch out and sleep," Stanley told him. "I might have to stay up with Olinger tonight, and I have an operation tomorrow on the ringworm man—a bone felon."

"That's a bad felyon," Blue Gum said.

"If your 'buncle begins to hurt, wake me," Stanley said. He stretched out under his blanket.

Blue Gum squatted on the ledge. We sat with Miss Lockwood and Wallum's goat, looking into the pine-covered valley, hearing the cries of the rain crows and hoot owls as they flitted about the mountain.

After Miss Lockwood went to sleep, Stanley awoke. He sat up. "How is Olinger?"

"About the same, I guess," Ham said. "That Indian hasn't come out of the cave."

Stanley looked at Blue Gum sitting on the crest. "How has he been?"

Scut grinned. "He walks around slapping his ears."

"He does have a bad case. I'll go see Olinger."

When Stanley came from the cave, he said, "He's sinking." He sat down and muttered, "What I can't understand is—he's afraid of Blue Gum, deathly afraid. And he wanted me to kill him, to give him some kind of medicine so he wouldn't live to have Blue Gum kill him."

"Why?" Scut said.

"I don't know. Blue Gum wanted him kept alive to tell something, and Olinger won't tell; he's a stubborn cuss."

"That little man was cocky while he lasted," Ham said.

"Why would Olinger try to rescue Blue Gum from the prison wagons and then get in this jam?" I asked.

Stanley said, "Suppose Blue Gum and Kurbstone had a big whiskey deal lined up with that red-whiskered man from Fort Smith. Suppose Olinger saw a chance for a big clean-up by throwing in with them? Maybe they were getting things arranged down here—in addition to looking for us so they could help Kurbstone. When Buckley captured Blue Gum by accident, what if Olinger, being a marshal, eased in with the deputies to rescue him. At first, no one would suspect Olinger."

"That makes sense so far," Scut said.

"And the holdup near Perryville," Stanley went on. "It was a big haul—money of the Choctaw Nation. Blue Gum admits to it. But what if he and Olinger came together again, and what if Blue Gum gave him the gold to hide? Olinger sees a chance to keep the money and get rid of Blue Gum. If that's right, then Olinger's greed is what puts him in the cave today. He knows too well when a man is badly hurt—he's seen too many—but he put off seeing a doctor to hide the money. It was a big stake—he could resign from his marshal's job, leave the Territory and be a rich man. But Blue Gum was too shrewd. When Olinger evaded his questions about the money, even though he was sick, Blue Gum brought him here and looked me up, to save him to talk."

"You may have busted the hull to make medicine with," Scut said.

"It was on my mind while I slept. It was what I awoke with. I don't see another answer."

Before evening came, the valley began to gloom. We sat watching it. The pines on the slopes stood straight but shadowy, their branches fringing from the tall trunks, and the darkness crept in. The wide-antlered elk ran from the swales. An eerie howling came from the wolves, and far-off foxes yapped, the sounds echoing from hidden canyons.

"Where can we sleep tonight?" Stanley asked Blue Gum.

"This ledge is good enough," Blue Gum said. "You sleep right where you are. Right by this cave."

Stanley stood up. "It may be good for you, but not for us. We'll be busy tomorrow. If I don't have Olinger on my hands tonight, I will when the sun comes up. And if your men get back, I've got at least two operations tomorrow."

"They always get back—so far. Where you want to sleep?"

"Up this high the chill comes early. Tonight will be cold. We want to fix our beds. Beyond the ledge the land is level. Have you got an axe?"

"Sho', we got axes."

"Then we want to chop saplings to hold pine needles. We're

tired. We want good, sound beds. If Olinger wakes up, call me. But I gave him morphine."

"Then you sleep where you want. But remember—me or Tukabatchee sit above you all night with a rifle."

"Fine. Where is the axe? We'll do the chopping."

When we awoke next morning, the valley lay heavy in fog. No creek was seen. We built a cooking fire beside the ledge. Miss Lockwood asked Stanley, "Did you sleep well?"

"Hardly. I was with Olinger all night."

"Did the men get back?"

"After midnight. They're sleeping in the cave."

"Maybe they couldn't find that ringworm woman," Scut said.

"They found another stage," Stanley said. "They hid more gold in the cave."

"The stage holdups are all very romantic from the other end," Miss Lockwood said. "I suppose everyone who comes to the West wishes to be held up. But if people could only see this." She looked about the smoke-blackened ledge. "It makes me shudder. Where can they spend the money?"

"That's the irony," Stanley said. "They can't. It's their seal of destruction."

Blue Gum came from the crest with his rifle. "Lawd, I'se tired."

"I couldn't sleep a wink," Ham said. "Those meringwether birds kept me awake all night. They've got a bleat like a nanny goat. Did they keep you awake?"

"I didn't hear no birds, only hoot owls. What's a meringwether?"

"They've got a long neck and they coast up and down the valleys sideways. Where've you been all your life, not to hear a meringwether?"

"I been mostly right here in the Territory."

"That's where they're thickest—especially in the Jack Fork country. Some fly clear to the Kiamichis."

"Hey!" Scut said to Blue Gum. "I don't figure you. Those birds kept us awake all night and you say you didn't hear a one. Yesterday you heard birds we didn't hear. You're in a bad way. You better drink some of that acid."

"I been thinking about that acid. Listen, you still got that bottle?" Blue Gum asked Stanley, a look of cunning in his eyes.

"I've got it," Stanley said.

"Then I wants it."

"I may need it this morning for an operation. I'll give it to you later."

"Then you be sure to." He turned and went in the cave.

"He's gone crazy," Stanley said. "Some day he'll run amuck."

At midmorning we set up our hospital. Stanley went in to see Olinger. When he returned, Blue Gum sat on the usual rock. "Are you the first patient?" Stanley said.

"I'se always first here." Blue Gum unbottoned and lowered his shirt.

"Take your hat off. How can I work under that hat?" Stanley cleaned the carbuncle. "When we leave, I want you to do this. Have your men work on the cut every day. Get more dead tissue out. You can make a slippery elm poultice for it, or use salt and turpentine. Egg yolk is good."

"Do you hear those rain crows?" Blue Gum asked.

"No."

"I hear some good preaching the other night," Blue Gum said. "At an arbor up by Mr. Jeoff Chandler's place. Ole John Jumper, he sho' whip the Devil around the stump."

"Did you sit in the arbor with the others?"

"I was hiding in the bushes. I been worried about myself. I been aiming to look up old Uncle Wallace—get him to pray for me sometimes."

"What worries you?" Stanley took a roll of bandages and began to dress the carbuncle.

"I gets scared, and I gets lonesome."

"Do dead people come back to haunt you?"

"I seen two or three lately."

"That's bad," Stanley said.

When Blue Gum left, Stanley whispered to Miss Lockwood. "Something is up. He may let us go. I suspected when he wanted the acid. Just to keep his train of thought moving, I told him how his men could care for him."

"What does he want with acid?"

"I believe I know. But while I doctor the others, empty the red bottle and fill it with water."

When Stanley finished his work and packed his instruments, Blue Gum came from the crest. "I wants the acid."

"Here." Stanley handed him the bottle.

"Now I wants you to go," Blue Gum said. "I wants you to get out of here. I don't want you to come back."

"What about our guns?"

"Saddle up and ride down the trail. When I see you get 'way past that narrow place below, I throws the sacks down."

"Get the horses saddled," Stanley told us. He turned to Blue Gum. "I want to see Olinger."

"Sho'. I want you to. You keep him alive for me."

As soon as we started and rode the horses beneath the ledge, Stanley said, "Olinger is almost gone. He won't last ten minutes, but I gave him more morphine. If Blue Gum empties the water on his wounds, he won't know it."

"Do you think Blue Gum will follow us?" Miss Lockwood said.

"No. By then he'll have his mind on something else. Let's take our time until we get the guns. Olinger will die in peace."

Chapter 14

ALTHOUGH the complexion of our journey had changed with the time we had spent in the Jack Fork ranges, we still had no cause for hope, even with the hot eyes of Olinger no longer upon us, for once we reached the Texas Road, danger still would lurk before and behind. Wallum's goat walked steadfastly as we rode from the deeper mountains into the thinning pines.

Since leaving the cave we had camped after half a day's march near a log cabin on a branch of the Muddy Boggy. We had eaten tahn fula, a corn dish, with an Indian family—Tom Fuller, white folks called it—and now we sat by a half-hidden fire beyond a split-rail fence.

Scut yawned. "All I want after leaving those meringwether birds is more sleep."

Stanley said, "Tomorrow we cross the Muddy and strike for

the Texas Road. But with Blue Gum's big holdup, the Choctaw lighthorse will search each mile and cabin."

Ham said, "Since I've been in the Territory, I've crossed so many rivers and creeks I've grown webfeet. I've lived with so many criminals that when I get to Texas, the first thing across Red River will be a sign as tall as I am—Wanted—Ham Esposita McGook, outlaw."

"Cheer up," I said. "We're not there yet."

"What will Kurbstone do?" Miss Lockwood said. "I don't understand why we haven't seen him."

Stanley said, "He gave this end of the road to Blue Gum and Olinger. By now he knows of Olinger's disappearance and may come himself. No matter how well his whiskey-train business has prospered, he still wants the goat. It means more money, and insures his job with the railroad, which is another means to smuggle whiskey."

"Why did Blue Gum let us leave with the goat?"

"After Olinger turned against him, he may not trust Kurbstone. He could fear a trap. Blue Gum is primitive—to him a thing is all black or white. If he doesn't find the money Olinger hid, he'll be all the more dangerous. But a meeting was arranged for somewhere. There'd have to be."

We awoke early next morning and had the horses packed when Ham and Stanley came back from a scout. "We don't go anywhere today," Stanley said. "The woods are full of Choctaw lighthorse. There was a murder on the Fort Smith road yesterday."

"Who?" I said.

"An Arkansas woman—she was in a wagon with her children. The eldest daughter was only fourteen. There are four others left—young boys and girls."

"How did it happen?" Miss Lockwood said.

"A Choctaw said the girl's father had gone to Texas to buy a farm. He sent back for his family. To save money and to keep their team, the mother decided to drive the wagon. She was shot by some wild bunch from the roadside—maybe because she wore a man's hat and they thought she had money. When the outlaws reached the wagon and found a dead woman, they fled. Other travelers buried her by the road."

"We'd better hide out," Ham said. "The lighthorse really look good. They kept two riders ahead, then came the main body—about a dozen. They even had flankers out. We hid the horses and Stanley threw rocks in the opposite direction to make a racket. Then the rear rider passed. They mean to get those killers. We haven't got a chance."

"What happened to the woman's children?" Miss Lockwood asked.

"The girl will drive on," Stanley said. "People in the other wagons will see that she gets to Texas. The Choctaw I talked to," he added, "said that the lighthorse have already combed the upper creek. He knows Jeoff Chandler. He told me to go to the old gristmill farther down. The mill keeper also knows Chandler. He sells him corn meal."

Miss Lockwood said, "Could this murder have been done by Blue Gum and his men?"

"No," said Stanley. "It happened yesterday morning. It's just another outlaw gang, probably from the grog shops on the Arkansas line."

"I should like to go to the mill," Miss Lockwood said. "Is it in a village?"

"No. A few cabins are along the creek, but widely separated. The people do have the One Member Church."

"What an odd name!" Miss Lockwood said.

"You know as much about it as we do," Stanley said. "We were anxious to avoid the lighthorse, so we didn't stay to ask questions. Let's move on."

The mill was a wide shed-like structure built on the bank of the creek. Near it, downstream, a swinging bridge hung like a suspended bow across the water. It was tightly cabled to the trunks of giant oak trees. At either end stood steps made of axe-hewn logs. Writhing grapevines covered the trees.

We stopped the horses. The big water wheel was standing motionless.

"Lesten Barr!" Stanley called.

A squat dark man appeared in the door with a wrench in his hand. "Yes?" he said.

"I am Stanley Hightower. I know Jeoff Chandler."

"Come in," Lesten Barr said.

Stanley and Scut and I walked to the door. The man stepped aside to let us pass. Inside, the mill was half in darkness. Stanley's eyes swept the shadows. "What is the cabin down the creek?" he asked.

"The One Member Church," the man said. He was broad-shouldered. His eyes never left Stanley's face.

"I see," Stanley said. He studied the interior. Square posts supported the heavy roof. The timbers and rafters were rough hewn and held together by wooden pegs. A workbench stood against a wall. Measuring tubs and sacks were piled on the floor. Wooden cogwheels and wooden augers lay scattered about. The thick solid-stone grinding burrs toward which Lesten Barr moved measured over a yard in diameter.

"You don't mind if I work?" Lesten Barr said. "I must balance the burrs today. I'll be busy next week." The big turning wheel of the pair was on top, above the stationary burr, upon which the grain was ground.

"You have a job ahead," Stanley said. "The space of a piece of paper between the burrs doesn't give much leeway."

Lesten Barr bent to dismantle the burr assembly. "What can I do for you?" he asked.

"Your neighbor sent me," Stanley said. "I came because you know Jeoff Chandler. I stayed with him last week. We are in trouble."

Lesten Barr raised himself and placed the wrench on the idle turning wheel. "Well?"

Stanley sat down on the bench. "That's it," he said. "The woods are full of lighthorse. We need a place to stay."

"I see," Barr said. Stanley stood up and we helped carry the heavy turning wheel to the workbench. "You can stay in the mill," Lesten Barr said. "The lady can stay with the family."

"Don't you demand our trouble?" Stanley said.

"No. Not if Chandler is your friend."

There was a slant-roofed enclosure on the side of the mill where we put the horses. Stanley and Lesten Barr walked to the cabin with Miss Lockwood. That afternoon we helped the Choctaw with his work at the mill. Stanley and he reinforced the supports of the burr assembly and replaced the wooden cogs. The rest of us worked at the slow task of smoothing the heavy grinding wheels.

When sundown came, we knocked off. Lesten Barr boarded up the windows with heavy planking, shutting out the last faint light. "I always close the place," he said. "Look." He led us to a trap door which opened over the creek. "I use this when I work on the water wheel. But it could be used to escape by."

We went out the door just as Miss Lockwood and the three Barr children crossed the swinging bridge. They carried our supper. "What is she wearing?" Ham asked.

Miss Lockwood came to the mill in a beaded doeskin jacket and skirt and knee-high leggings. "Well," Stanley said, "you might at least have dressed as a Creek."

"I am a Chickasaw," Miss Lockwood said. "Sadie Gunn let me wear the clothes. She runs the One Member Church. They belonged to her daughter."

"That church again," Stanley said.

"It's an interesting church," Miss Lockwood said. "Mrs. Gunn married a white man. They built it together—hewing the logs themselves. But an epidemic of fever and smallpox wiped out the congregration, even her husband. For years she has held services in the church each Sunday, but only for the very young. She has never admitted another member. She fears more pestilence would come. It is her superstition."

Miss Lockwood and Lesten Barr's children—a boy and two girls—set the pots and plates inside the door. The girls were slightly built and shy, but the boy—White Eagle, he called himself—was talkative.

The Choctaw said to Stanley, "He is White Eagle today, and Black Crow tomorrow. On some days he is Tom Fuller or Jimmie McCrackin. He was a photographer who passed by."

"I see," Stanley said.

"As soon as you go inside to sleep, bar the door. It will be better that way. Will you go back now?" Lesten Barr asked Miss Lockwood.

"No. I'll come later with the children."

Lesten Barr left to cross the bridge. When he was out of sight beyond the vines, Scut said, "This boy has said more in ten minutes than his daddy said all day."

"And with his energy," Ham said, "I bet he hasn't done a lick of work all day. He's already climbing the water wheel."

Miss Lockwood and Stanley sat in the wide doorway of the mill, watching the flow of the creek. "Do you have a good place to stay?" Stanley asked.

"Yes. In the loft with the girls—with candles and a shuck mattress."

"We'll miss you," Scut said. "You kinda took up with us cowhands."

She was silent for a moment. "I've thought of that."

Stanley stood up suddenly. "Are you ready to go back? It's almost dark. Barr says snakes are bad along the creek. I'll carry the pots and plates and we'll take the children home."

That night we were sitting cross-legged on the floor of the barred-up mill or stretched out on the long bench, finding ourselves strangely sleepless and yarning about how the cow ate the cabbage or indulging in some other deep subject like the whyness of the wherefore—anything to take our minds off our own affairs—when suddenly the trap door began to lift.

It couldn't have surprised any of us more than if the whole mill had begun to raise itself into the air to come to stop a thousand feet above the creek. We had a stub-length piece of beeswax candle set in a saucer on the floor, and by its flickering shadows we saw Lesten Barr emerge from the opening.

"Did you have to come in this way?" Stanley said from the bench. He holstered his pistol.

"It was best," Barr said, dropping the trap to step toward us. "I always keep a rifle above my own door. Never trust the darkness."

"Is there trouble?" Stanley asked.

Lesten Barr stood squat above the candle. "I didn't know until a few moments ago that you are a doctor. A woman far up the creek is in labor. It is so serious a preacher sent for my wife and Sadie Gunn. They are ready to leave. Will you come with us?"

"Yes," Stanley said.

Stanley put on his jacket and took his bags from the tow sacks. "Do we go out the trap door?"

"Yes. There is a log to the bank. Let me take a bag. The lady will go, too. She has a horse with the others."

"Do you want us?" I asked.

"No," Stanley said. "It would be too many. Will you stay here," he asked Barr, "now that I am going?"

"Yes," Lesten Barr said.

They disappeared through the floor.

After Stanley left, the next time our quiet conversation in the mill was interrupted, we were ready and knew what to do. We could have weighted the trap door down with the heavy burrs, but in case we had to leave the mill suddenly because of trouble at the front door, we didn't want to face that obstacle.

When first we heard it, there had been nothing direct or open about the sound. But there had been the stealthy scraping of boots on the water wheel, then while we waited, the trap began slowly to lift. But twice in a single night was too much. The very scraping sound had been ominous. We'd fought utter ruin all through the Territory, and this time we knew we hubbed it.

"Get ready," Ham whispered.

As the man's head appeared, one hand and arm shoving the trap door higher, Scut's rope snaked out. There was a yell, then as Scut jerked, the man lost footing and fell. The trap slammed down, the rope playing out beneath it, and Scut was dragged at top speed across the floor. He stopped his rush by making a sudden hitch about a post. But after the quick stop, the man might be suspended above the creek with a broken neck.

We hadn't really meant to hurt the man, for our plan had been to tangle with whoever climbed up and get him tied as soon as Scut roped him. But now as usual everything had backfired. Ham and I had already started for the trap, but in this new hurry we didn't even think to yell for Scut to loose his hold at the post, and the idea didn't cross his mind.

While Ham held the trap door back, I climbed down the ladder until my boots touched a vane of the water wheel. Then I stood face to face with a dead man turning at a rope's end.

We didn't know if he was a lighthorse, or if other men might be near, but I yelled up to Ham, "He's hanging. Tell Scut to turn loose. I'll be in the creek." When the body splashed in beside me, I got an arm out and swam and lodged it against the lower part of the wheel, trying to hold it up. By then Scut and Ham had climbed down.

"Good Lord!" Scut chattered, shaking all over. "I can't see his head. Is it still on? I got him right around the neck, didn't I? I never made such a throw in my life. Is he dead yet?"

"Shut up. Climb back and unbar the door. Ham and I will swim him to the bank."

When Ham gave a hand, we wallowed the man out, dragging him to the front of the mill. We were afraid of the consequences of all the commotion at the wheel, so first we stood dripping on the bank to listen. But the night was quiet, save for the sounds of the nervous horses.

Scut came from the door and we pulled the man inside. We

lit the candle and knelt over him. What we saw was the blue-black face of Bob, the Creek lighthorse who had spoken to Stanley the night we rode from the jail in North Fork Town. Ham took his knife and pistol.

Scut moaned, "Oh, God, what have I done?"

"Get those teeth out of my face," I said. "He's living. Tie his feet."

Ham worked with the rope. Bob opened his eyes and stared. When he got his wits together, he grinned, coughing. "That was a close one." He ran a hand about his throat. "You nearly broke my neck. If I hadn't got a hand on the rope, you would have."

"You nearly killed yourself and drowned two of us," I said. "Did you think you'd catch Stanley?"

"Maybe."

"Well, you learned a lesson."

"Where is he?"

"That's our business."

Bob coughed. "It's not mine. Not anymore."

"How did you know we were here?"

"Someone always talks. The best way to learn is not to try to. Here, don't tie my hands."

"That's not in the bargain."

Just then the trap door lifted again. White Eagle with a black crow feather in his hair climbed to the floor.

"If that door lifts again," Scut said, "I'll die in a gopher hole."

When Stanley awoke on the bench at noon next day, the old mill wheel was creaking happily in the swiftly flowing creek, and the big turning stone was grinding out its grist. Two Choctaws stood by their corn-laden wagons outside the big shed, waiting for a third man to unload more ears into a side chute in the wall. Within the mill three swiftly working Choctaw boys shelled the corn into brass-banded wooden tubs.

"Hey!" Scut said as Stanley stirred. "We hear you got a boy last night."

Stanley sat up and swung his boots to the floor. "I'm proud of that. Nine pounds—fat as a turkey. It's my first Choctaw."

"Well, look over there at the burrs. We're going to have corn bread today, fritters tonight, and grits and red-eye gravy for breakfast."

"Have you seen Miss Lockwood?" Stanley yawned, standing up.

"White Eagle was here," Scut said. "Climbing on everything. He said she's still sleeping. I bet it's that kid who keeps these wheels out of balance. His daddy says he's always trying to fix something. He built a toy mill down the creek but threw so much corn at the fish his old man bought him out. Gave him a hunting knife."

Lesten Barr had overheard, and he turned from the burrs. "Yes, he causes trouble, but he is a good boy. He will learn fast some day. Yes, he keeps the burrs out of balance. And he whittles new notches in the wooden cogs. He cuts the ridges off. He breaks down the water wheel." A deep chuckle came from his throat. "But I like it. It is all ours here. We enjoy him. He is a good boy."

Stanley went to the door. "Have you had any word on the lighthorse?" he asked Barr.

"Most have gone east," Barr said. "The men who brought the corn this morning told me. But I learned something. Pressure has been put on all the lighthorse to take you. Your chances are not much."

Chapter 15

LESTEN BARR, an indulgent father, had no idea of how good his son really was; neither did he know that not all the lighthorse had ridden off. One slept in a deserted cabin several miles distant, a log chain fastened about his waist, but fed and cared for by White Eagle.

That afternoon Scut and Ham and I mounted up for a scout. The rail-fenced farmlands lay in irregular patches among the brown trees or climbed to pine-green hills or flattened themselves near winding watercourses.

Men walked behind mules or horses or oxen in the fall plowing, and above the fragrant freshly turned earth mammoth flights of crows dipped and spread like black mantles. Dogs trotted behind the teams. While we watched from the trees, we saw the tops of steel plowshares glisten, or guessed the tops of wooden ones.

On other farms the corn shocks stood. Farmers split logs into rails for fencing, or cut the wood for winter burning in their cabins, piling it high in wagons, while others loaded ears of corn or stalks for fodder. Beyond the fences cattle roamed. The long rows of leafless cotton plants stood starkly, picked clean for household spinning.

"I've thought about Bob," Scut said as we rode. "If new pressure has been put on the lighthorse, was he trying to warn Stanley?"

"Maybe," I said. "But on the other hand, Bob might have to save his own hide. He wouldn't have a choice."

"Either way," Ham said, "he wouldn't tell us anything. All we can do is keep him safe until we leave. Then White Eagle can let him out of the cabin." We returned to the mill without spotting the lighthorse.

We spent two days more on the creek, and the last being Sunday, we walked to the One Member Church. The cabin stood in a clearing beyond the bridge. Two saplings notched and rawhided formed a small cross which rose above the door. Children shouted in the yard, including White Eagle.

"Sadie Gunn keeps the young while the parents go to the missionary churches," Miss Lockwood said. "Some ride twenty or thirty miles distant, and may reach home after midnight. But they come here first."

Within the church, a harshly blown cow horn sounded. In an instant the yard cleared. "We can go in," Miss Lockwood said. "Mrs. Gunn said to follow the children."

We moved into the cabin and stood with our backs against the clay-chinked walls. Hand-hewn tables and benches stood on the dirt floor. At the tables the impatient children waited. Then we saw Sadie Gunn. She sat in a rocking chair.

She was a huge woman, dark, with a tremendous large head. Her black hair was clumped on her neck in a bun. A red shawl covered her shoulders, and a curved cow horn hung by a leather thong about her throat. Her eyes were as clear as ponds when winter water has turned. She raised the horn to her lips.

The children at one table began to chant a hymn. "What

are those signs for?" Stanley said. Above each table a lettered cardboard hung. From the opposite side of the room another song began.

"The signs bear the name of their religion," Miss Lockwood said.

Scut muttered, "What does Mepid mean?"

"It must be Methodist," Miss Lockwood said. "The children make the posters from what they have been taught in their schools."

Stanley grinned. "In the Territory, Choctaw parents make the best truant officers. The Nation pays for each child they keep in school."

"Each group sings its own songs," Miss Lockwood said. "Mrs. Gunn says nothing at all."

"She doesn't preach a sermon?" Ham said.

"No."

"They change their religion pretty often," I told Stanley. "Everybody going to everybody else's table. But they sure seem happy—all but that paperwad Dead-Eye Dick in the corner. He must have Creek blood."

Food for lunch had been brought by all the Indians to Lesten Barr's cabin. We left with Miss Lockwood so she could help begin to lay things out on plank tables which had been placed in the yard. Kettles boiled outside, watched by Indian women, the smell of pishofa—hominy boiled with meat—heavy in the air.

When Stanley and Miss Lockwood went to the cabin, we walked around the yard and the cow and horse lot, taking things in. Nailed high to the cabin walls were curing hides of game animals—squirrel, deer, 'possum, and wide-mouthed catfish heads. In the fresh hay- and manure-smelling log barn, Ham pointed to the wall. "Look at that ox yoke. It's carved by hand. Look at that harness. I see where White Eagle gets his fingers."

Within the cabin pots and kettles stood before a wide stone fireplace. The furniture was plain. Most of it was home-built.

A spinning wheel stood before the big hearth. Bottles of dye lined the mantle—madder, oak, sumac, pokeberry, and others. Animal hides, fur out, covered the floor. Hide bunks stood against the walls. A picture of a girl in a coffin hung above the slabbed mantle.

"What's that?" Ham asked.

"It's their eldest child," Miss Lockwood said. "Photographers come down the Texas Road and work their way into the hills to the funerals. Many of the dead are photographed."

At one o'clock the cow horn sounded at the One Member Church. The children disappeared.

"They have class for an hour," Miss Lockwood said.

We went to the mill to spend the afternoon. Stanley removed the planking from the window. The creek glistened in bright sunlight. We talked and planned for tomorrow. Then as screams and voices came from the creek, we went to the window. Sadie Gunn sat under the grapevines in the rocking chair.

Two groups of children fought for possession of the bridge, which swung wildly. Some wore crow and turkey feathers fastened in their hair. They aimed small bows and arrows at others who pointed long sticks or cornstalks and banged away. The two sides fought with war cries and shouts.

"I get it," Scut said. "They're playing soldiers and Indians, like I used to play cowboy and Indian when I was in diapers. But how come just the soldiers get scalped?"

"When you were in diapers," I said, "what did you scalp?"

"Indians," Scut said.

With a head as big as a pumpkin, Sadie Gunn sat under the trees and rocked. It was as if she saw nearly four hundred years of history pass before her.

Next morning we struck for the Muddy Boggy, where the Fort Smith road came in. It had run toward the southwest through Skullyville, the Narrows, and Red Oak, through pine hills and then into the limestone country.

As we rode, I said to Stanley, "You told me part of the Fort Smith road was an old Indian trail."

"It was. And when the Chickasaws were driven west from Mississippi, they used it to come among the Choctaws. For a while they lived as one nation."

"Where did these Choctaws come from?" Ham said. "Before they left Mississippi?"

"What do you mean?"

"At the beginning, like in Genesis."

"They tell one story that a chief led his people to Mississippi from the westward ocean. He carried a pole which tilted eastward."

"We've got water witches in Texas," Scut said.

"Another is that two brothers, Chickasah and Chahtah, came from the swamps of Louisiana to found the tribes. Others said they came from a cavern in the Gulf of Mexico. The people have a story of their own early flood, as the Bible does. The tribes were related, just as the Seminoles are an offshoot of the Creeks."

"We've seen all these log fences," Scut said. "How come?"

"Tribal law gives a Choctaw the right to fence land. They're good farmers and stockmen. They're shrewd. Many years ago they learned that the Spanish and French and English played the Five Tribes against each other. As a result they became canny and wise. Their progress was slowed by internal struggles and wars with the Chickasaws, but with some of their first treaty money they founded an academy in Kentucky. Earlier they had asked the government for blacksmith shops and spinning wheels. They have many schools in the Nation."

"The reason those boys ran away from that academy out here was because they wanted to wet a hook," Scut said. "I did that, too—from my one-room log college, and those boys had stone buildings."

"We won't see much of the Chickasaw country," Stanley said. "Only the lower tip. The capital, Tishomingo, is west of Boggy Depot on the Washita."

"We know that river from the Chisholm Trail," Scut said. "We drove at the western edge of the Chickasaw land."

Stanley said, "The Chickasaws also have their academies. In the old wars they fought with the English against the Choctaws. When they were first discovered by De Soto, he wanted them to become baggage carriers. They fought a battle and drove him off, even some of his horses and hogs."

"You mean those blank-eyed conquistadors drove hogs?" Scut said.

Stanley said, "They had to eat. Spanish expeditions into New Mexico and Texas drove hogs. When you think of everyday things in terms of history, the big events stand out as something very final. But no matter where men have marched, someone drove hogs or sheep or cows. They are driven along the Texas Road today. In another year the railroad will carry them north."

"I'm encouraged," Ham said. "We're in history with Leviticus."

"The last Chickasaw war chief was Tishomingo," Stanley said. "He died in Arkansas on the Trail of Tears."

The Fort Smith road, which we now approached from the Jack Fork ranges, once carried the Butterfield stage on the route to California before the war. There had been twelve stations on the almost two-hundred-mile stretch through the Choctaw and Chickasaw Nations to Colbert's Ferry on Red River. But with hostilities, the line had been abandoned.

South of the road lay the old military trail to Horse Prairie, which was in a southward swinging loop of the Red. Eastward beyond it had run the Fort Towson trail from Texas Corner at Fort Smith—from the busy plaza on the garrison road below the church—leaving by way of Towson Road, or Towson Avenue. Fort Towson had been built near Doaksville, where the first Choctaw treaty in the Territory had been made, to protect the early migrants from the Red River Indians.

As we neared the road, we stopped the horses on a limestone ridge, for in winding our way among the hills and valleys toward the thin threads of civilization again, this rest had become more than a stop—it was the unspoken fear of trouble.

Stanley, stubble-whiskered once more, said, "I'm tempted to strike south or to Horse Prairie. But we'd be in good grazing land and a hundred outlaws and rustlers from Texas would hound us. It will be better to go to Boggy Depot."

"Do you infer," Scut said, "that us Texans are cattle rustlers?"

"When Union Army officers and Indian agents stole Cherokee and Creek cattle to sell to the government," Stanley said, "Texans rustled in the south for cows and slaves. The cowhand who sent you to pick up Bill Cookson gets his cattle from Horse Prairie."

Scut said, "I shouldn't have spoken."

"I hear a wagon," Stanley said. "Let's take the road for a few miles. It will beat the valley and creek windings. Leviticus is tenderfooted."

"Limestone did it," I said. "He can wear a sandstone mountain down to a nubbin, but not this limestone."

"When the railroad gets here," Stanley said, "these hills will produce good funeral markers. It will be good commerce, along with coal and cows and crops."

"What got you thinking tombstones?" Ham asked.

The horses moved down the hill. What we came to wasn't like the Texas Road; it wasn't as wide, but it carried a fair number of covered wagons. It didn't matter on what road you saw them though, it was always the same: the worn-out horses and mules, or the yokes of tired oxen pulling the high-stacked freight.

It didn't matter, for wherever it was, there were always the tight, strained faces above the wide seats of the wagons, or the dirty children peering from beneath the back bows—a family which may have come from a thousand miles to seek a land of hope and plenty. They came with more faith than some of us beaten-down cowhands who knew things as they really were, but back in the dim past our own folks had beaten their own hard ways on this and other roads as these were doing and some had ridden or walked beside burrows from Mexico, or had been driven onward across hot desert sands by the lashes of helmeted and mounted conquistadors.

These wagon people were free, and they passd through the Indian Nations in search of something, although in time even the seeking of the Five Tribes in their own new land must cease. Some among them had come to the Territory wearing bright turbans and Indian dress, but because their rifles had been taken before the long march and most of them had not even hoes or axes, some had again made spears and bows and arrows, for the promised food from the white man had rarely come, or when it did, often could not be eaten for worms and rottenness. In the new brush villages Indian boys with their steel-tipped spears had stood to listen to the alien preaching in the arbors. Now that had gone.

The Tribes we rode among could seek no more. The treaty wall about them crumbled. But they had not breached it. Instead, it was the white man who came again. And now the railroad. Even the last of their new days faded, lost in the shifting clouds.

A spell descended upon us as we rode.

"Do you feel it?" Miss Lockwood said. She was wearing her Chickasaw get-up. "I don't know what it is—only something that is very close. Something that comes near but is dead—but why is it still living? I'm not superstitious, but I feel it."

"The Indian, soldiers, settlers, and time," Stanley said. "The first Butterfield stage on the old mail route went from St. Louis to San Francisco in less than twenty-four days—from Fort Smith to here and on to Colbert's Ferry, to Fort Chadbourne and El Paso and across the burning desert to Arizona. At last it reached San Francisco, through Los Angeles. But even the color of those days seems long ago. I remember when I carried water to the chiefs in their council meetings and heard Opothleyahola speak of the island at the mouth of the Chattahoochee. Time—it's a wonderful cure."

"What do you mean?" Miss Lockwood said.

"Can you see the courage and heedlessness of the old stage drivers—the rutted trails, the mountains, their long night drives—can you see their lost graves along the desert roads? Mind you, they were not my people, but they were men. I never saw the old Butterfield drivers, since they didn't pass through North Fork Town, but I saw others and admired them."

"As I have said before," Scut said, peering toward the trees, "when the talk gets heavy, it's time to stop. I'm not tired from anything I've done on this trip, but I just want to sit by a road and watch it—or maybe camp. We've got all our lives to get nowhere, and I've become an old man. I wish I was back in North Fork Town singing 'Shall We Gather at the River.' "

Boggy Depot, when finally we saw it from across the creek, was something for the Territory to be proud of—not at all a desolate place like Perryville. Instead, it had livery stables and several inns, a large hotel, churches, the stage stand, the old stone official buildings, a number of stores and blacksmith shops and wheelwrights, and painted frame houses and log cabins. Mansions as big as Jeoff Chandler's sat among big trees.

We'd coasted in from Muddy Boggy like meringwether birds, at times for want of something better to do stopping to bog up or mire down from a continuous rain. Drovers from Texas knew the Boggy region as the graveyard of the cowman's hope, for they spent whole days dragging cows from the mud, or left them behind to be pulled out by Choctaw farmers rather than pay a fee to cross their land. The names of the creeks were enough—boggy.

Once more the forks of the Texas Road met the trail coming from the east, and the covered wagons rolled ever southwestward, but the late cow drives from Texas were slowing.

Stanley wanted to go to the post office and see a friend who lived in town. "We could beat around the bush till dark," he said. "But I'm tired of that. I'm tempted to ride straight in, lighthorse or not." After we talked, we decided that Scut would say with Miss Lockwood and Leviticus, so Ham and Stanley and I rode across the creek and into the village.

"How'd this place get its name?" Ham asked.

Stanley said, "It was a supply depot for the early Chickasaws. The old Chickasaw-Choctaw treaty was made here when the Chickasaws first came to the country. The town served for council meetings and a place to pay annuities. Later it was on the mail road and received a post office. For a time it was the Chickasaw capital with a Chickasaw academy. A Choctaw newspaper was printed here in both English and the native language."

"Was there any war fighting?" Ham asked.

"No. But it was a Confederate stronghold. We should see the old flag pole. During the war the Choctaws galloped around it to chant and yell their ancient war song."

After we crossed Clear Boggy we fell in with some southbound cowhands, so seeking safety in numbers, we rode with them. As we passed a street in front of a big white house before reaching the square, Stanley muttered, "Look by the corner." A tall sure man sat his horse, watching the traffic.

"Bench Buckley," Ham said.

"What brings him here?" I said.

"I don't know," Stanley said. "But by the way he looks, he means business."

Before the two-story hotel stood a bare-legged bulletin board with the mail and stage schedules tacked to it. Alongside the schedules and dates were poorly printed outlaw pictures and many times layered-over reward posters.

When we got off our horses and strode up, I pointed to one. "Look, that can't be old Wallum." Above Wallum's picture the heavy blurred black type said FIVE THOUSAND DOLLARS REWARD.

"Something's not right," Ham said. "This is some Texas cowhand's orneriness."

He reached to lift the bottom corner of Wallum's tacked-up likeness from beneath the reward figures, and then there appeared the picture of a goat and a full printed statement of how it had been stolen from the Katy. "Since this trouble came up," Ham said, "Wallum's picture must have been in all the papers. Some cowpoke cut this out and stuck it below the reward for Leviticus."

"He had an idea." Stanley pulled his slouch hat lower. "I'll go inside and get the mail."

"I'll get it," Ham said. "No use for you boys to take chances."

"Sure," I said. "You be our fearless hero again."

When Ham came back, he brought two letters, but he was pale as a ghost. "Guess who's inside."

Stanley snapped, "Who?"

"Our two old friends—Kurbstone and Betty Blye."

"Did they see you?"

"No. They were sitting in the dining room eating dinner and drinking coffee. That girl was sure dressed. She had that place upside down. They must have come on the last stage."

"Let's leave," Stanley said, taking the letters.

We mounted up and rode toward the livery stable. And you can guess it. Five black-clad figures sat on the top corral rail, but now one more had been added, and he talked as fast as the others. We left them and rode out of sight behind the livery barn for Stanley to read his letters.

The first was an old one from Amon Tilby. "It doesn't tell anything," Stanley said. "Only that he learned Kurbstone and Betty Blye planned to meet someone here at the depot. He thinks it's Olinger."

"He's wrong on that guess," I said, and then Stanley read Jeoff Chandler's letter.

"The other man is Blue Gum," Stanley said. "Chandler learned from some of his Negroes that they had talked to Blue

Gum during John Jumper's preaching. They said that before too long Blue Gum would meet someone here."

"Then that's how he caught us," Ham said. "We must have been spotted when we left Chandler's. He waited all day to close in, so he could cross the Texas Road with us and be safe at night. He's got brains."

"What about the lighthorse?" I said.

"Only what we know. They want me more than ever. Chandler says two Creek and two Choctaw lighthorse stopped at his place. Others are guarding the main trails to Red River." We hadn't told Stanley about Bob, and now since there was no reason to make thing worse, we still didn't.

I asked, "Are you going to see your friend in town?"

"No. He lives in one of the big houses, but with what happened to Collier and with Kurbstone planning to meet Blue Gum, I'm afraid to risk it. Let's go back. We'll ride up the creek and camp on higher ground."

"Could Bench Buckley have known about this meeting?"

"Perhaps. He could have learned from a prisoner or one of Blue Gum's gang. He could have left the Fort Smith prison wagons to come here after leaving McAlester. He may be after Blue Gum. At the same time, it's possible he doesn't know everything about Kurbstone's devilment. But let's move up the creek. Tilby said he'd have another letter on the stage a week behind this one. As delayed as we've been, I want to come back tomorrow."

Chapter 16

WITH MY BACK against a tree, I was sitting on night guard when a hand seized my gun arm and another reached around the trunk to clamp itself over my mouth.

"Get up," a voice growled. "Stand up and let me see who you is. I'se got this big pistol handy, so you keep yours. But if you reach for it, I cut you down."

The man had come like a quiet cat. I stood up to face him.

"You's the one," Blue Gum said. "Ole one-ear. Now you listen. I see a man today. He want to double-cross me about that goat you got. I don't want that goat, but if he double-cross me, I want it. I see another man, too—ole Bench Buckley—and he see me. I got away, but ole Bench will look till he find where I am and come shooting. I got to leave quick, and you's the main goat boy. You wake somebody and tell him I take you and they keep that goat for me till I get back. If that goat is gone when I come back, I kill you."

"Which one do you want me to tell?"

"Tell that doctor man. You wake and tell him. And tell him to stay right here or just move camp a little up old Boggy each day."

I went over and bent beside Stanley. "Stanley?"

He jerked his head on the cantle of his saddle. "Yes. What is it?"

"Don't move. Don't reach under your saddle. Blue Gum is in the trees, with his pistol on us. Listen . . ." I told him what Blue Gum had said. "Move camp a mile or so up the creek each day. When I get away, I'll look for you."

Stanley's head half turned. "Is his gun still on me?"

"You haven't got a chance. Forget it. I'll get along."

Stanley said, "If I can, I'll see Bench Buckley tonight."

"No. There's no reason for you to be caught, and if Bench knows, I don't want Ham and Scut dragged in. I mean it."

"Good-by," Stanley said.

"Don't sound so final."

I gathered my gear, then went out to unhobble my horse while Blue Gum mounted his in the trees to sit guard while I saddled. Then he said, "Now, one thing—you keep your pistol. Me and you can make it, or I can shoot you down. You use that pistol only when I tell you, you be all right. You know what I mean?"

"Sure." I mounted up. "Where do we go?"

"Ride right up this creek. I tell you when to turn."

It was a black night—in more ways than one. We rode northwest up Clear Boggy.

Morning found us well into the Chickasaw land. During the night we had turned west and with daylight, from the higher places here and there, we saw far ahead the distant mounds of the Arbuckle uplift.

Blue Gum said, "Let's stop, white boy." His black face

looked back toward the rising red sun, the dirty rag around his neck. "I like to see that ole thing come up. It sho' throw out the fire."

It did that, and it threw out rays that went up and up and never stopped—a prairie cowhand's sun. "Where is Tishomingo?" I said.

"It's about due south."

"Have you been there?"

"Lots of times. It's the headquarters for these Chickasaws. Only we don't go that way now."

Not fifty yards away half-a-dozen deer leaped from a swale, their stub tails high and white. Blue Gum laughed, opening his mouth like a bear trap, his gums and teeth showing. "That make me feel good." He jerked his rifle from its boot, firing at the deer as they bounded upward into the brush. One, two, three, four—they all went down. He had fired four shots. Two disappeared. "That make me feel good," Blue Gum said.

"How about me going over there to bring back some breakfast?"

"Sho'. You go fetch breakfast."

When I came back he said, "We go down where those deer stay to cook. A man find where deer stay, it a good place to hide." He cackled. "Everybody always wonder why ole Blue Gum get away. I just stay put and get fat."

There wasn't any use to talk to a crazy man, so after we ate, I stretched out and slept.

We had holed up that day and all that night in the brake, and with morning we rode westward again and crossed Blue River. At last after we swam the Washita, the Arbuckle Mountains pressed upon us, and now and again on low hills we rode between long parallel lines of limestone upthrusts which were like plowed furrows of stone, slanting outward from the soil like low fences.

Blue Gum slowed his horse to look before and behind. "You know, white boy, if a man die up here, all he got to do is dig his grave and cut his name right on top a rock. He don't move nothing. I call this country the Devil's Washboard. I bet it wear the hide off his knuckles."

"Have you been here before?"

"Listen, white boy, there ain't nothing I don't know about this country."

"How come you think so much of dying?"

"I got a feeling. But 'fore it comes, I stir up a lot of devilment."

"You were given free land after the war. Why didn't you keep it?"

"White boy, you expect Blue Gum to settle down to farming? What I want to farm for?"

"It's good enough for most people. The way you've led us, I haven't seen many farms among the Chickasaws, but what I have seen look as good as the rest, from the Cherokee to the Choctaw land. And most of the freedmen settled down to farm or build their own towns. Some have their own law and order. Why didn't you stay put?"

He jerked his horse toward mine, his face in a rage. "You keep yo' mouf shut. You keep yo' big mouf shut."

"I'll keep my mouth shut. I was trying to get some sense out of you."

"I got more sense than anybody. I got a lot of sense."

The cedars thickened as we rode among the rows of limestone. We dipped into low places and always before us rose the Arbuckles, seen close at hand like toy hills, or bold and rugged, top-rounded and cedar-covered, the valleys deep. At last we wound our way upward to the highest mounds and stopped. To the south lay the wide and level land, and northward the faraway and lost valley of the upstream Washita—"owa chito"—big hunt, the old Choctaws had called it, wandering far from their Mississippi land for the great buffalo hunts on the Western prairies.

I knew the valley, for on the Chisholm Trail we had crossed the upstream Washita at Rock Crossing. The Caddoes had their reservation near old Fort Cobb, and other reservations were near the river. With luck, I might escape Blue Gum and strike west to the old cow trail or go southwest to Red River Station, where the trail crossed to Texas. But I couldn't leave—there was our old camp moving upward day by day on the Clear Boggy. Here where we sat, the rounded hills spread about—the perfect hiding place for Blue Gum, and for something else.

"You told me you were smart," I said. "That no man would ever catch you again."

His black mood had changed. He guffawed. "Ain't no man ever catch ole Blue Gum. I die, sho' but ain't no man do it."

"You mean you won't ever be caught?"

"Ain't no man ever catch me again—that Bench Buckley did it one time. He fool me, but no more."

"Then look over there." I pointed.

On a rounded height almost as high as our own, only a few hundred yards away, his rifle booted, a tall spare figure sat a horse. Against the vast sky which spread endlessly behind him, he waited as immovably as a white outcrop.

Blue Gum turned in his saddle.

"That's Bench Buckley," I said.

Daybreak came, and we were out of the old Fort Arbuckle country, hidden in the boggy bottoms of the tree-lined Washita.

It had been a night of endless travel toward the west, ever winding and back-tracking among the rocky swift-flowing creeks. A few hours after midnight Blue Gum made a sharp cut back toward the Washita. Now we were due north of the mountains. We camped, building a smokeless fire to cook breakfast.

Blue Gum squatted and chuckled. "That Bench Buckley—he one smart man. But he won't catch this chile. He knows this rifle I carry. Ole Bench know too well not to come close to me. That why he sat off and just looked from that mountain."

"What was that road we just crossed?"

"That the Fort Sill to Boggy Depot road."

"You mean it goes straight through to Boggy?"

"It go pretty straight. But me and you don't go that way. We keep going across the Canadian, up to the Seminole country. What we cross next befo' the river is that road to California."

"You mean the old Fort Smith trail that came in at McAlester?"

"Right there's the place. That road sho' is tired when it sees the ocean. Get on your feet, boy. We got to prank ole Bench Buckley again."

"How do you know we did prank him?"

"Ain't no one stay up with me when I mean it."

We left the thick river growth and oak stands and rode across wide prairies.

"Who held Fort Arbuckle during the war?"

"Chickasaw battalions hold it. But Chickasaws never live out here much—too close to those wild Plains Indians. Those real Cross Timbers mark the limit."

"When did you get here?"

"I come long after that Cherokee Trail of Tears, part way by steamboat. I just a boy then. You know what those Creeks do to me in Florida? Those Army men tell them and those Georgia people—those big plantation men—you go down to Florida to those Seminoles and take back your stole' slaves. They take my mama and papa away, and we done lived there for a hundred years. My mama say when she see them come, 'Boy, you go hide in the swamp.' So my old people bring me out here and let me work my land with them."

"You mean you Seminole slaves worked your own land?"

"Sho'. That's why those other civilized tribes don't like us. They kept slaves in bondage. If there was left-over land, or some was rented us, or if we cleared land, that money was ours. We paid tax to the Nation just like the Seminoles. They run away from the South a long time back, and so did we. We had a lot in common. We like each other. They didn't like black men to be abused by nobody, especially Creeks. It like I come up to you and say, I'm a slave. I'm a good worker. I run away: Can I be your slave? And you say, Sho! There's a patch of land out there. Look at it. You build a hut there and help me work. I say, Sho! Then you say, Farm that patch of land if you want to, or catch you a fish. We get along fine."

"You mean it was still that way, even with the war?"

"That war change a lot of things. But it wasn't all war, it was that false treaty, when those chiefs sign what they didn't know nothing about from all that whiskey they was fed, and out here they got split up on all that and the white man's religion. Seminoles didn't have no business being here. They belonged back home."

"What about these Negro towns?"

"There was Negro towns before that war got started. When we come out here to live in this wind, we were put in the Creek Nation. Those Creeks cause a heap of trouble. They don't like free slaves. They say we ruin their own."

"Stanley Hightower said his mother kept good care of her slaves."

"How many she have?"

"Four."

"That all depend on people. But when you find four, five hundred slaves with some of these Cherokees and Choctaws, it wrong. Anyway, some of us go off to a creek and start a place we call Wewoka. That name mean Barking Water from the falls there. Then all those Creeks gallop up after us. They say we ruin the Territory. Then the Seminoles come riding against the Creeks. There's a good war a-brewing—then these Fort Smith soldiers stop it."

"Ain't Wewoka the Seminole capital?"

"Sho'. Ole council house and schools and everything, even that old execution tree. Maybe us slaves did do some good in this country. We start a good town. There was a bunch more treaties coming up anyway, and the Seminoles got their own land." Blue Gum scowled. "But ain't nothing come right since I got out here. Back home, there was warm days I woke with the sun in my eyes and killed me a bird for the bright feathers, or got me a deer with a bow and arrow. There was a ball court, or fishing, or I was on the swamp paths with a black girl running beside me. I been thinking those things lately. I ain't got long to live."

"What did you do in the war?"

"I fought with ole John Jumper—starving everywhere. I saw ole Stand Watie take all the clothes off the backs of those Pin women and children to put them on his own people. I saw so many of those refugee camps from one end of this Territory to the other I got tired of it." Blue Gum began to laugh. "There was just one thing I missed out on in that war—that was when that ole Yankee Creek chief, Opothleyahola, dumped all that Nation's treasury in a barrel to bury it. He say he going out West and start him a cow pen. I wish I had stood behind that barrel with a pistol. After that Round Mounds battle he let his wives knock in the heads of some of you Texas boys with their big hominy pestles."

"Did you like Stand Watie?"

"He was short and mighty bowlegged, but he was a tolerable man, even if he was a Cherokee. One time when they was all chased down by Red River, with thousands of Indians starving everywhere, Stand and this good-looking son of his got put up real comfortable in a big-sized house. While ole Stand was gone, Saladin got liquored up and make insult to womenfolks. He come back home that night with his warwhooping and found Gen'l Watie sitting on the porch. Ole Stand jump up and pound him down. A preacher man run up and says 'Don't, Brother Watie, stop, he's drunk!' Ole Stand stop punching and look up from the ground and say 'Preacher, so am I!' Then he start pounding again."

After we crossed the prairie, we stopped in a blackjack stand to let our horses blow. We sat among the trees and rested.

"White boy," Blue Gum said, "why don't you let me even up those ears?"

"What do you mean?"

"Whack that other off. Then you match up fine."

"They'll do."

"Boy, you ever kill a man?"

"No."

"Didn't you ever want to?"

"Maybe I did."

"A man want to do something, why don't he do it?"

"It's not just what he wants to do. It's what comes to him to do."

"What you getting at?"

"I've got a reason to kill. I've got a right to kill."

"What's on yo' mind, boy? Why you talk crazy? Who you got what you call a right to kill?"

"Old Wallum—he killed my daddy."

Blue Gum laughed. "Yah-yah! You mean that ole goat man? Then why don't you kill him? Why you drive that goat to Texas?"

"If I kill Wallum, what? One of his men kills me. Then one of my friends kills that man. There's no end to it."

"You is sho' right there," Blue Gum said. "There ain't never no end. A man start him a good killing, it bounces like a tornado across the ground. But this man killed yo' daddy. Why don't you want to kill him?"

"All I know is, I want to make Wallum eat that goat."

"You don't want him to eat that goat, not the way you took care of it."

"I don't mean for him to eat it that way. I'm just going to take it home to him."

"Well, that's yo' business. You think ole Bench Buckley going to catch me, don't you?"

"He'll catch you. He's set his mind to it. You haven't got a chance."

"You don't know Blue Gum."

"I know you. I've got friends who know you, too. What happened to those other men you had?"

"Two got killed trying to rob one of those stages. That ole Indian boy, Tukabatchee, still sit up in the cave with the last one. He got shot up pretty bad. One of these days I got to get me some new men." He stood up and yawned. "Lawd, I'm sleepy." He walked to the edge of the blackjacks, their leaves brown and sere, the gray grass of the prairie blowing in the sweeping wind. "What's that?"

I got up and walked to stand beside him. "What?"

"That over there—in the big trees."

Between two oaks at the edge of the woods, a tall figure sat his horse.

"That's Bench Buckley," I said.

"How come he know I was here?"

"He didn't even look for us in the mountains. He knew where you would come, and there he is."

"Then he won't come too close so long as he know I'm Blue Gum. Yo' name is Scrape, ain't it? Scrape, you stay right here where he can see you. Let Blue Gum rest and sleep awhile. I'se might tired. You just stay here so he sees you, and he be afraid to come up."

"He's not afraid. Do you want my pistol?"

"No. You just stand and watch him. I'se mighty tired. Mighty tired. Just let me sleep."

A few hours later Blue Gum awoke. It was pitch dark. He sat up, grabbing his pistol. "Bench Buckley? Where he go? Where he go?"

"How do I know where he went? He left a fire over there, and he built another one behind us."

Blue Gum stood up. His shadow bulked against the trees. "Then I fooled him. Scrape, you're a mighty good man. Me and you get some place together."

"Don't count on anything, not with Bench Buckley."

"I going to fool him good. I going to fool him good." Blue

Gum began to gnash his teeth and peer into the white starlight above the rustling branches. "Scrape, you pretty good boy. We going to fool him. Listen to that clacking wind."

"What do you want to do?"

"What that new fire over there for? Look, there's another one. He got four fires around us, that ole devil."

"Let's ride across the prairie, then strike north for the river. He hasn't had time to get back to the first fire yet."

"Oh, yes, he has. He got time to get anywhere." But we mounted up and rode out to the prairie and struck north. Blue Gum said, "Maybe we cross this big water and ride back east to where Little River come in. We be back to Creek country then. Ole Jesse Chisholm marry him a girl at that trading post. Ole Jesse dead now. He die of cholera. Po' Jesse."

"Do Seminoles have lighthorse?"

"They got the best lighthorse of all. That's why I don't stay up there. Before we get to Little River, we pass through ole John Jumper's country. He got a big church house. He got preaching and eating arbors. Maybe he have a camp meeting. Maybe we hear him pray. Ole John fighting another treaty now. He say it give our land to those wild Indians. He say we just fade away. I been seeing a lot of those ole chiefs tonight—ole Micanopy and Osceola and Chittee Yoholo and Billy Bowlegs. We chase ole Billy back and forth in the war. Osceola never get here—he get tricked in Florida and die in a dungeon. Yaha-Hajo die in Florida a long time ago. He get killed by soldiers on Oklawahah River. Ole Black Dirt, he build the first Seminole town out here. I see all those men. Those were the prettiest feathers in that swamp. Scrape, I'se sho' tired."

"Bench Buckley built those fires to worry you."

"You think so? Then I fool him again. Instead of riding down this river, we ride up. We cross over and maybe go up the North Fork to ole Kickapoo Town."

But within an hour Blue Gum had changed his mind. At daybreak we were again on the sandy Canadian, across from the Seminole land. We got off our horses and stood, watching the far north bank. "Look over there." Blue Gum pointed beyond the river. "That land's the old Nation. Up at Wewoka on that brown rock creek folks is happy and laughing. In all their cabins smoke come from the chimleys. Down around that big bend there John Jumper wake up. I'm going home, Scrape. Them lighthorse won't get me. Let's have a good breakfast this morning—a real good breakfast. Ole Blue Gum hungry today."

The river was wide and sandy. Through the walnut and sycamore trees on either side a thin shimmer of water twisted through the glistening bed. Blue Gum said, "I'm going to lean back against this tree and rest. Scrape, break things out for the cooking. Man, that country look pretty. Scrape, ain't you mad at me? You ain't afraid of me?"

"It wouldn't help me to be mad—or afraid either."

"You a crazy boy. I'm sho' glad we're out of those black-jacks. We got some more ahead, but I know where I'm going. Those trees reach at me like fingers. A man got to take a good axe to get through those trees. That coffee smell good. Did you see something move on that far bank?"

"I can't watch the other side and fry sowbelly and potatoes. We got one can of beans left. You want to open it?"

"Sho'. Throw it here. This old hacking knife cut it right open." Blue Gum chuckled. "Last time in North Fork Town, I hear something funny. Ole man I know there always dig snakeroot for a living. I say, 'Hello, you still digging snake-root?' He say, 'Yes, I'm a snakeroot digger and a tie hacker.' First time I ever hear that word. It come with the railroad."

"You just wait," I said. "A lot of things will come with the railroad. I'm glad I came through the Nations when I did. Did you ever ride on a railroad?"

"I never did. I don't want to be shut up that way. If I go places, I want the open."

"I rode from Chetopa into the Territory."

"That town Chetopa named from an ole Osage chief. How you like that train ride?"

"It was all right. But the way it swayed, I nearly fell over when I walked. It makes you think."

"Everything make me think nowadays. Everything. Scrape, what make people keep doing things? What make that railroad come? What make me run around? What put you here right now?"

"I'm not smart enough to know. And I don't want to. Are you ready to eat?"

"Sho', boy. Let's shovel it up. Look at those good brown potatoes! Look at those hot beans and sowbelly!"

When we finished eating, Blue Gum stood up. "That's the best breakfast I ever ate. You get things cleaned up and then we ride. I get a good laugh on ole Bench Buckley this morning, him 'way up there by Kickapoo Town. My stomach sho' feel good. We got more coffee?"

"One cupful. You want it?"

"Sho', I take it."

When we were ready to ride, Blue Gum chuckled. "White boy, I'm going home. I'm going to show you some places." He threw a big boot over the saddle of the roan and looked back. "Good-by, ole Chickasaw country. I done left you behind. Let's get going, Scrape."

We rode from beneath the big trees to a clump of red sumac and into the cottonwood saplings and among the yellow leaves of the willows on the bank. In the river bed the sun glinted on the narrow path of water.

Before moving down the slope we stopped the horses. "Look over there," Blue Gum said. "Look at that Seminole land. See how the yellow grass shines on that rise." He sighed. "Oh, Scrape, that ole dry land. It ain't like I told you at all. What make a man tell such big lies?"

Across the river a tall figure moved. He had stepped from behind a cottonwood tree, raising his rifle. A sudden splat sounded close. Blue Gum fell to the slope. I swung off the horse and knelt beside him. Blood had already come to his thick lips. "Are you hurt bad?"

"Sho', Scrape. He got me." He turned his head. "That ole rascal got me. Straighten me out. I beginning to hurt bad now."

His hat was six feet away on the sand, and beneath his brush jacket a crimson stain darkened his chest. I got him straight and he said, "Bring me that ole rock from over there. Put it under my head. I want to see the far land." He coughed, the blood on his lips heavier. "Where ole Bench go?"

"He's standing half behind that tree, watching. Do you want any water?"

"I don't want nothing. I just want to look. I want to look over the man that killed me to something I never saw before."

"I know what you mean."

"You a smart boy, Scrape. You learn just like I do. You think ole Bench'd shoot me down?"

"He was bound to."

"I guess he was. I guess so. But he still afraid. He won't cross that river. He won't come."

"He doesn't have to. He did his job getting here."

"He knew what I'd do. He knew all the time what I'd do. He was just waiting. Put that rock a little easier."

"Let me ride and get him. Maybe he can help."

"No. I done made up my mind. Ain't nobody can help me. I want you to go. You a good boy, Scrape. I'm going to give you my horse. I want you to go to your friends. You go right south and hit that California Trail. It take you back to McAlester, or you keep south and hit Clear Boggy. You go by some of those big Chickasaw schools and it take you to your people."

"I'm not leaving you like this."

"Do what I say, or I cut you down. This ain't a stole horse. It's a bought horse. There ain't no better, or Blue Gum wouldn't have him. I hates to leave that horse. Reach in my shirt pocket and I sign my X on that paper I got. Then you keep it. It make you legal. Look at that pretty land over there."

I put the paper in my pocket. "I ain't going to leave you."

"You do what I say. Me and you got along fine. You been a good friend. When I see ole Bench, maybe lots of your troubles get easy. He still watching, so do what I say. I want him to come over here. Go to my horse and take that rifle from the boot. Hold it high—'way high—so he can see it. Then throw it away, as far as you can. Then take this pistol off me and let him see you throw it away. Then take the horse and leave. Then me and Bench Buckley look at each other. I got maybe an hour before that big sun goes out, so you leave."

I did what he said. "Is there anything else you want?"

"No. When Bench Buckley cross the river, I tell him something. It make it all right for you. You don't worry no more. You go on to Texas."

I got a lead rope on his horse and mounted mine. "I'd stay if you wanted me."

"No. A long time ago I saw bright feathers. Maybe you have better luck. Maybe old Bench lay me out at John Jumper's church. Maybe ole John pray for me and bury me in the churchyard. Did you ever see one of John Jumper's meetings?"

"No. But I saw meetings down in Texas."

"Ole John do a little visiting and preaching early in the day to warm folks up. Maybe he have a thousand people there, maybe two thousand. They come walking and praying or on horseback and in wagons. The big preaching arbor is full of people, and all the eating arbors. And then about nightfall, after everybody gets full, Brother Big John he gets wound up and he begins to whip the Devil. He run him around the stump and he beat him. Everybody jump up and cry Hallelujah! Then John get everybody working against the Devil. When he got him whipped, everybody start singing and shouting. They start dancing up and down and clapping. That firelight is sho' pretty—all my people dressed up bright and dancing—hopping up and down. Scrape, if you ever see John

Jumper, ask him to pray for me. If you ever see Uncle Wallace, ask him to pray. Me and you got along mighty well. Tell Bench Buckley to hurry."

There wasn't anything to do but ride off, and I did. But I stopped in the trees and waited, looking back. When Bench Buckley rode across the river, I turned the horses toward Clear Boggy.

Chapter 17

NOW THAT the length of our trek across the Territory neared its end, if we made it, Ham and Scut and I held a council. We were at one of the hide-outs above Boggy Depot. What had we gained by this journey? If it had been anything, we didn't know what and maybe we'd never know. But one thing was certain, we weren't the same boys who had left Chetopa.

Ham said, "All we did was lose time from cows. We've done a good job doing that. And no matter where we go, we add one more critter to the outfit. After Leviticus we got one from Belle Reed, and now we add another." He looked at the red roan and at Stanley, where he sat with Miss Lockwood by the night fire.

"Something's happening between those two," Scut said. "While you were in the Chickasaw country, Stanley stalked around as black as a thundercloud. She talked to him about some old German piano player named Vogner before she calmed him. But I never heard her say what this professor did for a living except pound the ivories. Maybe he worked in a saloon."

"Scrape, you don't help a bit," Ham said. "Since you show up with this outlaw nag, it means Bench Buckley will come riding."

"I showed you that bill of sale. And Blue Gum got the horse from Tom Starr. Anyway, I'm no worse than Miss Lockwood with Belle's mare."

"Pick out your hanging rope," Scut said.

"What do we do now? Go slow or make a break for it? A bird could fly from here to Red River in fifty miles and we've got only two stage stops left between Boggy and Colbert's Ferry. If we don't make a run, it will take three or four days, the way we'll creep around."

"On general principles," Ham said, "I'm opposed to hurry."

Scut yawned. "So am I. Let's get some shut-eye."

So now, on our moving day from Clear Boggy, we tighten our belts and take a good look at each other. From the beginning, we'd all hitched up together like something blown in from a tornado. It is fourteen miles to Nail's Crossing on Blue River, but to us much more than that, the way we'll wind in and out of hills and valleys to avoid the lighthorse. Stanley is stubble-faced, a determined fire in his eyes.

Miss Lockwood says, "Whether we make Red River or not, I'll never forget what we've done."

Standing by his horse is Scut—old Chief Big Grin—and Ham, his dark face showing nothing. We mount up and strike for the south, still within the border of the Choctaw Nation. Among the tall oaks, I fall in beside Stanley.

"Since you left Blue Gum, have you caught up on sleep?"

"Sleep doesn't matter. What worried me was being so far gone I was stopped by those Chickasaw schoolgirls on Clear

Boggy. They were out hunting nuts. They really found one. I was asleep in the saddle and didn't know who they were."

"You've got a way with women," Stanley said. "Cherokees and Chickasaws."

"I sure have. The girls took me to Wapanucka Academy and made me eat dinner. I felt like a sultan in a harem. Have you seen that place?"

"No," Stanley said, his eyes hawking into every thicket.

"It's built in great blocks of limestone. It's about the biggest building I ever saw. It's got more windows than a martin box. The boys said some strange cowhands have been to Boggy Depot."

"They must have been Wallum's men. We haven't been there since you left." I rode close to town to see my friend, and he told me about the cowhands. He said I've had no mail, so I think things up the road are tight. The lighthorse may be watching Chandler and Tilby. Stop!" He grasped my arm.

We were along a clear flowing branch which edged the base of a cedar-topped hill. A few stunted trees stood in staggered lines beneath the summit, and among the ledges splotches of brown grass waved in the wind. Near the crest a band of riders waited.

Stanley snapped to the others, "Quick! Get beyond the creek. They haven't seen us." When we were hidden in the oaks he asked, "Aren't they cowhands?"

"They look like it, even from here."

He said grimly, "I shouldn't have mentioned cowhands. They must be Wallum's men."

"If they bum for makings, they're cowhands. That means it's us and the goat. Listen, take Miss Lockwood and leave."

Stanley said, his eyes on the brown hill, "They're bumming. No. We stay."

"Then what do we do?"

"Sit tight till they leave and think of Nail's Crossing."

We got off our horses, and leaving the rest of the outfit

behind, crept through the brush to get a clearer view of the riders. They seemed to be in no hurry to move from the hill.

"Whoever leads them is smart," Stanley said. "He has everything on the west side of the road in view, and he's probably got men on the other side. I don't see how they missed us, unless they reached the crest at the very moment the curve of the branch threw us into the open. Scrape, what will you do if we do get to Texas?"

"If I get by Wallum, I'll see if Slick Pilifer will keep me on."

We were holed up in the trees for hours before the riders left. The morning was pretty well shot, so we decided to eat from what scanty store we had left in the sacks. After nooning we set out again. We made better time and traveled closer to the road, always within hearing of the howling wagons. Scut said, "That sound is going to wake me up for the next fifty years."

"The first fifty have been bad enough," Ham said. "But just look at old Scrape. To him, nothing matters. He's got to go on."

"If it's any consolation," Stanley said, "We're near the hills where a battle took place between the Caddoes and the Choctaws back in the days when the old Choctaws made their big hunts. The ground is still covered with bones and spear points and arrowheads."

"Lo! the poor Indian," Ham said. "He never was worse off than this outfit."

We traveled on with the road until we stopped near Nail's Crossing on Blue River.

The old Nail home was east of the Blue, above the crossing on the steep banks. It was a wide white house, with brick chimneys at either end. To the rear were smaller chimneys. A roofed porch extended along the front, and scattered log outbuildings dotted the area. An oak-post fence with ornamental pointed tops enclosed the yard. A stone stile was used as a crossing from the mail road.

Stanley and I edged our horses from the trees, taking the picture in. Stanley said, "Mr. Nail died a few years ago. I don't know who runs the place now. Shall we try for information?"

"I don't see many wagons on the road, and no cowhands. Let's try it. If things sound good, maybe tonight we can make a break for the border."

We moved on, then stopped at a hitch rack beside the stile. Except for a few dogs and ducks and chickens the place appeared to be deserted. "The men may be at the crossing," Stanley said. "There once was a small bridge over the river, but it has been washed out several times. They could be working there."

"Do you want to go to the house?"

"Yes. There's a chance a letter might have come."

We left the horses and crossed the stile. A yellow dog came near, barking, then suddenly turned tail and ran. "This place is eerie," Stanley said. "There's always activity at a stage stand. I don't understand the silence." He stopped as we neared the front steps, giving a loud "Hallo!"

Behind a lilac bush which shielded a portion of the porch—and himself—a tall man stood up—Bench Buckley. He waved a hand toward the road. There was a storehouse near the fence, and from it walked two men. They were Creek lighthorse. Bench Buckley motioned to a circle of empty chairs. "Sit down," he said.

I don't remember how I felt when I sank into the chair on the wide porch of the old Nail place. Too much had happened since we left Chetopa to feel much of anything but numbness. Everything had gone wrong—as wrong as if we had discussed every moment we were to make to decide the right thing to do, and then had done exactly the opposite. There are times when a man's head can be as thick as a limestone block, and this was it. I didn't know anything. I sat down.

For a moment Stanley stood before Bench Buckley without speaking. Then he, too, sat. He looked at me with some kind of drawn amusement on his face, but I was too far gone to figure it out. Then he looked back to the officer. Bench was a broad-shouldered man, but with a quick litheness about him even as he took his chair. He had the coldest gray eyes I ever saw in a human face.

"How are you?" he asked Stanley, swinging one long leg over the other.

By now the lighthorse had joined us. "I'm fine," Stanley said.

The brush-jacketed lighthorse spoke. "Hello, Stanley."

"Hello, Bob. Hello, Tani."

I didn't know who the short Tani was, but I had good reason to remember Bob. He grinned. "Did you tell Stanley?"

"No."

"I thought not, but it's just as well. I wanted to see him only to talk about old times. But the news was bad, and you boys were playing for keeps. I needed rest anyway."

The two lighthorse sat down.

"What's this with Bob?" Stanley asked. When I told him, he grinned. "You can't blame us for trying," he told him.

"Lesten Barr had a good laugh," Bob said. "He knew all about White Eagle's mischief."

Bench Buckley said to Stanley, "Have you heard what has happened?"

"If it's this important, I suppose not. I've had little opportunity to hear anything."

"You are a free man," Bench Buckley said.

Stanley was silent. Then he said, "How?"

Bench Buckley said, "Did you ever know a man named Kurbstone?"

"No. I'd never seen or heard of him until I was arrested in North Fork Town. Then later he and Olinger put some whiskey kegs in my equipment for the lighthorse to find. I believe he killed Collier, or helped Olinger do it."

A frosty gleam came to the gray eyes. "Kurbstone is dead—killed."

"How does that make me free? But who killed him?"

"His wife."

"You can't mean Betty Blye?"

"Yes."

"Why would she do that?"

Bench Buckley was looking across the fence to the roan. "How do you like him?" he asked me.

I put my hand under my brush jacket to my shirt pocket. "I've got a bill of sale."

"I know. Tom Starr once owned him. Before that, I did. Tom stole him from me. On the Canadian, just what did Blue Gum say he would tell me about Kurbstone?"

"He didn't mention Kurbstone. I didn't know he meant to tell you anything about him. What did you do with the body?"

"I took it to John Jumper."

"That was square."

The eyelids didn't even bat. "And Blue Gum didn't say a word about Kurbstone?"

"No, sir. He just said he would make it easier for us."

Bench Buckley turned to Stanley. "Blue Gum told me that Kurbstone killed Bill Cookson. Olinger helped him. He was near the cow camp when the boys put Cookson in the hearse. He stood watch in the alley while Kurbstone went in the back door. The door was unlocked."

Stanley nodded. "Yes, it was. Did Blue Gum say why he wanted to tell you this?"

"Kurbstone planned to double-cross him, as Olinger had. Also, he took a liking to the boy here."

"Why did Betty Blye kill Kurbstone?"

"The way it happened, perhaps she still thought a great deal of Bill Cookson. When I returned to Boggy Depot, I went to the inn to arrest Kurbstone. They were alone in their room. I knocked at the door and told Kurbstone I was arresting him on a Fort Smith whiskey charge, and for investigation in the murder of Bill Cookson. That was all Betty Blye needed. She jumped from her chair and pulled a derringer from her garter holster and shot him. When he fell, she clawed like a tiger. She got the truth, not I."

"She's good at that," I said. "I saw her tangle with Rowdy Ann at Newton about Bill."

"You boys are free of complicity," Bench Buckley said. He told Stanley, "You ran a good trail."

Stanley indicated the lighthorse. "The reason is there, along with a few other complications. Were those your riders in the hills today?"

"No." Bench Buckley stood up. "Good day, gentlemen." He left and climbed the stile and crossed the road to the trees and mounted his horse. Then he jogged north. He hadn't mentioned Leviticus.

Tani said, "He wanted us to come with him." Tani was bowlegged and with his squat build, he looked more like a plains Comanche than a Creek.

Stanley said, "Why? And in the first place, why did he come at all?"

"Bench says that a man who is desperate enough to run from a crime he didn't commit is desperate enough to kill. Anything could set you off, even your own lighthorse."

Stanley said, "Yes, I suppose so."

"We'll pull out in a little while," Tani said. "We came with the Choctaw lighthorse, who are out spilling liquor. When they get back, we'll ride on with them to Boggy, then strike for North Fork Town. Do you want to come?"

"No, I'll stay on the Blue tonight. Is Tilby safe?"

Bob lit a gnarled stump pipe he took from his jacket pocket. He puffed and said, "He's safe. We put a lighthorse with him." He puffed again, the tobacco catching and the smoke swirling away. "I'm glad this is over. It's been a bad business. And with the railroad coming, the next outbreak will be worse. It will be worse everywhere."

The returning Choctaw lighthorse trotted up the road from down Texas way. They stopped at the stile. A line of covered wagons passed, moving ever onward. The bull whips of the booted freighters snapped near the oxen like exploding rifles. A few dogs ran in and out among the teams, and milk cows followed the tail gates at ropes' ends.

The Creeks stood up to go. "Say," I said, "about this goat I've got."

Tani turned at the steps. "We weren't sent to find goats." He slapped his hand on Bob's back and they walked laughing to the stile.

Stanley sat in his chair without speaking. At last he said, "We'd better get to our horses before we pay rent to the stage stand."

The trees and the river were near. Stanley was free, but I still had Leviticus. "There's something funny about those men and that goat," I said. "Why don't you go back with the lighthorse? There's no use for you and Miss Lockwood to be stuck in our hard luck."

"No," Stanley said. "We keep moving. Tonight we camp as usual."

We rode back to the Blue to join the others and then wandered upstream a few miles before we staked out for the night. Stanley didn't say anything about what had happened at Nail's until the horses were cared for and we had a small fire burning in a rocky cul-de-sac. Then he strode to Miss Lockwood and broke the news.

Doggone, that was something to see! That girl from the houseboat on the Holyoke laughing and crying and throwing her arms about the neck of that Poor Lo, and he bending down to kiss her. That was the happiest out-of-grub camp in the Territory that night. At last those two stopped their shenanigans and faced us.

"We may as well tell you now," Stanley said, "that if things worked out, we planned to be married. Now we will be."

Scut slouched with his hands on his hips. "Ain't that sweet.

Just listen to those twittering crows in the trees. All you did was get out of the frying pan into the fire."

"What are you going to do for a living?" Ham asked. "You can't run backwards and forwards on the Texas Road all your lives."

Miss Lockwood laughed and took Stanley's hand. "Remember," Stanley said, "I'm a doctor. We thought we might go to the Creek capital at Okmulgee and start a small hospital. Or when the railroad comes, if the people of North Fork Town move to the terminus, we would like to begin there. The old town life has been lost in the Territory, and many people live alone in the hills with their farms and cattle. I know them, and they trust me."

Ham said, "You said that place might be called Eufaula."

"Yes. Are you happy?" he asked Miss Lockwood.

"I can't believe it," she said.

Well, even though you may get the devil stomped out of your own hide, sometimes when you see what you've done for people out of your own trouble, it can cheer up the most lost of souls, as it did with me and Scut and Ham that night around the fire. It was worth all our trouble to see Stanley and Miss Lockwood with their future. So we cheered up and tried not to think of our own. One more march, and we might make it to Red River. But in spite of how we tried to shrug off our worry, the same thought came back—the men on the hill.

The north wind was up suddenly, like a cat howling. A few flakes of snow began to sweep through the trees. Then it spread wide like the wings of an eagle. Stanley said, "Let's plan for tomorrow."

Scut and Miss Lockwood drew blankets over their shoulders. Stanley and Ham and I sat hunched in our hats and slickers. Before long a ground film of white lay beneath the spreading branches.

Stanley said, "We can try the Texas Road to Carriage Point and the ferry, or we can avoid the road. We can cut west by old Fort Washita or strike to the southeast across Island

Bayou. But no matter how we go, the Red will still be before us. With luck, we'll make the river by nightfall."

Ham said, "Then up steps Wallum and says 'What are you doing with that goat?' "

"What's at Fort Washita?" Scut said.

"Only a few ruins remain on the hill," Stanley said. "Even the pole stockade has fallen. At one time, a settlement was near by, but I think it's gone. The Fort was in Confederate hands, but it had been built earlier to protect the Choctaws and Chickasaws. It was on one of the California trails, where emigrants gathered to gain numbers. When the Confederates left, the settlers burned it. They thought it might become an outlaw stronghold."

"If the settlement's still there," Ham said, "we might try for something to eat." His stomach growled. "This no-food business is getting serious."

"What's to the southeast?" Scut asked.

"After we cross Blue River," Stanley said, "we come close to what's left of Fort McCulloch—only a few old bastions and redoubts. It was abandoned by the Confederacy for more northern strongholds. Then we cross Island Bayou."

"Since leaving Chetopa," I said, "we've followed the Texas Road when we could. Let's stick to it. When we near Colbert's Ferry, we can turn right or left to others if we have to. Anyway, we can still swim our horses. I vote to stick to the road."

"Scrape, you were bent to make a run this morning," Ham said. "And you see now how far we got."

"Sure. And it brought some pretty good luck, at least to Stanley. Maybe we'll have more tomorrow. At least now only half of the outfit is outlawed. And the best thing is that we can look for trouble mainly before us, and not behind."

"What's at Carriage Point?" Ham said.

"It was Fisher's Station on the Butterfield route," Stanley said. "But later it took its old name again. It's on Mineral Bayou, near Island Bayou."

So we decided tomorrow's course. "And we ain't got anywhere yet." Scut yawned. "Well, we will gird our loins with the rising sun and go forth. Scrape, you ain't croaked a word in a pigeon's wink."

"I was thinking about all the people on this trail. Up there in the Cherokee land . . ."

"You mean that girl," Ham said.

"I didn't mean her. I meant even at Chetopa—Booger Red and those preachers and Kurbstone. I meant Willard Law and Captain Jamison and the old Cherokee—I see those people the way I would if I looked in a stereoscope at Newton or Abilene."

From off the Texas Road, somewhere in the trees among the sifting snow, the sounds of singing and a banjo came:

"Oh, Susannah!
Oh, don't you cry for me,
For I come from Alabama with my banjo on my knee."

"He came a long way to get here in a snow storm," Ham said. "But it ain't a nickle in a frying pan to what some of them did."

"They'll always do it," Stanley said. "And when they kill themselves to get where they're going and build up all they want, they leave for another place. Or a new generation will tire of what it's gained and move on. These restless men or their sons will never stay, they go on and on into oblivion, yet taking something with them. How many will ever stop to hold a single palmful of earth? The white man never does."

"Some will," I said. "They haven't been here long enough to know it yet."

"No," said Stanley. "They will never settle."

The snow swirled against the sides of the trees. Stanley said, "We'd better sleep."

Scut took first watch, then woke me for the next. He turned in and I sat by the low fire. The snow fell effortlessly, quiet and peaceful. Or the flakes danced suddenly in the wind gusts.

The sleeping figures stirred under their tarps, and the whitening backs of the horses became more distinct. Then a weird sight emerged from the falling flakes.

Hundreds of Indian children marched in a long line, carrying their small bows and arrows. They were like those we had seen at the One Member Church, but by some trick of the snow they suddenly became as the little people of the Cherokees, for they marched naked save for breech clouts or aprons, their gliding figures on some ancient quest, purposeful among the trees.

But as the boys passed, they grew to become young braves with slender girls beside them, yet somehow they all seemed to be thrust farther back into the past, even though they had grown older and should be nearer and clearer now.

But even as the braves with their bows and arrows moved back to the ancient home of their people, still others who had become worn and old in that other world emerged in an alien land at the end of the Trail of Tears.

They came nearer, the people of all the Nations, wandering in swamps and morasses where fathers struggled to hold their wives and children above the pathless waters, or stumbled behind horses or wagons on rutted roads and lost trails in deep trees, kneeling to bury their dead, the gaunt old men and women like skeletons in despair, while infants and children sickened of starvation and disease.

The old faces stared through the snow.

Ham's eyes were there, and he came through the snowflakes. "You didn't wake me," he said. "If I hadn't woke by accident, you'd have been sitting all night. Go get some shut-eye."

"Maybe I am sleepy," I said, standing up. "Keep your eye on Blue Gum's horse. He's been restless."

Chapter 18

OH, YES, you would have thought us a smart bunch next morning, being there on the Texas Road, seeing how we got tricked by a bunch of Texas cowhands. So much had happened on the long trail through the Territory that we didn't know if even Bench Buckley or the Creek lighthorse had misled us about the goat—that is, if they had known the outcome a full day before we did.

After we broke camp and hunted a fording place near Nail's on steep-banked Blue River, the horses splashed across and we cut back to the road. A stiff south wind had come up overnight and the spotty snow disappeared. The ruins of old Fort McCulloch lay hidden to the left, but as we rode on, siding the tree edge of the road, a close-grouped body of Wallum's shouting riders burst upon us.

Stanley dashed his horse forward, his pistol cocked and pointed. "Hold it!" I yelled. "Hold it! It's Slick Pilifer!"

Slick jerked his horse up beside the bay. "It's a good thing you held it. You might have got us all killed."

Stanley shoved his slouch hat back. He said coldly, "That was my intention. Or at any rate to get you."

"Well." Slick looks at me. "So you finally got this far. And me leaving a late roundup to chase you down." He was put out and provoked but dressed pretty well as usual.

"Don't cry on my shoulder," I said. "How come you're here in the first place?"

"I'll get to that later," Slick says. He shifts his eyes uncomfortable like, not wanting to meet mine.

"You bet you'll get to it," I said. "And quicker than you think. I've had a hunch for a long time that you were back of some of the trouble we ran into. How is my mama?"

"She's doing fine. I rode down to see her."

"Did you tell her about my ear?"

"Yes."

"What did she say?"

"Nothing. She just went to the window and looked out, then she turned back pretty proud and said, 'Mr. Pilifer, would you have some coffee?' "

"Then I guess it's all right."

"I guess it is," Slick says. "Scrape, it's up to you. Before I left, I asked her to marry me." There was a big guffaw among Slick Pilifer's cowhands, but he bowed his neck and stuck to his guns. "She said it would be your decision. Scrape, you and I could go a long way in this cow business."

"If you didn't get so ornery," I said. "But right now I've got some questions to ask. How did you get in touch with Captain Jamison?"

"Oh, that?" Slick squirmed in his saddle.

"Yes, that. You sure are innocent."

"Well, it was this way. I thought it would be a good trick if I pulled something on you boys. So while you rode on to Baxter Springs, I sent a hand to Fort Gibson to see Jamison.

My intentions were good, but things just worked out wrong. I didn't know you'd get into trouble on your own hook."

"Go on. I sure like to see you squirm."

"Well, I told Jamison to shanghai you into the Army—just for laughs, you understand—and take you around the country. But when he found you with the stolen horses, he had to arrest you. He couldn't do otherwise until you were proved innocent. At first, he didn't know who you were. When he found out, he wrote me from Fort Gibson."

"Where is he now?"

"In Washington. The old Cherokee chief died there. He's buried at Arlington. Scrape, I want to talk this out. Let's get off the road and sit."

All of us moved into the trees and sat on the ground near the horses. We rested under a big brown oak—a tree that must have been a sapling before the Texas Road was even a deer or buffalo trail. Slick grinned and pointed to Leviticus. "Is that Wallum's goat?"

"Yes. I'm taking it back to Texas. I don't know what the old rascal will do to me."

"Don't worry about Wallum," Slick said. "Wallum's in jail. That's not his goat, anyway."

"Not his goat?" I said. "What do you mean?" After all these weeks of worry, my stomach turned sick. The way they looked, Scut and Ham felt the same.

Slick got up and took a folded newspaper from his saddle pockets. He held it open. It was a St. Louis paper. Two big pictures were on the front page—Wallum and a goat. A black headline across the top said, "After All the Fuss, Which Is the Goat?"

"What's the date on that paper?" I said.

Slick got more uncomfortable. "Oh, it's a few days old."

"You bet it is. It got to Nail's Station yesterday morning by stage. That's why Bench Buckley and the lighthorse didn't do anything when I was there. You framed things even with them."

Slick sat down among his cowhands. "Well, when we finally

met with the law, we all thought it would be nice if I broke the news first—in a family way, more or less, since I'm to marry your mama. We've scoured the country for some time, looking for you."

"That was your bunch on the hill between Nail's place and Boggy yesterday. But why isn't this Wallum's goat?"

"John D. Rockefeller and J. Pierpont Morgan hired the Pinkerton Agency to make an investigation for the Katy. They were afraid Wallum would take the railroad off their hands. It turned out that Wallum's goat had been mixed up on a transfer at Sedalia and was shipped by the Union Pacific to California. This goat got put on the train without a waybill. It was to go to a dead man's relatives in the Cherokee land near Chouteau. But the relatives had left the country. Your goat came down on Wallum's bill of lading."

"That's why Kurbstone never looked at the address on its neck," Ham said.

"You mean this is our goat?" I asked Slick.

"It sure is. John D. Rockefeller can't keep it, and J. Pierpont says he doesn't have room on his little place. August Belmont and Levi Parsons, on the Board of Directors, don't need it. I want to ask you, Scrape, what will you do with it?"

I hunkered under the oak, watching Slick. "I guess just sit and look at him. That's all I can do. How come Wallum is in jail?"

"Because I swore out a warrant and took a necktie party along to make the sheriff honest. Folks in that county have taken enough from Wallum, and when Jamison wrote me about your mother's X on the deed, it was all I could take. I've got enough vigilantes organized to keep the county under control until Wallum is tried for murder and you get your ranch back."

Stanley said, "Scrape, your trouble is over."

Slick got to his feet. "Let's head for Texas. Drive that goat to the road. Someone from the wagons will pick it up."

"No," I said.

"What?"

"I'm driving the goat home, no matter what the law does to Wallum."

Slick laughed. "Now, get in the saddle, boy. We're burning daylight. I'm on a roundup, and there's a wedding coming up."

"Is there?"

Slick stares, his face livid. "What do you mean?"

"You said it was left up to me. Well, I'm not sure about a lot of things. Anyway, I want you to squirm a while. I'll let you know some day. Until I get home, take my mama some posies. She's had a bad time."

"Oh, the plague take you!" Slick howls. "I'll tell her I did my best."

He hopped into his saddle and tore back toward Texas with his cowhands.

So with all of us free once more, and not quite believing the suddenness of it, or why it had happened, we walked the horses down the Texas Road, for once no one in a hurry to get anywhere.

"Are you still sticking with us?" I asked Stanley. "You've done enough. You've got a long ride back home yourself."

"We want to go to Red River," Miss Lockwood said.

"We'll reach it this afternoon."

"Oh no," she said. "Stanley and I want one more camp. We can buy provisions at Carriage Point, so tonight we'll all stay on one of the bayous."

"Food is the best word I've heard in a week," Ham said. "And especially now. But I don't feel right. I don't have troubles."

Scut broke out with "Shall We Gather at the River." "What are you still singing that for?" I said.

"The old Red's closer," Scut said. "And about my happiest time in the Territory was singing hymns back at North Fork Town. I'm going to buy me an organ some day."

"You do that and me and my Cherokee will come visit."

On the sides of the wide rail, and in the middle, the wheels of the covered wagons rumbled. In the hard, springless seats, there was something different on the faces of the tired travelers—an expression now of hope and eagerness, and not the tight strain they had worn over all the turning miles.

Miss Lockwood gazed back up the road. "Look! As far as you can see—the wagons!"

We provisioned for the night at Carriage Point, on the divide. Mineral Bayou flowed back to Blue River, and Island Bayou on down to the Red. We followed it a few miles to make camp. While we cared for the horses and Ham got the fire started, Stanley said, "The bayou marks the boundary of the Choctaw Nation. Tomorrow we'll be in the tip of the Chickasaw land."

"What's at Colbert's Ferry?" Ham asked.

"It's quite a place," Stanley said. "When he was a young man, Mr. Colbert settled on the river, and a few years later built his first ferry. He owned a good many slaves and several plantations. The Butterfield stage used the ferry, and today most of the wagons and freighters do. He does a good business."

As the evening shadows fell, I went down to a clear pool on the tree-lined bayou for water, and among the vines I saw the trumpeter swan. It was white and tall and graceful, and it stood by the water, watching. But one shoulder had been shattered by a shotgun blast, and its wing tip touched the ground. It had better have been killed by a clean arrow, and best that I kill it now, for its wings would never spread again.

The bird hopped about the pool, one wing beating the air. It circled once more and stopped to face me, then it held its long neck upward and stood with a proud eye, its head as high as mine.

It was gone—it was all gone, the day of its flight, and it would never return. The Choctaw racing upon the ball court, the Cherokee and the Chickasaw in their struggles and council, the Creek in his pride, and the Seminole hunting game in his swamp—it was gone.

There were the schools now, and the white man—more driven than ever—and there were the manual arts of the schools, and driving ever southward, relentless with its steel miles, the railroad came. Better that they could have waited and found their own civilization rather than be here, even this their new land shrinking with each treaty.

The proud bird watched, a gleam in its eye. I raised my pistol and fired.

When I got back to camp, Stanley said, "What did you shoot at?"

"I saw a bird," I said.

There had been a few strong rustlings in the trees during the night, and soon after sunup, as we broke camp, the awakened south wind of yesterday struck full blast. When it began then, the cold snap had passed; now we were caught from the other direction.

"You look bright-eyed and bushy-tailed today," Stanley said.

"I'm going home," I said.

We saddled and packed the horses and rode up the east bank of the bayou to the stage station. The smoke from the stone and clay chimneys lay straight out, pointing to the north like spears. We left the horses at one of the watering troughs while we bought supplies at the store for the homeward trek, once we had crossed the Red.

We came out bent sideways into the wind with our tow sacks, and after packing we filled our canteens at one of the stone wells. We looked at the divide of the bayous and southward toward the haze and sand-blown valley of Red River.

Back with the rest, I asked Miss Lockwood, "Hadn't you better start for North Fork Town? The wind will be rough."

She said, "Stanley says it's only thirteen miles to the river, so we'll be there before noon. Then we will try to get back to the Blue River station after nightfall."

"You'll make better time without Leviticus," Ham said.

"When we near this river sand," Scut said, "you'd better tie a bandanna across your face like heathen cowhands do."

We took a look at our gear, and then we were out on the road again and off among the wagons, our heads bent in the gale, going south to God's country. A few hours later when we saw Mr. Colbert's big house and outbuildings, we still had our teeth in the wind.

"He's got a real place," Scut said.

"It's fertile ground." Ham looked about. "If only it stays where it was put."

"Colbert is enterprising," Stanley said. "After he started the ferry, he built a steam sawmill, a gristmill, and a cotton gin. He keeps up most of the roads hereabouts, and even talks of building a wagon bridge across the river."

When we reached the ferry, the road was lined with at least a hundred waiting wagons. Tree growth had been thinned at the steep landings on either side of the river, and somewhere in Texas a plantation owner must have had every acre in the county plowed that morning, for the whole sky was just a beating cloud of dirt and sand.

"How do we cross?" Ham said. "Line up with the wagons and take our turn?"

"Yes," Stanley said. "Get in among the wagons and move when they do. Mr. Colbert takes extra horses with the wagons."

There was some sort of commotion down at the ferry approach. A wagon had fallen over the bank. "Think we'd better help?" I said.

"Go on," Scut said. "I'll hold the horses and stay with Miss Lockwood."

We left them and walked down the road and through the crowd of drivers and long-skirted women and curious children. We shoved our way to the bank. Mr. Colbert stood in the sand by the overturned wagon. He was a light-complected jovial man, and he couldn't have been a day over forty-five, or even that much.

"Don't worry," he was saying to the driver and his family. "I've sent for the oxen. We'll get the team unhitched and have you out in no time."

The emigrant turned a despairing face upward, his eyes hounded.

"Well, I'll be," Ham said.

Just then the man's troubled gaze caught sight of Stanley. He seemed to find some security in Stanley's face, although he remained just as miserable. "Doctor," he said, "I need a friend."

It was that wagon-squeaker from up above Chouteau, and the boy Stanley had operated on in the woods stood by his mother, waving a grimy hand up the bank. "Hey, I got well!" he cried. He lifted his shirt to show the scar.

"Fine!" Stanley called down to the boy. "That's fine. How did you fall over the bank?" he asked the man.

"I was backing up to get in line better. I came in on the wrong side and while I was backing, the wagon tilted over the bank and took the team with it. Friend, let me tell you something—and heed it. God put a man in one spot on earth and meant for him to stay there. Wherever you live, don't ever move."

"You should have been here weeks ago. What held you up?"

"After you left, the big rain came. We bogged and couldn't get out of the timber. Then the first day on the road the mules ran away and smashed a wheel in the trees. I had to get a new one made at Perryville."

Ham grinned. "Did you roll it back?"

"No. I tied it on the side of one of the mules and he fell in a rut and broke his leg. After I shot him, I had to find work to buy another. I got a job stripping coal at McAlester."

Stanley said, "Don't tell us the rest of it. It breaks you up too much."

An attractive woman rode through the crowd, sidesaddle. "Is anyone hurt?" she asked Mr. Colbert.

"No. Just shaken up a bit."

"Who is that?" I said.

"I think it's Mrs. Colbert," Stanley said.

"Will you and the child come to the house?" Mrs. Colbert asked the woman.

The spare man beside the wagon shook his head. "Lady, she ain't going anywhere. She stays right here till we get this wagon to dry land, and then I'm talking to her."

When the wagon was on high ground again and safe and sound on four wheels, with the team hitched up, the man said to his wife, "Do you see that ferry?"

"Why, certainly I see it," she said.

"I left our good home in Ohio," the man said, "to come to this ferry. I fought hell and high water and wound and back-tracked this wagon with nothing but trouble for over a thousand miles to get here. Do you know what that is?" He pointed across the grit and gravel blowing in the air above the river. "That's Texas. That's what I've come to. Do you see that black cloud? That ain't a cloud, that's land moving in the sky. That's Texas up there. There's nothing left across this river for you to set foot in."

"It's time for us to get on that ferry," the woman said.

"Oh, no," the man said. "It's time for you to get on. I'm not moving from here. I listened to your Texas talk for five years, and I promised to bring you. Well, I got you here. Now just reach in the air and grab a handful of Texas."

"What do you mean? Ain't you going on with me?"

The man took an old wallet from his hip pocket. "Here's my coal money—fourteen dollars." Then he reached into a side pocket. "Here's fifty-four cents—it's the last of my snake-root and tie-hacking money. You take it all. It leaves me broke, but I don't care. I got you to Texas, and if you want to live in that devastation, just drive this wagon onto the ferry. But the minute you do, I start walking back to Ohio." He looked at the windy sky. "I didn't leave home to come to that."

"All right," Mr. Colbert said to the woman. "It's your turn on the ferry."

The man turned and plodded up the road.

"Just a minute," the woman told Mr. Colbert. "Let me think." She looked at the boy, at the sky, and at the man. She said to Mr. Colbert, "My man did tell me the truth? That's really Texas over there?"

"That's Texas," Mr. Colbert said.

"Is it always like that?"

"Sometimes. It depends on where you live in Texas. Out West the wind is bad. Here, you get used to it."

"I want to ask you," the woman said. "If you was a woman like me, what would you take—a man or Texas?"

"Madam," Mr. Colbert said, "I'd take a man."

The woman gazed up the road. "That man means to go back. He never did this to me before. Look at him walk." She glanced once more across the river. "Well, I can tell my neighbors I saw Texas."

She turned the team and drove the wagon back up the road.

"Benjamin!" a raw-boned freighter beside his oxen called amid the roar of laughter. "You talked yourself out of a fare."

"Maybe they'll be happy in Ohio," Mr. Colbert shouted back. "They wouldn't have a chance in Texas. Who's next?"

Meanwhile, a wildly rushing stage had arrived at the stand above the slope. The horses had been changed and now, the driver blowing his horn, the four-in-hand jolted and careened down the narrowing road to the river. Stanley said, "The stage has priority, even before a goat like Leviticus. It takes the place of the Ohio wagon."

Ham nudged me. "Will you look at that?"

As the stage slid down the bank to the ferry, the lanky driver riding the brake handle, a black-hatted figure stuck its head and arms out of a window, gesticulating to another who sat across from him and did likewise. Six more black-clad men were mounted on good horses which galloped behind the stage.

"It's packed full of preachers," I said. "The black priests of old Chetopa and all the others they picked up. What do they mean to do in Texas?"

Stanley said, "I hope they left someone in the Territory."

A big red-haired woman stuck her head throught the door between the two preachers in their separated windows. She wore a wide yellow hat with four straight-up white ostrich feathers on top, and a blue traveling suit. She waved a purple handkerchief.

Ham said, "She remembers us!"

It was Booger Red. I yelled, "Where are you going?"

"To a little country town called Dallas!" Booger shouted.

"You mean you quit railroading?" Ham yelled.

"I'm starting a joint for cowhands. Stop and eat with me!" Then as the stage rolled upon the ferry, she was lost to view.

"She'll get along," I said.

As all the wagons moved toward the river, we walked back up the crowded road to Scut and Miss Lockwood, then took our own place in line. At last it came our turn to board the ferry. We'd all been pretty silent for a while, because we seemed to run out of something to say. I looked at Miss Lockwood and she looked away. The wagon before us was on the ferry now.

Stanley put out his hand. "Good luck, and thank you."

"Sure," Scut said. "And we hope you're happy. When you have triplets, name them Scut, Ham, and Scrape."

Miss Lockwood blinked. "What if they're girls?"

"We're not particular," Ham said. "Call them Scrapelet, Hamlet, and Scutlet. It wouldn't matter to us. We'll see you some time."

We rode aboard the ferry with Leviticus and the great red roan. We got off the horses to walk about the planks and look. The barge was attached to a steel cable strung across the river, and eight stalwart Negroes began to pole into the wind. But one wasn't a Negro. It was Benjamin Colbert.

Midway across the water, as we looked back upon the Territory, Stanley and Miss Lockwood waited on the bank. Behind them the flat land spread and on beyond, even as we watched, the low hills seemed to grow and rise. They were blue with time, yet for us some of their mystery would always live.

Ham said, "I just figured something. It was worth it."

"I guess it was," Scut said.

"With all their trouble," I said, "they tried for a little while."

"How come you're poling?" Scut asked Mr. Colbert. "You own this outfit. You own this ferry."

"Some of the men wanted off today," Mr. Colbert said. "And others are working in Texas to keep up the road to Sherman."

"You mean you keep up Texas roads?"

"It helps everyone. It helps the people and the stage lines. It helps my business." He stuck his pole in the water and put his weight to it, moving as easily and as surely as the Negroes. At last the ferry stopped.

We mounted up and climbed the Texas bank. Leviticus stared indifferently upon the Territory. He was that mountain of white I had seen before me day and night.

The far-off figures of Stanley and Miss Lockwood waved good-by. They swung their horses and jogged back up the Texas Road, their shapes becoming smaller.

"They'll have the wind with them," Scut said.

"Well," I said, "we've seen the last of the civilized Indians."

Mr. Colbert looked up from the ferry. "No, you haven't." He laughed. "I am a Chickasaw."

High overhead, from the distant Cherokee land, in other winds the V-patterns of the wild geese winged south.

AUTHOR'S NOTE

The Bright Feathers attempts to depict the tragedy of the Five Civilized Tribes, and their later struggle to adapt to the white ways. This is all developed as the three youthful cowhands cross the Indian Territory over the old Texas Road.

As for the time the trip took, I'd say perhaps two months. It began late in September of '71, and ended early in December. The time element is all tied in with the actual progress of the railroad construction, and the plot was developed to allow the preliminary railroad activity to reach North Fork Town by the time the boys arrived there from Fort Smith.

The direct route of the Texas Road across the Territory appears to have covered something like two hundred and seventy-five miles, but the boys made a number of lengthy side trips, adding up to roughly six hundred and fifty miles for Scrape and somewhat less for the others.

All the Indian tales are true and verifiable history, or are based on fact. I, as author, take no side in the various opinions expressed in regard to the character of John Ross, the Cherokee chief. I give the beliefs of each faction, and the reader may decide what he will.

The Indian who gobbled when mad at his wife used the old taunt or war cry; the incident of the Indian who returned to Red Oak for his execution did so according to custom. William MacLeod Raine used a similar incident in one of his books about this region; the source is in the Chronicles of Oklahoma. Disease could wipe out the entire membership of an isolated church, and from such events came the One Member Church tale.

The steamboat on its way down the Arkansas faced the exact navigation hazards mentioned. And there is the old shelf across the river at Webber's Falls, and boats were pulled over it. In 1923 my father was scouting around from Fort Smith for a location in Oklahoma. He took me and my brother with him, and we crossed the river at Webber's Falls. Due to the lack of a bridge (as I remember, it had been washed out) we forded the river on the very shelf Scut pulled the steamboat over. Then we stuck in sand and water and the car had to be pulled out by a team of mules. The old shelf was once six or eight feet high; it is almost nothing now.

And even Belle Starr's candy recipe is genuine—a woman found two among old newspaper clippings, and gave them to me. Perhaps the punctuation, which I used, was Belle's.

There was no outlaw, however, named Blue Gum. I based the name on Blue Duck, one of Belle Starr's crowd. Other characters, such as John Jumper, were real.

As for the title, perhaps the word "feathers" represents happiness and security. As a slave boy, Blue Gum had known happiness in the Florida swamps with the girl running beside him while he hunted birds for their bright plumage. The future events of the Trail of Tears, and his subsequent outlaw life in Indian Territory, were to destroy this security and Blue Gum's other values until he found them again with Scrape.

The site of old North Fork Town is now covered by Lake Eufaula in the Arkansas River Navigation Project.

J.H.C.

Shawnee, Oklahoma

ABOUT JOHN H. CULP

The author was born August 31, 1907 in Meridian, Mississippi, worked on ranches in Texas and Oklahoma, taught school, ran a music shop, and served in the Air Corps during World War II. He now lives in Shawnee, Oklahoma, where he is at work on another novel.

In THE BRIGHT FEATHERS, Mr. Culp has constructed a saga about the country and the people he knows best, not only through thorough historical research, but from his own first hand experience:

"When I was a boy in Fort Smith," he writes, "a number of us always took our blanket rolls to school on Friday noon, and when school was out we headed for the Ozarks or the Cookson Hills in Oklahoma, or southwest from Fort Smith into the Choctaw country. We'd always return home like a pack of tired dogs by Sunday night, and with more adventures under our belts than Scrape and Scut and Ham could shake a stick at."

Miss Lockwood
S. Hightower
Capt. Jamison
Scut, Scrape, Ham and Leviticus
CHISHOLM TRAIL
California Road
WICHITA MTS
N
W
E
S
0 10 25 50
Scale in Miles